Savior's Odyssey

Dennis Gregory

PublishAmerica
Baltimore

ISBN:978-1-61582-807-4
PUBLISHED BY PUBLISHAMERICA, LLLP
www.publishamerica.com
Baltimore

Printed in the United States of America

Other books by Dennis Gregory:

The Last God, fiction
Camelot Again, poetry

*Some scenes in the book are not suitable for younger readers.

For my brother, Drew
who had all the qualities of the real Jesus.

*Give me life in all its color and madness,
give me copulation and galloping horses.*

—Alexander the Great in
a novel by Shan Sa

Drink no longer water but use a little wine…
—Saint Paul, I Timothy: 23

It is hard to kick against the pricks.

—Jesus Christ
Acts 9:5

Jesus the Christ did not die on the cross, he escaped and lived on.

I know, I am the poet, Demetrius, his best friend and I was with him every step of the way.

He was so good, so filled with the Buddha's wisdom he learned in India, with his looks of a Greek God and words of love he won the peoples' hearts.

Jerusalem had never seen such a hero. The older Jews in power were soon jealous and wanted him dead.

When Jesus heard he would be crucified—he escaped the cross and traveled back to his home in Persia. This he did years ago and he and his wife, Mary Magdalene, are growing old here. I am their friend growing old with them.

In Babylon now he is called Prince Jezep, the Persian name for Jesus.

We listen to the caravans telling tales of his miracles and we laugh because it was never like that. Stories stretch over time.

Great stories grow into legends and legends flower into religions. They say he has sparked a religion in faraway lands.

But that is far from here.

He sits in Babylon, unknown, and empty as a wineskin.

The dancing girls, the wine and the lion hunts are empty substitutes for real living. A great hero like Prince Jesus needs to ride through life and touch many people and be remembered through the ages.

He sits waiting, his life is one long sigh.

His great soul yearns for one more quest...

Chapter 1

Jerusalem, Friday, April 7th, 30 A.D.
Around 2 in the afternoon...

Jesus blinked up at the hot sun, stinging sweat dripping in his eyes.

His arms ached from the ropes tying him to the cross.

His strong legs turned sideways were tied to the wooden post, his muscular arms were outstretched on the crossbeams and he was breathing hard in the blazing sun of Golgotha.

But something much deeper troubled him.

The sleeping potion was wearing off and he was wide awake. The escape depended on him being drugged and looking dead.

He shook his head brushing the flies from his face. His stringy brown hair stuck to his square rugged cheeks and beads of sweat crawled down his forehead. He felt like the sun was leaning down on him alone.

He trembled, 'if my escape is discovered they'll have to kill me outright'. He closed his eyes tight, fear racing through him, 'Pilate has to save face, bribe or no bribe.' His thoughts were jumbled, his eyes twitching from side to side.

'I need more wine,' his heart was pounding.

He looked down at the Roman guards seeing the tops of their tarnished iron helmets, he groaned for attention.

Flavius, the husky, young Roman captain, standing at the foot of the cross, glanced over his shoulder, his stern, dark eyes squinting from inside his helmet.

The large soldier nudged the red-robed guard to his right and barked the order, "He needs more wine." A bucket was passed. The other centurion bent down and grabbed a sponge and dipped it into the bucket of warm wine mixed with the sleeping potion. He attached the wine-soaked sponge to the end of his spear and held it up to Jesus.

The red drugged wine stung his lips and was bitter as vinegar but he drank deeply. It burned his cracked mouth. His glazed eyes sagged down at the Roman and his lips formed the Latin word, "Plus." The Roman hauled it down, dipped the sponge in the wine again and stuck it on the end of the spear, it was dripping red as he raised it to Jesus' mouth once more.

He sucked on the sponge and could taste the bitter drug in the wine. In a few moments he began to feel heavy on the cross.

The soldier turned away and straightened up facing the onlookers, Jews and families of Jews, many women and all were sobbing. The Romans' forceful stance and pointed spears kept them pushed back.

Jesus gazed up at the circling crows slicing around the bright sun, he closed his eyes a moment and smiled feeling his breathing coming slower and slower.

Chapter 2

Roman soldiers gave him drugged wine to drink—he tasted it.
Mathew 27: 33-34

The Romans were guarding this laborer's son they jokingly called 'King of the Jews'. The wooden sign above his head proclaimed he was a king but it might well have read, 'Clown of the Jews' for all the entertainment he'd provided that day.

The mock trial by Pilate, the dragging of the cross through the streets, the parade through town, Jews weeping and Romans cheering, what a show!

But the Romans near the cross knew it must appear like any other crucifixion. To be sure of his death-sleep they lifted more wine to his parched mouth. The warm wine spilled down his chin. He coughed, his stomach was churning.

He was sweating rivers in the blazing sun, his naked chest was shining wet. The goat's blood they'd secretly poured on his hands and feet had dried and the biting flies were scratching his ankles like the devil's own fingernails.

He flicked his stringy dark hair away and managed to fix his stare on the people beneath his cross. The drug was working so he could barely make out their faces.

There was Mary, his mother, with her bright eyes and the black cloth draped so angelic over her head. She beamed at him with her perfect smile.

Beside her was Mary Magdalene, his wonderful wife, so beautiful with her light long hair, she was trying to smile. He loved her with all his heart and hated that she had to go through this, he would make it up to her with perfect love the rest of their lives.

The two women knew his escape was working, he saw their hidden smiles.

Seeing his wife and his mother made him glow inside, he had to hold back a smile, powerful Jews were everywhere.

Standing next to them was Demetrius, his dear friend the poet, dark and curly-haired, his sharp green eyes were laughing up at him because they both knew things would turn out fine.

They'd been in worse places in their adventures across the world.

The poet was standing there with the white-satin cloth of Persian royalty over his muscular shoulder, the white cloth went all the way to his knees, front and back, Persian Style. A wide green sash was tied around his waist. His leather sandals were laced up to his knees. He shined next to the dirty peasants around him.

Demetrius, like himself, was half Greek, half Jew, but unlike his own strong bulk, the poet was slim as a running athlete.

Jesus could barely hold back a smile. They had traveled the wide world together, to Persia and India and now back to Jerusalem.

He felt for his friend who had left the comforts of Babylon to return with him to dusty Jerusalem to preach.

A true friend was Demetrius pushed beyond patience. He knew that he ached to return to the cool gardens of Babylonia.

Jesus saw the poet's smirk that said, 'now look at the fix we're in'. But they both knew the escape was working and knew they'd soon be back in the green coolness of the gardens, floating beneath cool waterfalls, drinking wine at night toasting to dancing girls.

The poet shook back his curling black hair and put his hands together in a prayer to his friend hanging ridiculous on a cross. He looked around at this gruesome place and it made him hold his nose and grit his teeth.

The prince had to come to this pigsty to preach. After their trip to India he was afire with the wisdom of Buddha and it had to be Jerusalem, their homeland, that prompted it, but what a pit this was compared to the palaces of Persia.

He knew the escape would work and, God-willing, they'd be back in their palaces by the next full moon. He turned and looked toward the east.

Jesus looked once more at his dear wife, Mary Magdalene, she mouthed out, 'I love you'. She was his angel and the only reason he endured any of it. She was standing with the other women. He could not take his eyes off her, his beautiful light-haired love. Eyes pure and blue as the first morning of the world.

And there was disciple John, a raving, red-haired fat man in muddy white robes. He was the only one of them who had made it to his crucifixion, only because he was completely daft.

The Lord felt sad that none of the others, not even his brother James, had come to see what they believed was his last day on Earth. Friends he'd shared everything with for years were off sniveling in the hills, the cowards.

But here was disciple John, God bless him.

He looked down at the raving fat man with tangled red hair, his dirty robe draping in the dust. Red-bearded John dropped to his knees babbling, "MASTER! I hath forsaken thee, please forgive me!"

'Forsaken? No John, all but you have forsaken me, the rest have fled like chickens.'

Jesus nodded down at him and then glanced away, 'crazy as a goose, God help me if John writes anything about me. Scripture according to John would be a total disaster.'

The drug made him drowsy but his huge arms still ached. How long must I hang here? The ropes burned his arms, scratching like dull knives across his white flesh.

Chapter 3

The bandits who were crucified with him also taunted him.
Mathew 27:44

He looked to his right and to his left at the poor bedraggled souls crucified beside him.

They had robbed the temple of a few shekels to buy bread, an unforgivable sin to Caiphus, the head Sanhedrin Priest, for that they were crucified.

They had been dead now for an hour and hung like limp rags on their crosses. Before they died they had seen the Romans tying his arms instead of nailing them, pouring fake blood on his hands and feet, and giving him wine to drink.

After watching Jesus and his easy treatment, they were grabbed up and nailed screaming to the crossbeams. He had to watch them nailed upon their crosses and then raised straight up their posts jammed into the ground beside him. Their screams had been unbearable, their heads, black hair and beards, whipping back and forth, cursing heaven and hell.

Magdalene and Mary the others had to leave the ghastly spectacle.

Before they died the robbers noticed Jesus was merely tied on the cross and in their pain had cursed him, spitting out, "Why are you not nailed and bleeding like us—You Jew Swine! False king! Rotten piece of pig shit!" "And to hell with all you Roman Bastards!"

The Romans did not suffer their ravings very long. After a few minutes of their vile curses, they broke their legs with large iron mallets, and both quickly slumped down with gurgling sounds frothing from their mouth, they were dead in minutes.

Breaking the legs caused the body to fall onto the lungs causing quick suffocation. He had paid the Romans dearly, especially the head centurion,

Flavius, to skip this part of the ordeal, actually to skip the entire crucifixion altogether.

His whole crucifixion was a hoax, thank God, and Jesus prayed to fall asleep.

He stared at the robbers' on either side hanging there. They had died an hour before and he could still hear their screams.

The crows were starting to peck at their eyes. He turned his head away.

A fly landed on Jesus' nose and it itched to madness, he shook his head, trying to shake off the rest of the unbearable cloud of flies buzzing around his eyes and nose, crawling in his dark beard. They were all over the goat's blood on his feet and hands, nibbling like tiny fishes.

He looked around at Golgotha. He saw mounds of bleached human skulls and bones, piles of them all around the floor of the small gorge, some bone piles were high as a man. Romans had crucified people here for years.

Beggars picked through the recently departed bodies searching for clothes, necklaces, anything that might fetch them a Shekel for bread. The poor souls, he felt for all of them, the dead and the living.

Human bones were strewn everywhere. Jesus closed his eyes. The stench was like rotting animals mixed with vomit.

He groaned loudly, "Why have you not shaded me?" He looked down and saw disciple John, scratching his words on papyrus. "Why have you forsaken me? Is that what you said, Master?" Jesus rolled his eyes, "No, you fool, I said, "Why have you not shaded me!"

God knows what drivel he was writing. John scribbled and then raised his hands to Heaven gesturing wildly.

Jesus looked away and let his glance fall down to the red-robed guards standing around the bottom of his cross, with their old pot helmets and their spears pointing outward toward the crowd. The soldiers had played their parts well, bribe money well-spent.

He peered down his broad, sweating hairy chest. The sun was flexing its blazing muscles.

He grew sleepy. A numbness like a river of ice flowed through his body. The pain in his legs was gone. His arms light as feather wings.

People were blurry shapes drifting away in a fog.

13

Disciple John was writhing around, his arms waving to high heaven.

The Roman guards stared at the bearded, red-haired madman in his muddy robe jumping around. They jabbed their spears fending him off and then looked up their nervous eyes questioning Jesus, he calmed them slurring, "Forgive him, for he knows not what he does."

John was waving his reed pen around, writing in air.

"I'm getting all your words, Master- what did you say? Forgive them, for they know not what?"

Jesus rolled his eyes, and mumbled, "O shut up!"

His body was feeling like a sack full of iron, the drug was finally working, thank God. His arms and legs slumped down. The Romans glanced up at him and to assure them they could now see Demetrius to collect their money he mumbled, "It is done,"

And his head slowly dropped.

Chapter 4

**You are looking for Jesus of Nazareth who was crucified?
He is not here in the place they had laid him.
—Mark 16:6**

Jesus opened his eyes in darkness, the dank smell of wet dirt filled his nose. His throat was dry as hot sand.

The black tomb felt ice cold to his bare skin and his head felt like it was crammed full of sheep's wool.

A hand lifted his chin and he tasted cool, glorious water.

"Jesus, wake up! It's Demetrius, we have to get out of this cave RIGHT NOW, the Jewish police will be back any moment. Wake up, my friend, you're still drugged."

"Where am I?" he mumbled sitting up on the wooden cot.

He raked his long fingers through his wet, straggly hair. He shook the sleep from his eyes and looked up blearingly at the dark form hovering over him, "Demetrius!" He reached and hugged him then looked around seeing milky moonlight outside the cave.

"How long have I been here?"

"Two nights. Please Issa! we have to get out of here!" the poet was gazing outside nervously.

Jesus looked up with a broad smile,

"Thank you, my friend."

"Issa, we must go."

Jesus wobbled to his feet still wearing his white burial shroud. Demetrius threw a dark robe over his shoulder, "Get out of that linen and put this on."

He wrapped the brown-hooded robe around him and they hurried out of the cave. Passing into the moonlight he gazed up at the night sky sprinkled with stars.

The sleeping potion was still slowing him down. They hurried across a wide depression in stone and up into an olive grove. Jesus turned to his friend, "You have not called me Issa since we were in Babylon"

"You have so many names. Issa reminds me of us in India."

"But here you are not my servant, call me Jesus".

"Alright, but I am always your servant, my friend."

"And I, yours." they smiled at each other like brothers.

They walked barefoot through the dark grove, Jesus felt the rocks jab his bare feet as he stumbled along behind the long-robed Demetrius. He had been laid to rest without sandals. They both wore dark brown robes to hide them in the night. He blinked and looked up at the moon, it was spreading silvery light across the ground illuminating the olive trees around them turning the tops chalky white. Demetrius walked ahead of him, his short-sword drawn, searching the night. Jesus stumbled along behind him. Wool filled his head.

Suddenly a stench like an old cattle-yard hit Jesus' nose. The smell of vomit mixed with dead rats.

"Demetrius, what is that smell?"

"Golgotha." and he motioned with his short sword to their right. A hundred paces to the right was The Place of Death.

The thin, pale moon shined on piles of skulls, they looked like prickly white hills in the shadowy light. The yellow slice of moon hung low behind this grim graveyard, in the darkness Jesus could see the outline of his own cross and the two other crosses beside. The crucified robbers were only shreds hanging off the beams.

Golgotha at night felt heavy and haunted. The cooing wind carried along a million silent voices cursing heaven, cursing hell, cursing everything.

Jesus stopped a moment and said a prayer.

They both held their nose and hurried on through the groves.

Chapter 5

"Stop right there!"

Right in front of them four soldiers stepped from behind an olive tree.

They wore short, white tunics and round, bronze pot helmets, their swords were drawn and pointed at the two of them.

Outlined in the moonlight their faces were ugly and scowling, typical police.

A fat one who appeared like the leader barked out, "Who are you?! What are you doing here?!"

Four swords were pointing at them.

Demetrius stepped forward bold as a bull and bowed low in a long dramatic bow. He straightened up clutching his robe at his chest and boomed out play-acting, "Gentlemen, good evening, it is I, Demetrius, the famous poet of Babylonia and this...my fine gentlemen, is the great and famous Jesus of Nazareth, King of the Jews, King Jezep of Persia, we are out for a stroll in the moonlight."

He stood aside gesturing grandly to Jesus standing very still in his hooded robe. The poet gave a grand bow, heart pounding, praying inside.

The silence between drew out taut as a bowstring.

They burst out laughing, sliding their short swords back into their sheaths. Relief.

The head Jewish policeman, the pot-bellied one in a gray uniform, turned to the others, waving with his sword, "Look, men, it is the King of the Jews and his jester or more likely two drunk and crazy shepherds." then his eyes got thin sizing them up, " but you look a bit too old for shepherd boys?"

"Yes sir, you have us there, we are old shepherds—no one but sheep will have us."

Louder laughs.

"But alas our sheep wandered away, they didn't appreciate our overtures of love." More belly laughs. And when they died down the fat leader gripped the top of his sword sheath and slid his short sword back into it, his blubbery mouth spoke, "We can't be too careful tonight, they say the followers of that radical rabbi, Jesus might try to steal his body to make it look like some divine damn thing or another. They are saying he will rise from the dead in three days and stealing his body might start up the legend, that is their big plan we have heard."

"Imagine that." smiled Demetrius gazing incredulously back at his friend.

"What? Doesn't your friend speak?" said the leader.

"Say something to the fine policemen, my friend, the King of the Jews must have something to say."

Jesus bowed his head and looked right at them and in his deepest, quietest voice tried to end this charade, "Everything is fine, boys, we bid you goodnight then."

Jesus had the cloak over his head and his face was hidden but his smile was wide and shined in the dark. His smile was contagious, they smiled back at him and hearing such a commanding voice all three gave a short bow of their head to Jesus. The large leader spoke, "Alright shepherds, we hope you find your sheep, Shalom. Come along men."

"Shalom." The two said together.

The four policemen passed by them and marched back toward the tomb. They knew the soldiers' quick pace would get them to the open tomb very soon and the ruse would be up, so they started running into the darkness, their dusty robes flapping behind like ravens' wings.

Chapter 6

"How much further, Demetrius?" Jesus gasped.

"Over that hill in front of us."

They finally huffed up the hill, Jesus looked down and there it was glowing in the valley below—a white tent the size of a large house. The tent of John of Arimathea, the man who'd arranged his entire escape, a saint to Jesus.

The tent was a cloth mansion glowing from within.

The tent had two peaks both rising fifteen feet high, under the stars they shined like two snowy mountains.

In the lantern light of the tents shadows of the people shifted around like ghosts.

As they walked down the hill he heard an outburst inside, hurt words were going back and forth.

The prince heard the sweet voice of Mary, his dear wife, and his heart leaped like a morning fountain. He heard her shouting and then sobbing, "I pray Demetrius got there in time but what if he didn't, the police are everywhere, they will kill him if they find him walking around, God protect him."

Jesus shuffled down to the brightly lit tent and shouted, "Mary, my love, I'm here!"

"Praise God!" the shadows ran to the opening of the tent and there she was, his beautiful Mary. Her shining smile, her blond hair shimmering in the moonlight, her arms lifting, running toward him. They met hugging warmly as all the clouds of Heaven and they kissed like they had invented kissing. They could not stop. The cold breeze blew their clothes and hair and still the kiss went on.

The others emerged from the tent and surrounded Jesus and Mary, all their arms enfolding around them, "Praise God! It is you, Jesus! Praise God in Heaven!"

"And here is Demetrius!" and arms surrounded him too.

Jesus finally pulled away from his love and under the sparkling stars hugged everyone, then his mother stepped from the tent. He caught his breath, "Mother."

Jesus left everyone and walked to her, tears streamed down their faces, they hugged deeply. She looked up at him, her blue eyes filled with brimming tears of joy, "Thank God you are alive, my son." He smiled, "Yes, mother, thank God."

With his arm around his mother he turned to the regal bearded man standing near, "Joseph, great friend, a thousand thanks for saving my life!" The prince reached to hug him and also his dark African servant, Gideus.

His wife Mary walked up and put her arms around his waist, they all walked into the tent and everyone went inside and sat down on deep oriental rugs. Wine was poured from the pitcher, leaven bread broken and passed around, cheese, grapes and olives were in bowls around them. The prince looked around at everyone, smiling at each one.

There sat Joseph of Arimathea, his old Jewish friend. His white hair and beard were full and his nose like a parrot's beak, his eyes twinkled young as a child's. Joseph had built the burial cave and arranged the escape. He offered Jesus a goblet of wine, "Come my friend, let us drink to your new life!"

Jesus reached for the silver cup and raised it high, "Thank you, Joseph and God Bless you all!

He started to bring the goblet to his mouth but stopped and raised it again.

"Here's to going home to beloved Babylon! May our next adventure be as great as this one !" His rugged smile was comical and charming as ever.

Mary and Demetrius sitting on the floor lowered their cups and glowered at him, Mary looked at the poet and then back to Jesus, scolding, " My love, there will be no more adventures, this one was quite enough."

The eyes of the great prince sparkled and he laughed, "You never know, my dear, you never know." and then he drank down the whole wine cup and set it on the small table.

"This wine is better than that hot Roman swill!"

"But praise God you drank it", laughed the poet, "it knocked you out and saved your life!"

And they all laughed.

One by one they fell asleep. Jesus and Mary Magdalene curled up on thick rugs entwined in each other's arms.

The next morning the prince and Mary, were gone early. They had slipped away unnoticed. The two were gone all day and returned that night. When Joseph asked him where he had been, with a mischievous smile Jesus answered, "We had to say goodbye to some old friends and were they ever surprised to see me."

After one more night of wine and stories, Jesus and his wife Mary, and his mother and the poet woke to a beautiful dawn. They hugged John of Arimathea, and his servant, Gideus and climbed into an old horse-drawn cart.

They clicked 'giddy-up' to the two horses and rolled east toward Persia and the gardens of Babylon.

BABYLON
Chapter 7

Young men shall see visions and old men shall dream dreams.
—Acts 2:17

Jesus closed his eyes, 25 years had flown by like an owl at sunset.

He lay back scratching his short silver beard.

He was Prince Jezep now and he lay back on his golden sheets in Babylon gazing at the high ceiling.

He lay there as he did every morning pondering his life, waiting for nothing.

His thoughts turned to his dwindling family. He thought of how his real father, regal Heraclion had walked the halls of his Babylonian palace giving orders, hugging him, guiding him in princely ways, and then he thought of the wonderful years with his sweet mother, Mary.

They were both in heaven now, the two had been so in love. Heraclion had been his real father. She married him after his stepfather, Joseph had died in Nazareth—so many years ago. Thumbing through history.

Reclining on his shining royal bed, Prince Jezep thought back on the easy living these many years with his wife, Mary Magdalene and his poet friend, Demetrius, who was never far off, roaming the desert in his chariot.

The poet also had been dubbed a prince by old Heraclion. After returning from their long-ago journey to India Heraclion had called Demetrius his 'other son'.

And he lived as fine as himself and Mary.

Prince Jezep smiled and sipped wine from a goblet thinking of the wonderful nights filled with temple dancers swirling their hips and clinking finger bells before them, sweet years of laying on couches talking of love and lions, of philosophy and a girl's sweet smile. He and Demetrius had poured the years of their lives into goblets and drunk them down with a laugh.

He had watched swaying gardens grow up green and lush around him.

He'd walked each day with his sweet wife, Mary, who he loved with all his heart.

Walking in gardens holding her hand, kissing her in the moonlight on top of castle towers, listening to her melodious voice, stroking her long, blond-white hair, she had filled his life with the finest love a man could ever dream of.

He had felt the joy of fatherhood.

So many years earlier Mary gave birth to Emmanuel, his son and two years later, Sarah, their lovely daughter. She was dark-haired and beautiful to behold.

Emmanuel, their son had grown to a young prince, the image of Apollo. Their daughter was a proud, dark-haired princess with all the beauty of her mother, Mary Magdalene, and the sweetness and light of her grandmother, Virgin Mary.

Voluptuous and pure was Sarah. Her Greek name was Katrina, that was her playful name.

Noble Emmanuel, now twenty-five, had ridden out of the royal gates in an ivory chariot seeking his own fate.

Sweet Sarah-Katrina married a bald merchant and sailed west settling in southern Gaul. She was a royal princess living humbly somewhere in a distant village.

His son was seeking his fortune in Alexandria, Egypt. Like his father, Emmanuel was another Alexander the Great driven to greatness.

For indeed Alexander was in their blood-the legend king was their great, great, 7th great grandfather going back three hundred years.

Prince Jezep, had blazed across Asia in his youth like the great Alexander but unlike the God King who had conquered people with sword and died young—Jezep always conquered with love and wisdom and had lived on, sometimes he thought for too long.

He took another long drink of wine and thought of Demetrius, his best friend who had never married, he always said he loved the dancing girls too much, "Besides," he would say, "I'm married to them all!"

"Wine and poetry are MY children" he always said with a laugh and his poems would carry on his name. The prince smiled thinking of his best friend.

Chariots archery and swordplay filled the poet's days. Love, wine and poetry filled his nights. At times he envied his friend who lived for pleasure and did not feel the distant pull of fame. He envied his soul, always so relaxed and free.

Now as an older ruling prince, Jesus of Nazareth, now Prince Jezep, son of the former king Heraclion could have anything in the world. His power and wealth were boundless. And this power was a heavy rock around his neck.

Having everything filled him with nothingness.

On this golden morning sprawled across his Persian bed the emptiness felt especially heavy on his chest. The sunny days were the worst, a beautiful trap mocks you.

His purple robe lay open showing his broad chest of silvery hair, a necklace of gold coins lay across the curling hairs of his chest, he gazed up at the ceiling and sighed, "I'm the great Prince, and now what? Indolence, numbness, death?" His stomach was scrunched-up papyrus.

"There has to be more!" He roared and it echoed through the hall.

He reached across to the table beside his bed and slipped his fingers around the silver goblet of cold, red wine and gulped it all down in one swallow.

He drank and still the hole in his chest was never filled.

His stomach trembled just a little as he looked out at the sun-drenched room. There were floor-to-ceiling windows and the morning light sliced into the room, the curtains of yellow silk breathed softly in and out.

He took the pitcher of wine and filled his goblet once more. Red wine spilled across his trembling hand. Drunk by noon, he felt saddened.

Chapter 8

Entreat the Lord, that he may take away the frogs from me.
—Exodus 8:8

His thoughts went to Mary, his wife, his sweet Cleopatra.

He thought of her royal barge today drifting down the Euphrates River, she was floating down the calm Persian waters gliding by date palms and bull rushes unchanged since the Garden of Eden.

He thought of her reclining on her royal cushions on her hundred-foot barge, being cooled with peacock fans in the hands of tall, black Nubians. She would always eat red grapes and every other grape she would toss to the muscled rowers pulling the floating palace down the river.

He smiled thinking of Mary, his feisty one, how they had met in the street long ago in Nazareth, the day she was being stoned by the townsmen. He had saved her life with a challenge. Once a street woman, now she was royalty. He remembered a poem by his friend,

> One day rich, the next day poor,
> This fickle life, nothing's sure.
> One day poor, next day riches
> God looks down and laughs in stitches.

'Ahh my dearest Magdalene' he thought, 'her quiet blue eyes and thin beautiful face, her light waterfall hair splashing onto her perfect shoulders, light bronze from the Persian sun. Her red rouged lips, full, made for deep kisses, and her warm tongue.

Her perfect breasts, two round fruit soft as goose down. 'God I love her sweet breasts, her kisses' warm as a pillows. How I love her.'

The wine let him dream.

25

He drifted back to their wedding day, her stepping shyly from the boat on Galilee and walking across the sand to him in her flowing white dress. Their full, deep kiss on the sand, he could still taste her luscious open mouth.

Prince Jezep, sat back against the carved, cedar headboard and set down the goblet on the bedside table. He closed his eyes.

"What next?"

He stood up, straightened his robe and walked over to a full-length mirror at the end of the room.

He was broader than the mirror, his arms were still huge and strong, but he felt his age, he saw the lines in his cheeks, the black and silver beard, 'Where is that innocent face now?' he thought.

"Admiring ourselves are we?"

He turned and there at the door stood Demetrius.

He was smiling like the morning sun, older now but still an Apollo. His white tunic flung over his shoulder with the warrior skirt of a Persian prince.

"Looking at this old body? Yes." said the prince, "Admiring? No. How are you my friend? Great to see you!"

They walked toward each other and hugged then pulled back, the poet spoke out, "Issa, how old you look this morning!"

"Yes, I'm feeling my age, thank you." noticing that Demetrius, almost the same age had long black hair and looked twenty-eight years old. Thin and healthy, shoulders of an athlete, 'damn that Demetrius, looking so young.'

"How are the verses today, lord poet?"

"Coming along. Last night I wrote one about you taming a lion." Demetrius flopped down in a cedar chair and stretched out his long legs, reaching with his arms getting comfortable.

"Lion you say?" mused the prince as he walked over to join his friend.

Jesus sat on the edge of his bed facing his friend who was relaxing on the royal chair. Demetrius flicked his tunic over his shoulder and reached for the pitcher of wine pouring himself a full goblet of the red.

"So, great prince, you asked for me and I rushed here from archery, what is on your O so divine mind?"

Jesus took a sip and set his goblet down.

"What year is it, Demetrius?"

"By our Persian calendar or the Roman's?"

"I mean how old am I?"

"Well, unless you skipped a year or two you are a year older than me and since I am 56 that you would make you 57, and by the look of that silver in your hair perhaps you *did* skip ahead a few years."

"Quiet, you." Jesus smiled.

A sudden wind blew the long, silk curtains out like a billowy dress into the room and the bright sun rippled its fingers across the white and gold marble floor.

"Remember India? Jerusalem? Our days of glory?"

"Nostalgic we are, wine does that to you and yes, I remember."

Demetrius with a smirk, "But I also remember we were 20 and not almost 60."

He sat back and looked to the ceiling. Jesus stared at him with a musing smile then raised his full goblet to his friend and toasted too loud to sound sincere, "To new adventure, may it come to us soon."

"You've been drinking this morning I see, Adventure is it?"

Demetrius smiled at his friend remembering years crossing deserts, chasing lions and those years sloshing along the muddy roads of the Holy Land and that shaky escape from the cross, Demetrius clinked his goblet with the prince.

"Very well, to adventure, but be careful of what you wish for, my friend, it might show up to bite you on the rear."

"I hope it does."

Just then the desert wind blew the curtains high billowing into the room.

Chapter 9

"Now started the most terrible and destructive fire which Rome had ever experienced."
—Historian Tacitus, eyewitness to the Great Fire of Rome.

Orange flames licked the face of the city.

Blazing teeth of fire chomped away at people by the hundreds. Flames roared higher and mad shrieks mingled with the sound of crackling flames.

Rome was burning.

White buildings fell crashing down in smoke and flying sparks.

Flickering cinders fluttered high into heaven like a million black moths and for miles around dark smoke blocked out the noonday sun.

For seven long days the fire raged, and for days the sun was an orange disk hiding behind dark smoke.

By day, the hot orange and yellow teeth of flames raged madly on. The blazing summer sweated even hotter as the fire ate up the city from within.

The fire matched the sunshine in brightness and its ferocity mocked the sun itself making it seem pale by comparison.

By night, it was a three mile-wide bonfire one hundred feet high lighting up the Seven Hills, turning the darkness into daylight. The City of Rome became a gigantic flaming lighthouse seen a hundred miles away.

First it burned the town shops, its flames eating up wood and thatch-roofed houses, devouring them, crackling through wood and human bodies like a burning fuse racing toward a bomb.

Then it devoured mansions and marble temples, stone so hot it exploded like Greek Fire, no structures could resist it, they crumpled over like dying men.

People caught fire and became running torches. And when they fell screaming in flame they were burned black in their tracks. Those not burned were crushed by falling buildings.

First the flames swelled and burned through the city then the fiery arms reached into the hills burning trees for miles around, vineyards and villas were eaten up by the crackling crimson beast, its hunger never filled.

Shrieking women ran everywhere, pulling their hair and yelling themselves hoarse. Slaves and citizens, nobles and commoners ran panicking into each other, falling down to be eaten alive by a mouth of painful fire.

At night shadows of fleeing people flashed by on the walls. By day charred black bodies were left strewn around the ground and on marble steps stuck forever in frantic, contorted positions.

Black pieces of wood were sticking up everywhere releasing white smoke.

Day after day flames sprang up outflanking people, toying with them with terrible yellow paws. When people tried to escape to another quarter of the city, the fire followed and found them, eating them alive screaming at heaven.

It went on unbearably and the endless fires grew bolder by the hour.

Chapter 10

Nero fiddled while Rome burned.
—Historian Tacitus

On the third night of the blaze, amid leaping flames, the emperor Nero appeared on an actor's stage.

He was grinning down at the terrified people below, a few slowed to look up at this strange apparition, then a crowd formed, smudged faces looking up in amazement.

The short, chubby emperor was dressed in a long white robe perfectly clean and trimmed with gold ribbon. His balding head was encircled by a gold headband around his forehead. His face was round like a baby's and his devilish gray eyes sneered down at the gathering crowd, his mouth had a cocky grimace. Against his shoulder he held a small harp and amid the fire he began to sing, sounding like a high-pitched cat, *"Rome like Troy was filled with joy"*, his voice was shrill and scratchy.

He ran a plectrum across the strings, they rang out discordantly as he sang, *"And Troy like Rome burned like a toy"* People looked up in total disbelief. Amid the chaos, they saw their emperor—the one charged to help his people—was singing like a silly girl.

Like a sick cherub, Nero grinned, giggling as he sang, *"And fools rush around and are burned on the ground in Rome in Troy, o joy o joy"*. He was cackling and strumming mad as a Magpie.

When people in the crowd finally grasped what he was doing, some spat at him and threw handfuls of blackened earth up at him. He was atop the Palantine Stage but not high enough to escape rocks and chunks of marble hurled at him. Showers of rocks and dirt and small burnt boards were thrown and the crowd began shouting him down, he backed up to dodge the rocks and insults but kept singing from the back of the stage and as he sang they cursed him to high heaven—

"Damn you, son of Hades!" "Crazy king!" "Sick Nero!" "You sing while we burn, curse your soul forever!"

Small rocks whapped into his robe but uncaring he fell back laughing and singing his crazy song. *"Rome and Troy, joys,o joys, cook the girls and save the boys"* over and over he mocked crazily as he sang in drunken jibberish.

He strummed the harp and laughed madly, the fire burned all around the stage as the people kept cursing him but were finally pushed back by thugs hired by Nero. Official soldiers were nowhere to be seen, only hired unshaven ruffians who followed the emperor's every order.

As he ran from the stage a Greek slave stepped out, shook his fist and shouted, "You dog of an emperor, you started this fire to build your own cursed temple to yourself!"

Nero reappeared suddenly, wiped his brow and shouted an order to a gaggle of raggedly-dressed men with spears and clubs, "Kill that man!"

The slave was struck down by a bearded thug slamming the blunt end of his spear against the slave's head and when he fell to the cobbled street, the man turned the spear around and with the iron point stuck him through his back. He screamed as the thug twisted it around and then jerked it up out of his body. Blood oozed everywhere.

The man lay still on the white stones, his mouth open and silent, forever.

People kept running in all directions to escape the thugs and trying to escape the flames that were devouring the greatest city on Earth.

On the seventh day half the city lay black and smoking but the fire was mostly out.

The Seven Hills surrounding the city were blackened and all was gray ash to the horizon. Vineyards were gone, forests gone, all was just smoking stumps.

Streams had dried up leaving only cracked mud.

Charred bodies were thrown onto carts and rolled away. Sobs and lamentations pierced the air of the Eternal City.

Smoking ruins were all that remained of a large part of Rome.

The fire had been started by the cursed followers of Christ, that was what the emperor put forth.

Chapter 11

Mathew was a large, burly man who always wore dark-brown sack cloth to show his humbleness and devotion to Christ.

He had been a disciple of Christ.

Mathew had known Jesus and walked with him for three years before the lord was crucified. He had miraculously seen the savior 3 days after he died, he believed in him with all his heart.

Mathew was beardless and though past 60 had a young, overly-white, glowing face. He had a full, wild head of light-brown hair and burning brown eyes.

Jesus had named him leader of the disciples and now years later, Mathew was still a leader hiding in abandoned buildings leading his shabby flock.

He had been faithful to the savior now for more than 25 years and cared with all his heart about his fellow Christians, now hiding in a burnt-out warehouse in central Rome, He turned to them with the worried brow of a father, "Is everyone alright? Anyone burned?""

The crowd of ten robed men and five women and a few children nodded, "Yes, we are fine."

"fine," answered another, "alright".

The men and women were sitting down before Mathew, huddling in the blackened building. He was the chosen leader of the group of new Christians who met under the streets. Their meeting places were underground called catacombs. Their symbol was a fish, its head drawn to point toward secret meetings.

Smoke from the horrid fire still clouded the air of the city.

Everywhere Roman soldiers peered into the darkness of buildings poking their spears here and there, searching for any suspicious movement. Mathew's group of Christians huddled low speaking in whispers.

He spoke quietly,

"God sent this wrath to the Romans, his kingdom is coming soon."

All nodded.

A bearded one near him spoke, "That is what we believe but the emperor does not share our views, he blames us for the fire."

Each person looked at each other fearfully. He continued, "They know we have long preached that Rome would be destroyed by our God, now they think our God really has burned the city to the ground."

A women in dark robes screeched from the back,

"Nero set that fire! We all know that, he blames us for his evil work."

Heads nodded and men jumped to their feet in agreement. Mathew spoke, "Calm yourselves, my friends, we have no real proof that Nero blames us."

"Nay, there is proof."

A cold voice spoke from the back of the room.

A thin old man stepped from the shadows in the back. He had chalky skin, gaunt with a thin wispy beard flowing down the front of his black robes. His eyes were stern as death. He pulled a piece of papyrus from out of the front of his robe and read it slowly, *"It has been revealed to your Divine Emperor—Nero, that the disruptive sect known as Christians started the fire of Rome, they are spreading the word that their god, Christus, did this to punish Romans. It is therefore decreed that all Christians are enemies of the empire and will be executed for the burning of our beloved city.*

The mysterious man, finished reading, rolled the papyrus back up and stood facing the small crowd. His thin face full of dark clouds, he spoke again in a low rasping voice, "This notice is posted all over the city. They are searching for us even now.'

Dread pulled like a lead weight on every heart. They all looked to Mathew.

A woman's voice shouted out, "Mathew, what shall we do?! We are all going to die!"

Mathew spoke calmly,

"Fear not, my friends, do not lose faith, Christ will return to save us."

They all huddled together and mumbled, "Amen."

They gazed out the open door that had been burnt off along with the shutters of the windows, through the dark, burnt building they could see into the bright morning street.

Suddenly a chill raced through each of them, in horror they saw Roman soldiers in full silver armor and short, red crested helmets rushing toward their building. The soldiers were running straight toward them, spears lowered for the kill.

Chapter 12

Demetrius, downed his goblet and set it on the marble table.

"So Issa, you would leave sweet Babylonia for another cursed adventure?"

Jesus downed his wine and set his silver goblet down on the table, "Yes I would! There are endless wrongs out there and my soul is aching for a quest. What of Rome, what is going on there these days?"

Demetrius stretched out in his chair, "Who knows, Rome is so far away."

"Is Nero still the emperor?"

"Yes, and I have heard he is a raving tyrant. I'm getting hungry. Let's go find some food."

The prince let the adventure talk drop for the moment.

"Food, good idea, sire poet."

They both stood up straightening their robes. The poet humored him, "Let's talk of your great adventure while we feast."

They started laughing at nothing at all, slapping each other on the back, walking out the door in the direction of the garden.

As they entered the lush garden they saw the servants had done their job well.

The long, white marble table before them was filled with yellow and orange cheeses, large bunches of red grapes and dark green melons deliciously cut open. There were fat breads, frosted cakes and a black, roast pig with a peach stuck in its mouth.

The fragrances of the table filled their noses and they looked at each other smiling like boys.

The food was on silver platters on the marble table and there were two large pitchers of wine and silver, bejeweled goblets placed here and there on the table.

Standing nearby, nearly hidden in the trees were two tall slaves one black and one white, both waiting to serve. They looked at the two princes walking up and all smiled at each other. They were friends, slaves in name only, they were paid well and treated generously. Prince Jezep acted a world away from the other lords of Babylonia, who treated slaves like slaves.

The marble feasting table rested in the center of a patch of bright green lawn looking like a neatly trimmed, oval carpet. Surrounding the emerald grass, white birch trees were arching over it with light fluttering branches. The trees hung down above the table like a tent of leaves. Thicker trees and bushes spread out from behind the light birches and filled the courtyard clear to the surrounding walls.

From behind the table birds flitted everywhere chirping loudly. Large rocks had been placed around and little stone benches were nestled here and there in the small forest courtyard. The forest was surrounded and cupped by high walls not far away. Skies were always pale blue.

Thirty feet behind the head seat at the table, through the trees were rocks with a small, gurgling waterfall ten feet high pouring into a pool filled with golden fishes, a stream flowed from the pond under green bushes, winding through moss-covered banks where the stream split flowing around behind the large table in a stream encircling the oval lawn and the feasting table like a two-foot wide moat, the stream flowed on off to nowhere.

A hundred colorful birds trilled in the trees and bright blue, regal peacocks glided through the courtyard forest around the lawn and table. When the two princes appeared the peacocks raised their bright blue heads and spread their enormous fans wide. They continued strutting away. Two gazelle fawns grazed in the miniature forest and courtyard. A young, tame lion sat in a far corner licking the back of his paw.

Jesus gazed at the table, and slapped his friend on the shoulder, smiling away, "Is this not paradise?"

Demetrius smiled, "Yes, my friend this is Heaven, let's eat."

Chapter 13

They hopped the garden stream, stepped around the long table and sat down, Jezep at the head of the table, his friend at the seat to his right. The prince brushed a low-hanging branch away saying, "Mary will be here soon and we will all feast together, but first we drink."

They both reached for their goblets already filled with fine wine.

They sipped and shook their heads and smiled at each other. They gazed at the feast before them and smiled even wider.

"Where shall we start, O great Prince?"

"First the Grace."

"Of course."

"May God in Heaven bless this table and all who sit around it."

"Amen" came a women's voice and Jesus looked up stunned as always to see her. Each time he saw her felt like the first time.

It was his wife, Mary Magdalene shining like a goddess in a light blue silk gown.

Both men stood up, "Hello, my love." said Jesus.

"Hello, Mary," said Demetrius.

"Hello, hello, my princes, please sit down,"

Jesus stood still at her stunning beauty. Long shining white blond hair flowing around her shoulders, bright, sparkling blue eyes, and wide, perfect deep-red lips.

She wore a blue, see-through silk dress. Demetrius smiled wide watching her walk toward them, Jesus kissed her briefly as she gracefully glided down into her chair to his left.

"And how are my two favorite men today?" Mary cooed.

"Fine, fine, and how was your row down the river?" asked the prince.

"Wonderous, please pass the grapes, my love, I saw a Hippopotamus, it opened its mouth wide and bellowed at me as we rowed by."

"Grand!" Jesus looked at his friend then back at Mary, "tell us more."

"And we saw at least twenty lions drinking at the river, It was amazing twenty!"

"Lions you say…" he grew quiet, remembering lions for years, running through the broad plains of his mind

"So, Mary, tell us more of your day, tell us of the lions…"

She went on and Jesus knew why he loved her. Her red lips, luscious and full almost singing the words, musically telling a story about a mother lion licking her cub and then nudging it out into the river. 'So touching' thought Jesus noticing her breasts through the light blue silk, how they were like sweet cantaloupes, her every movement was all that was feminine, and she had a strength that matched almost any man alive.

"My dearest, what is wrong, you haven't eaten a thing since I sat down?" she reached and held his large rough hand in her soft white fingers.

"You are my goddess and your beauty fills me." said the kingly one.

She put down her chalice and leaned over and kissed him long on the lips.

She then turned to Demetrius across the table, " So Poet, how about a poem."

"With pleasure, my dear, he stood up beside the table under the trees, his voice flowed soft and easy as ripples on a stream—
"When the wine in the sunset,
is a ruby in your eye, when the voice of an evening
makes us cry, when the laughing in our heart
makes us fly
in that eternal moment,
we'll live forever
you and I."

Jesus and Mary both clapped.

"Great! Good one!, more! please—another!"

He smiled over them and with a hand gripping his shoulder tunic, he began again—

"A rose is not a rose
until you smell it, A tale is not a tale
until you tell it, A song is not a song
until you sing it
and love is not here
until we bring it."

Jesus and Mary stood up from the table clapping.

Chapter 14

**The Lord is my helper and I will not fear
what man shall do unto me.
—Hebrews 13:3**

All of Rome smelled like wet, burnt ash.

One third of the magnificent city was blackened earth and charred wood. The emperor's orders were to arrest every Christian in the city and drag them to jail for execution.

A large Roman Centurion gazed into the darkness of the burnt building where Mathew and his friends were cowering, they saw his glowering eyes, he shouted—

"Are you Christians?!" he yelled in Aramaic, the language of Christians. Silence. He shouted once more, ARE YOU CHRISTIANS?! Next time my spear will do my talking!"

Mathew climbed out of the burnt building and stood in front of the huge guard, He answered boldly, "Yes, we follow Jesus Christ."

The Centurion grabbed him by the arm and gave curt, loud orders to the other soldiers, " I have him, go in and grab the others, they are all Christians!"

The other Romans, charged through the open door space into the dark room grabbing up the crying women and the squirming men who were all squirming and pulling away, hanging onto doorways calling on Jesus to save them.

The Romans pulled out all of them from the building, threw them to the ground and tied ropes around their ankles, to tie them in a long string, beating them on their backs and buttocks with their spears. They screamed in pain and the women wept and cowered on the ground.

"Please, do not hurt us! Please, we beg of you!"

"Shut up you bitch hounds! Lucky we don't have our way with you right here in the street, perhaps we will!"

The Centurion leader knew their language and yelled, "Get on your feet you Christians dogs, the lions are hungry!"

The Roman soldiers laughed, their faces half-hidden behind their helmet guards.

Mathew and the others' ankles tied on a long rope were led through the cobblestone streets toward the jails of the coliseum.

Big burly Mathew was in the lead and suddenly fell to his knees, clasping his hands in prayer to the skies, "Please, Lord Jesus, our messiah and savior, come save us we beg you, come save us all."

A Roman lifted up his brown leather boot and kicked the large man in the side of the head and he rolled over in the dust.

"To hell with your Jesus! You'll meet him soon enough after the lions!"

With the help of two other soldiers he dragged Mathew to his feet and kicked him in the groin, "Move, along, you Christian swine!"

The others followed in line tied together at the ankle by thick hemp ropes.

Romans poked them with their spears and white-robed Roman citizens standing on temple steps and in buildings, jeered and spat at the Christians shuffling along.

A haggard, older Christian woman, with thin gray hair, tears streaming down her face looked to the sky, raised up her wrinkled arms and cried out, "Save us my Lord, save us!"

As she spoke a large, jagged stone flew from the crowd and made a loud a crack as it hit her head. She crumpled face-down onto the street, her head lay sideways on the pavement, her head and mouth were oozing blood. Her withered body quivered a moment then she lay still.

Her friends turned in horror and reaching back for her. One woman managed to sit down holding the dead woman in her lap, swaying back and forth weeping, tears burning her face.

The head Centurion grunted, "Cut the dead one loose, leave her for the crows!"

A soldier stepped out and with his short sword cut her ropes from the others in line and kicked her small body to the gutter. He yanked the other woman to her feet and they marched on.

Chapter 15

"Lord, who hath believed our report?"
—Romans 10:16

Tales of the fire spread across the world.

Riders on horseback, carrier pigeons, fires on mountaintops, men onboard ships, and on foot spread the news.

The underlying message was—the Eternal City was weak and wounded. Millions across the empire grew bold and dreamed of sitting on a throne. Roman Slaves dreamed again of Sparticus and his slave revolt years before.

The time was ripe again.

A small breeze of freedom can turn into a hurricane overnight.

Across the world in each non-Roman's mind, the logic was clear—Rome's legions must tend to rebuilding the city and cannot hold the empire outside of Rome. The city is weak!

Many a wild-eyed firebrand grabbed his sword and jumped atop a big rock calling on his comrades to strike.

Italy heard the news first, the cities of Pompeii, Tuscany, Brindiseum and then, Corsica and Sicily, every city and country town in the entire boot soon knew of the disaster. Italy trembled, their guard was down, their under-belly exposed to the bloody swords of barbarians.

In the dark forests of Gaul hairy tribesmen in bearskins frantically wagged on and on in strange tongues urging revolt.

Spain heard it as riders on horseback charged over the hills and down into the white alabaster towns shouting out the news, throwing out rolled papyrus scrolls from horseback into every villa.

News reached the shores of Britain and blue-painted Wode warriors in the forests of Britain; all around Stonehenge and the plains of Scotland cheered and danced around bonfires giddy with the news. Even the Isle of Eire heard and beat their swords on wooden shields. They were poets and harps were strummed with tales.

Every Briton hated the distant heel of Roma on their necks.

The Britains plotted revolt and would later carry it out almost to success led by the brave woman warrior named Boudeca. A mother's revenge for her own rape and that of her daughter. Her wrath would shake the empire to its core.

Cities in Northern Africa heard. Greeks soon knew, as did all the islands of the Mediterranean along the shores of Asia Minor.

In Macedonia the ancestors of Alexander the Great gripped their swords dreaming of past glory. A glory that had raged in the flaming heart of a heroic young king 300 years before.

When the frontier provinces of Jerusalem and Judea heard of the fiery catastrophe, the Jews let out loud cheers and armed themselves for another excuse to kill Romans and gain their freedom. Soon enough they would dare a revolt to their fiery doom.

Though they followed many messiahs in many bloody uprisings against Rome—No Hebrew leader ever got out of the neighborhood and the woeful Jews only managed to get themselves crucified. One Jew in particular stood out in many minds. He had preached of peace and prophesied rightly that those with a sword would perish by it. He spoke true.

Egypt heard it and bald-headed Egyptian soldiers in their wicker chariots cursed in vain to rise up against the Romans and avenge their Queen Cleopatra. Augustus Caesar had forced her to put a poison snake against her breast 80 years ago. But now they were mere mosquitoes to the mighty elephant of Rome.

In the end, all the countries in the empire proved the coward and re-adjusted Rome's chains around their neck.

They bowed to the practical and sent the usual sheepish tributes of loyalty.

A messenger with news of the fire finally reached the gates of Babylon, to the palace of the House of Heraclion and to Prince Jezep, Jesus of Nazareth.

An old friend that would break it to him.

Chapter 16

Prince Jezep sat fidgeting on his marbled throne.

He was nervously rubbing the gold arms of his chair. His purple robe under his arms was wet with sweat.

This morning a traveler from Jerusalem had arrived with an important message about Rome.

The prince stared at the tall closed doors. His long silver hair hung down over his purple-robed shoulders mingling with his speckled black and silver beard. His noble face stared out like the sphinx.

To his left on a smaller throne Mary sat knitting on a loom. She was making a many-colored coat for her prince. A large white parrot sat on a perch beside them squirreling with gibberish. Garbled words would seep out, "Evil is here, beware, beware". The prince turned and frowned at the bird. "That bird is too smart." he grumbled.

The shining white steps before them spread down and out like a giant white fan into the wide room.

The royal ceiling forty feet high and the room was wide and long, mostly white and green marble, one of the last elegant palace chambers in the old city. All was silent but for the parrot prattling away, "beware, beware."

Mary turned to Jesus clenching his fists.

"Relax, my love, who do you think it is, the Roman Emperor coming for tea?

"Quiet, Mary, please!" Jesus snapped and quickly glanced over at her mocking smile. He sat back in his throne his hands gripping the end of the arms, waiting.

'Clang, Clang!' the doorknockers echoed from the huge doors before them.

Jesus glanced at Mary then shouted, "Enter!"

Two muscular black servants swung open the twenty-foot high Cedar doors.

When he saw the man Jesus froze solid.

The man was wearing a hood over his face but the prince recognized him instantly. He could feel him like a cold wind, like seeing a snake on a path.

The figure was darkness itself.

He was thinner now and shrunken, like a tall black shadow shaped like a man. His very soul was made of ice and Jesus could feel it twenty feet away. It suddenly brought back that horrible afternoon long ago. Golgotha, it stuck in his throat like a clod of dirt.

The skeleton man stood there cloaked in a hooded black silk robe wrapped around his impossibly thin shoulders, the robe fell straight to the floor swirling like black waters around his shiny cow leather boots. His face was ghost-white and thin as the devil, he peered out from the black hood, and he had a hawk's curved nose. He gazed up at Jesus and Mary with large hollow eyes under arched eyebrows, his greasy black beard stuck tight to his white cheeks the tight beard coming to a devilish point below his chin His voice sounded like a cactus, "Greetings My Lord and my lady." he bent his head almost mockingly.

"Hello Judas.' Jesus almost gagged.

Mary looked up for a moment then gazed down quickly at her loom, wishing she were on her barge floating down the river. She did not look up and muttered, "Hello, Judas."

He swished across the floor and stood at the foot of the steps to the throne, he gestured in Hindu fashion slithering his hands from his forehead to his lips to his heart. Jesus felt he was being mocked.

"Judas, excuse me if I do not get up to greet you, our history is so long, I am choking on it."

"I understand, please do not get up, you are a prince after all."

"WHY are you here!? No one is supposed to know I am here and who I am. If Caiphus knew I was still alive…it would mean disaster."

"I know, I know," his long face shaking from side to side, his finger shaking in front of his face to erase everything being said, even the fact of him being there.

Jesus remained seated, not knowing whether to sit or step down and hug this old friend or have him seized as a criminal.

"And you, Mary are looking beautiful." he said in a slithery tone.

"Thank you, Judas," she said, still not looking up. A chill shot up her spine.

"Judas! Answer me, What ARE you doing here? When I know that we will talk of the old days…you were supposed to be gone forever after the cross!'

The servants in the room quickly turned, feeling they had just heard forbidden words. The servant girls gazed up from the corners wondering.

They all knew the legend of Jesus and the cross, 'what had a cross to do with the prince?'

Everyone in the hall gazed at up at the throne, their faces full of questions.

The prince looked around at those in the room but continued, "Speak Judas, what is your message?"

"I have come to inform you, O great Prince, there has been a fire in Rome and the great city is half-destroyed."

Jesus' bearded head turned to Mary and she looked back at him in utter stupefaction. Jesus turned to Judas, "This is true?!"

The servants, guards and even the snake charmer in the far corner looked at each other, mouths gaping at the news.

The center of the world almost destroyed!? All went silent.

"Yes, it's true. I have ridden a thousand leagues from Jerusalem to tell you this, for I know your secret and it is most important you know of the fire, as a prince *and* as the one you truly are because there is more here that concerns you." Jesus sat straight up and suddenly turned to everyone in the room, "Everyone, leave us, please, we must talk of this, but fear not." The crowd of people in the great hall scurried through the open doors and closed them quietly behind.

Chapter 17

"Where is Demetrius? I was sure he would be here."

Judas asked, still standing beneath the two on their thrones. He had not expected to see such pomp.

"He is out in the desert chasing lions"

"Excellent, still the bold hunter. And still the poet I imagine."

"Judas! We had an agreement, you would never come to Babylon, my father paid you well for that, there may be those who followed you and will discover who I am, Caiphus might still have people who would kill me and harm Mary."

"My old friend, calm thyself, when I tell you more of this fire of Rome—*you* will proclaim to the world who you are, or I do not know the true Jesus."

Jesus remained seated, resisting the urge to order him gone. The world was shifting beneath his feet

He was still stunned at seeing the one who had pretended to betray him at the last supper as part of a secret plan—Jesus sensed evil in him, he was hiding something.

Danger lurked, they both knew—if he was discovered still alive it would kill the spirit of his new followers.

Jesus Christ still alive as a mortal man, living in luxury in Babylon — It would break a million hearts and they'd return to worshipping idols and licking the golden calf.

Jesus and Judas stared at each other; they knew the significance of the secret.

"Excuse me, gentlemen, I will leave this men talk," said Mary, She stood up and smiled down at the tall shadow standing menacingly before her,

"Goodbye, Judas." She leaned over kissed Jesus on the cheek, her lips in his whiskers, she gathered up her cloth and walked behind the throne of Jesus disappearing through an open doorway.

Jesus spoke up,

"It is a tragedy but why should I be interested in Rome burning?"

"Because, my Lord, your followers are being blamed for the fire and they are being executed for the deed."

Jesus went still as a dying breeze.

He stared through Judas and then put both his hands up to his face his fingers pinching his eyes, he looked up wearily, "The Christians?"

"Yes."

Jesus hung his head, his large hands hanging limp over the arms of his throne. He was a dishrag and remained silent for a long time.

"My Lord, are you all right?" questioned Judas stepping forward.

Jesus quickly raised his palm, "Stop!" he straightened himself on his throne. His bearded head staring straight out, his eyes staring far away…

The day of the sermon on the mount flashed into sight, standing on the hill on that bright morning, looking down across the green valley into the upturned faces of all those hopeful souls gazing up at him, believing in him, following him, giving their life to him… they were his children and now they were dying for Him.

A tear wandered down his face.

Judas was looking up, his mind coiling like a snake.

"They are being killed because they are my followers, I am the reason for this?"

"It is so, my Lord."

More tears dropped, he closed his eyes pinching his nose again.

Judas drove the message in deeper; " They will all be crucified."

"O God, no!" Jesus groaned and took a giant breath.

"Yes, my lord," Judas stood up and continued, "and they are to be thrown into the coliseum and ripped apart by lions, the rest crucified around the edge of the stadium and at night Nero will light them on fire as human torches."

"STOP! I have heard enough!"

Jesus' clutched the arms of his throne and his face grew stern and white as marble, gazing down at Judas, speaking slowly in words of stone—

"I must go to them!"

"What are you saying?" Judas flatly said as if reciting well-rehearsed lines.

"Yes", said the Lord with all the pain he could release, "It is because of me they are being executed so it is I who must save them. What else can I do?"

Jesus wiped his eyes and looked at Judas, "I must go to Rome, I am the cause of their deaths and I must stop this terrible thing, I caused this pain, a must heal it."

"But, my friend, you are older now. Can you possibly have any effect?"

Jesus turned in his tracks,

"No one is old in the eyes of God."

"Jesus, you said exactly what I thought you would say."

The Master looked down at Judas who bowed and then turned in a cape of black wings and was gone.

Chapter 18

Lie with me.
Genesis 39:7

Jesus woke in his large feather bed holding Mary tight.

His right arm reaching under her arm, tenderly cupped her breast, his other arm held her sleepy blond head like a giant pillow.

Their bodies were spooned together; joining her, nudging warmly together, Jesus felt perfect.

'If there is Heaven on Earth', he thought, 'it is this.'

The sun rose a little higher, the room was glowing brighter and the curtains were a waterfall of golden light. In his half-slumber, Jesus heard a horse snorting outside in the courtyard and then hoof beats clomping away into the distance.

Judas. Jesus frowned at his rudeness, leaving before they put everything in place. His eyes were open and questioning, his face was lost in Mary's sweet silver-blond hair.

"Was that Judas?" mumbled Mary.

"Yes, my love,"

"That is strange?"

"Strange indeed, there was something about him, something not quite right."

A moment later sleep lifted from him and it hit Jesus like a charging bull—the god-awful talk of the Christians in Rome being killed.

It sent a chill through him as if his skin were falling off and he was only bones, he had to clutch his soul lest it fly out of him leaving him empty forever.

Thinking of leaving on a long journey without his love gave him a deep jab inside. He rolled to the side and was suddenly wide-awake staring blankly at the ceiling above their bed.

"I love you, Jesus." Mary whispered sweetly. She was still half-asleep beside him.

The words plunged into him, thinking of how very soon he would perhaps never hear those sweet words again. She could not journey to far away Rome. His heart was racing like a runaway chariot.

Staring up from his pillow, the bearded Jesus shut his eyes tight, tears welling up painfully for he knew he must leave his only love in the whole world.

He must depart this perfection, this love, to go off thousands of miles away on some crazy quest. He must leave his true soul mate to follow his fate. It killed him.

It slammed into his bones. She felt it instantly, "What is wrong, my love?" She turned to stare at him propping her pretty blond head up on her pillow, staring into him with her soft, blue eyes, the only home Jesus had ever known.

In all his lonely wanderings her eyes had been his only nest.

She grabbed his head in her two hands and with the eyes of a woman scared that her man has weakened, her rock dissolved, she stared deep into his eyes, "Tell me, my love, what is wrong?"

And the a man who had traveled the wide world, pulled her tightly to him his tears melting into her sweet blond hair and with all the bravery he could clutch onto spoke calmly, "I must leave and go to Rome and I may never return."

Mary Magdalene shook her head slowly and smiled, "Never, my dearest, not without me. Where you go, there I go also,"

He suddenly felt like he was released into a sunny meadow.

He looked into her eyes reached his hand behind her head, pulled her lips to his and kissed her sweet mouth.

Their kisses did not stop, only becoming warmer and deeper and faster coming, mouths joining deeper, he grazed along her soft neck, her mouth opened, her breath sucking in, his mouth moving downward as if tasting strawberries, her arms went wide and her chin went back, her mouth opening wide moaning louder, giving herself completely, clutching him and scratching, their bodies moving together, joined in a rhythm as old as time and in perfect peace they breathed each into each other and when warm Nile poured out, they slept in perfect peace for an hour.

Chapter 19

Jesus stood tall in his ivory chariot. The morning sun glittering off the gold.

When Mary said she would go with him to Rome it lifted his heart to heaven. Her warm love had turned him into Hercules.

Beneath the steps of his palace he held the reins of his chariot, his head flowing with the long silvery hair of a God. His black and silver beard was combed and he smiled a bold smile up to Mary at the windowsill.

He would go on one more lion hunt before the long journey to Rome.

His face was like brown papyrus, his dark eyes were piercing clear and flashing beneath bushy eyebrows. He looked like Zeus come down to Earth with his white tunic thrown over his left shoulder. His chest broad and tight, his stomach flat and rippling, the neck of a bull, a chin of marble. Truth was, he would never look old.

Chasing lions and wrestling kept him strong. Loving Mary kept him young.

He smiled easily clutching the reins holding back his two black horses, Bucephalus and Hermes, his huge hands held back their prancing and rearing with ease. His muscles flexing as he pulled back the reins.

The prince stood in his chariot in front of his marble palace. He would chase the lions today with Demetrius if that wild poet ever showed up.

Mary looked down from the high bedroom window in their palace, her thin blond hair floating in the breeze, an easy smile on her perfect, light face. She waved down to her prince and threw him a kiss on the wind.

From the dusty street in front of the palace steps the prince waved up to her. After their talk of Rome that morning he needed a day of revelry.

He needed to forget and at the same time remember the Christians and the journey to come.

He needed a run through the desert to clear his soul.

Mary needed time to cry into her pillow.

A roaring cloud of dust burst around the corner and roaring down the street was the churning chariot of Demetrius.

He was hanging onto his horses, out of control he was howling like a wild wolf! Careening in his chariot he was barely hanging on behind his two runaway horses, his chariot hit the side of a wall, bumped into some people and in a cloud of white dust his chariot, raring horses and all, pulled up next to Jesus, crashing into his chariot sideways, a loud crunk! And little wood pieces flew off.

The poet fell over the front of his chariot but straightened back up. The prince barely held onto his startled horses as all they reared up and bit at the horses of Demetrius thrashing into them.

"Yasooouu!" yelled Demetrius jostling in his chariot, He was out of breath, he threw his long dark hair back and laughed, "Are we ready for the hunt?"

Jesus laughed—

"I am, but are you?"

Grabbing the reins the prince shouted to his horses, "Hiiyahh!"

The two friends in their gold-trimmed chariots charged down the wide stone street, Jesus in the lead. Ragged robed men, old women, donkeys and yelping dogs jumping out of the way. A cart overturned and vegetables flew everywhere.

They passed out of the tall gates charging far into the desert, horses running wild, dust trailing behind.

Chariots racing, heroes alive looking for lions, searching the horizon for anything, bird, beast or wandering god to chase and stir their awakening hearts.

Together they charged, bumping chariot to chariot, laughing and throwing their longhair back in the wind. Laughing into the sky. Older men young again.

After a few miles lying beneath some shade trees they saw a sleepy pride of lions. There were maybe ten of them, big tan males with fat furry manes licking their paws and a few sleek female lions pawing at their cubs. The prince and the poet charged toward them whooping like boys! The lions, unsure at first, remained sitting as long as they could before begrudgingly stirring and finally lumbering up to start running away with flat, clumsy paws.

Jesus picked one out and he was off. The chase was on.

A big male lion running in front of the chariot calmly terrified, Jesus shaking the reins shouted to his horses, "On Hermes! On Bucephalus! Faster! Faster, make that lion sweat!"

Jesus fixed on the huge mane and the beast's tawny muscles rippling as he ran, he saw his tail whipping around madly, his paws reaching out in huge bounds leaping faster and faster easily outrunning the two horses.

The lion veered off to the right and loped behind a sand dune. Jesus pulled his chariot to a stop waiting for Demetrius to catch up.

Chapter 20

In a few minutes the poet pulled his chariot alongside his friend.

"That was great! You ran his tail off." They laughed together and stood in their chariots smiling at each other.

When the dust floated by, Demetrius, bare-chested, and muscular, pulled out a leather sack of water, and offered it to Jesus and they drank deeply.

The poet wiped his mouth with his forearm and corked the skin. Standing in the silence of the Persian Desert Demetrius looked up at his friend the god, and asked, "So I hear you have found your quest."

"Then you know of the trip to Rome."

"Yes, and about the fire and the poor Christians, God Bless them, and Judas? He was HERE?! And now gone? What was that about? We have not seen him in 30 years and you did not tell me? What did he look like? What did he say? Tell me all."

"Slow down, let us walk over into the shade and talk,"

Jesus pointed to a tree growing out from a dune, a 'lion-spot' with sand dug up all around and claw marks on the tree where lions had sharpened their claws on the bark.

Perfect for two human lions to sit in the shade and talk of great journeys to come.

They made clicking sounds at their horses and they pulled them over to the shade not far away, they pulled back the reins, halted and stepped off their chariots. The well-trained horses wandered not far away pulling the chariots about forty paces away and stopping.

The two friends ambled into the shade of a tree leaning against the cool sand dune.

Chapter 21

"Fortune favors the bold"
—Virgil, Roman Poet.

They had just sat down when the huge lion walked from around the dune and looked directly at them, swishing his long tail.

They could see the tiny pink bumps on his panting tongue.

A big gold-colored lion with a huge scraggly mane with a head as big as a small Hippo. His two top fang teeth were protruding down below his lower jaw. The giant cat glared at them, opened his hairy jaws wide and let out a heart-wrenching growl. Demetrius slid backward on the ground and lay flat against the dune, his hands gripping the ground. He garbled out cracked, raspy words, "Issa, he's ready to charge! I hope you still have the power."

"Brother, so do I." he answered staring at the beast.

He stood up calmly.

"God, be with me now?" he mumbled.

"Amen." answered Demetrius.

They had no spears and could never reach the chariots in time.

The desert wind had stopped, the lion's loud purring thundered into a growl, the poet's stomach turned to ground-up grain.

The lion whipped its giant paw backwards against the ground like a bull ready to charge.

His muscles stiffened, its broad paws dug into the ground showing sharp claws. His brow scrunched down over its flaming yellow eyes glaring right at them, a devil was in him. His long sharp teeth were dripping with thick strands of saliva, his tail was swishing around signaling a deadly leap.

Growling loudly summoning up all of hell it chilled the air around them, he was ready to lunge.

Jesus was standing up straight, staring into the lion's yellow eyes.

"Demetrius, don't move." he whispered.

"Don't worry."

The poet froze against the dune, his heart in his throat. He'd seen lions kill, it was not a pretty sight.

The lion lowered its huge body, elbows up high, it would be over in seconds.

The horses were whinnying and jumping up and down, tipping the chariots around, they ran off about 100 paces and stopped. The lion turned his head toward them for a moment but turned back fixing on the men, the sure prey.

A man-eater, he had no interest in horses. Jesus walked step by step slowly toward the lion, man and beast—eyes fixed dead-on. 'Are you with me, God?' he pleaded.

Staring eye to eye, Jesus broke it off and gazed up to Heaven for a moment He closed his eyes, whispered something and then looked right back at the lion. "Are you with me?' Then slowly, giving his heart to Heaven, Jesus stretched his large arms out to the side, his palms up and open, surrendering his whole being to life, the lion, God, standing to his full height, flexing his bare arm muscles yielding completely, giving himself. Feet spread wide strong as an oak, facing the yellow beast.

The lion stood still as air, he stopped panting a moment, its muscles tight and tense. An eternity passed. Hearts pounding their last.

The lion relaxed.

He closed his panting mouth and turned his head away then back at Jesus. The beast shut his eyes a moment and then straightened back up, evenly on all fours. The lion shook his huge head and turned, plodding across the desert.

Jesus stood still, watching the beast lope across the tundra melting into the watery distance.

He turned quietly and walked to sit down beside his friend who was still lying there with his eyes shut tight. He opened his eyes and spoke, "We could have been devoured you know"

His hands were shaking still clutching the ground.

Jesus replied calmly, "It is not our time, my friend."

The poet sat up and handed him the goatskin of water saying, "You still have it.'

"Thank God," and took a long swig of water. He tapped the stopper back in with his huge fist.

They stood up and walked slowly back to the chariots.

Chapter 22

One hundred long silver trumpets blared and long rows of kettledrums pounded as emperor Nero in his ivory chariot rolled through the gates of Rome.

His small round head was encircled with a green laurel wreath and his impish, cherub face bowed to the roaring crowds around him. His purple robes flowed down behind his rolling chariot as the four white horses pulled him forward, he was leading a procession of red-robed, silver-clad soldiers, an entire legion of men through the gates of Rome.

Behind the legion walked one hundred slaves throwing loaves of bread out to the people, this whipped their cheers up higher.

In his chariot with his four white horses pulling him along he proudly pranced toward the senate steps, around him were fifty thousand citizens and twice as many slaves cheering and throwing flowers at their emperor.

The temple of the senate was one of the few remaining buildings left untouched by the massive fire that had blazed a month before.

The crowds cheered only because slaves were tossing out bread. Some slaves threw coins.

The slaves were also letting loose large herds of goats and sheep into the waiting, grabbing crowd.

The people had not forgotten his impudent harp playing during the fire and hatred for the little madman rippled beneath the surface of the white-robed crowds. The gifts were not working.

Nero kept their hatred beaten back by fear. Five thousand, plume-helmeted soldiers armed with sword and javelin kept the peace just fine.

Ten thousand more sitting in the barracks assured it.

His chariot pulled up to the bottom of the flower-strewn steps. He stepped off and turned around to the sea of citizens. He raised his arms high to loud cheers and even louder boos. Unfazed he began walking up the steps to the senate building and the waiting senators.

Behind the emperor five thousand soldiers clanged to an abrupt halt, the slaves stopped behind them and all became silent.

He walked alone up the steps.

He got to the top and turned to the ocean of people standing before him, he held up both arms high to more cheers and even more boos.

The walls around the square were forty feet high made of white marble. Beyond the square were miles of blackened buildings and beyond them burnt ashen hills.

The Eternal City still stood proudly but only inside the hearts of the people. It was a black shabby mess for miles across and blame for it needed to be assigned.

"Fellow citizens" started the little man, his shrill voice echoing across the giant square, "I come to punish those responsible for the fire!"

"You are to blame!"

An abrupt voice echoing off the distant wall, he frowned a moment but continued, "We have discovered it is the Christians who started the fire and they will be executed in the coliseum for this sin against us all!"

The cheers swallowed up the boos and all looked around to discover anyone fleeing or moving, anyone betraying themselves as a Christian. A few people broke and ran, they were grabbed and dragged to the center by enraged citizens who threw two men and a woman down in front of the lines of soldiers. Soldiers jumped up sticking their javelins into their bodies. They screamed and then were silent, blood streaming on the cobblestones as the crowd whistled and cheered.

More Christians were recognized and grabbed up by soldiers and in a few minutes bleeding bodies, both men and women, were spread all over the square.

Forty more were rounded up and stood shivering and crying but most placed their palms together defiantly praying as they were roped together at the ankles and marched away doomed.

The emperor continued, "These are but a few, but we will find them all and punish for what they have done to our fair city!" Nero waved once more to the loud cheering and then stepped between the columns of into the marble building and was gone. Behind him thousands of voices cheered but many booed the emperor Nero who had fiddled while their city had burned.

Chapter 23

Resist the devil and he will flee from you.
—Timothy 4:7

Two thousand miles away on the side of a mountain a lone figure was inching up a thin trail to the summit.

The cold wind constantly blew his dark robe sideways.

He had to stop every hundred paces to catch his breath. He was miles up on the slopes of the Persian Holy Mountain, Mount Ziggurat. He was wearing a heavy brown wool robe with a pointed hood. He clawed along the mountain path with a wooden staff.

"I must reach the top before nightfall." He talked to himself and to God at the same time.

He could feel the rocks jab through his thin leather sandals, his head was bent downward, his beard was dripping with sweat. His breathing came heavy.

Jesus sat on a big rock to rest and looked down across the wide valley. There in the middle of the desert stood Babylon shining in the late afternoon sun. Square and blue, with a hundred dazzling palaces within.

His palace was in the center of the city and shielding his eyes he could make it out, a tiny square speck, behind it was a patch of green grass. 'Mary will be having afternoon supper in the garden now' he smiled, stroking his beard.

He turned back gazing up at the high, brown rocky peak over a mile above him—there he must climb.

Once long ago in India he had seen God on a mountain and now he must seek him again.

A vulture tilted by near his head, its wings tilting in the up-wind gliding around the side of the mountain.

A wind kicked up and whipped grains of dust into Jesus' eyes and they stung a moment and he stopped.

He was almost two miles up from the desert floor and he gasped for air, when he squeezed his eyes tight tiny green and purple worms danced in the blackness of his eyes and he began hearing angelic music coming from the heavens.

He pinched the bridge of his nose and saw more dancing lights in his mind and he grew light-headed.

When he opened his eyes, a shadow on the trail turned into a long black snake and wiggled around, as he shook his head and stared, the snake reared up and glared at him with burning ruby eyes, it hissed, "Turn back or die, Jesus, all is hopeless." Then it dissolved.

"No Satan, I will not listen."

The snake dissolved before his eyes.

The lord frowned and never missed a step.

The sun slowly blinked and went to sleep behind the distant hills and the mountain grew dark around him. He climbed higher and higher on the narrow trail. He pulled his cloak tight, the temperature was dropping and his arms and legs were turning a light shade of blue and were feeling numb and stinging.

He walked around a bend in the trail and suddenly he was in front of a dark cave, it was head-high, a low opening but wide as two men across. He peered into the cave and in the dim silver twilight he saw a big, gray wolf lounging on a rock shelf staring right at him with glowing yellow eyes.

He bared his sharp teeth and growled. His front paws were crossed calmly. Jesus stopped and stared straight at the wolf, the wolf's eyes were glowing blood-red, his nostrils flared out, he spoke in a raspy voice, "Do not go any further Jesus, if you know what's good for you." and then like a dream the wolf melted away into the rocks and the cave was empty.

His heart pounded faster, 'that was real', or perhaps it was his own fear trying to stop his quest, his fear rising these demons up before him.

He stumbled on, hugging the side of the mountain on the crumbling trail to the top.

The wind suddenly knocked pebbles down from the cliffs above and they struck Jesus' head and a white flash swooped down and a giant owl flew by and scratched its talons into Jesus' head, he yelled in pain and he looked up and saw big white wings flapping away, the white bird screeching—

"Go back! go back! go back! go back." the screeching trailed away into the dark twilight and the owl was gone.

Jesus touched his head and felt a warm trickle of blood, "That's real! Thin air or not." he wiped the blood away with his fingers and walked on heading straight to the top of the mountain.

It was dark without a moon when he finally reached the summit.

Chapter 24

**I saw a light from heaven above the brightness of the sun,
shining round about me.
—Acts 26:13**

At the top was a small clearing.

A dim silver shaft of light shined down in the clearing. On the far edge of it was a cleft of reddish stones jutting up at the very top of the mountain, darkness behind.

Jesus started to walk across the dimly lit floor heading across to the top to finally rest and begin his prayers. He felt bone-tired; his fingers shook as he walked.

Halfway across the open space a chilling wind blew into this face, he pulled his robe in tight.

Suddenly in the darkness rising slowly from behind the rocks came a large, round blinding light, a horrible moon, wide and absolutely terrifying.

Jesus trembled and dropped to the ground, his face flat on the dirt floor. He could not look at directly at the light.

The massive round light pinned him to the ground like an elephant with one foot on his back. His stomach was a fist of pain. A silent power held him down.

He stared at the ground in deadly fear. All the strength in his arms could barely hold him up a foot off the ground; he stared down in deadly fear. He was pressed downward, gazing at the red dirt.

The heat of the large, round light above him burned his exposed neck like the sun but at the same time froze him like mountain snow, he was face down, paralyzed.

Night was all around but the light hovered above him silent yet deafening, its brightness lighting up the clearing like daylight, his body formed a shadow on the ground where he was facing down held up by his shaking arms.

He could not turn his head. He cried out, "O GOD!"

It was an immense, blazing light and his heart shrunk to the size of a prune and he trembled but knew he must look up.

With all the courage he could gather he turned his head slowly upward and glanced out of the corner of his eye, he saw it or Him—a perfectly round, clear white globe twenty feet across with endless depth, it was humming yet perfectly still and quiet, calm yet terrifying.

Jesus knew it was the Living God.

His soul was mush. His heart shrunk to the size of a pigeon's, his fingers clutching the dirt like an eagle's talons. Desperately trying to hang onto the world.

Suddenly he felt his heart disappear completely, who he was and all boundaries of himself dissolved into nothingness, he merged with the light and with eternity and left the world, He was living light! More alive than he'd ever been or imagined! Lightning was shooting through him, a force was pinning him to the ground. He felt huge invisible hands reaching into his chest, cupping his heart with motherly warmth, brushing him like a baby.

His eyes were clamped tight and tears poured out from the sides of his eyes.

God was a bright, unbearable moon bearing down on him, surrounding, burning and consuming him, accepting him. It weighed a thousand pounds on his back and kept burning his neck, scorching him. He clenched his teeth not a sound did he utter.

Fear was gripping his dry throat as he saw the ground around him light up bright as day. From the corner of his eyes he saw the nearby hills lit-up like morning, yet beyond them it was deepest night.

With all his courage, with the full bravery of who he was, a Son of God and Alexander the Great—he turned and gazed into the face of God.

His eyes were blind with light, he blinked in pain, tears streamed from his eyes, every ounce of strength drained from him, his arms collapsed under him, his cheek felt the hard gravel as he crushed into to the dirt, the side of his face in the dirt pinned to the ground, but he held on, gazing into God's Holy and Terrifying Face.

The light was pure and almost blinding with a bluish halo shimmering around the outside of it and then soothing words came booming from the center of the light, the silent yet deafening words of God—

"MY SON, FIND THE STRENGTH AND I WILL GUIDE AND PROTECT YOU."

A moment later it was over.

Chapter 25

Suddenly all was dark and cold.

Jesus lay face down in the clearing shaking in the dark. His eyes were buried in his arms. He could not move, only shiver, he wept and he wept.

The words of God had entered him. He knew his answer had come. No images of God, no visions of an old white-bearded man on a throne—this was God and His light had spoken to him.

To question it would be ridiculous and petty.

This blessing gave him the confidence of God. Whatever he chose to do now and forever he knew could not fail.

He knew what he must do.

He fell asleep in the clearing, thoughts of the glowing God keeping him warm.

Chapter 26

The dawn turned the mountains glowing pink.

Jesus awoke shivering at dawn, his fingers white and frozen. He lifted his head and pushed his now silvery long hair, back and pulled his brown robe tightly around him.

The dawn was turning the mountains glowing pink, the miles-long slopes dotted with brown shrubs. He rubbed his eyes.

The light he had seen last night still blazed in his mind and the words were engraved inside him, 'Come up with the strength and God will guide me and protect me', that was the message.

He felt calm and suddenly hunger grabbed him slowly digging like a knife.

The air was thick and it sang a low humming song he could only feel.

An owl winged by and dropped a piece of bread near him. He ran to pick it up, dusted it off and bit into it. As he chewed the bread he noticed a donkey standing on the trail below, it had a leather flask around its neck. Jesus walked down to the brown little beast and saw that it was a leather flask of water.

He knew God was still there, and would always be there.

After devouring the bread and drinking the flask dry he patted the donkey on the head and started striding down the mountain.

The trail was wide and easy with the turns and he took long, bounding strides. He felt free flying down Mount Ziggurat.

He was at the bottom in twenty minutes. It was barely ten o'clock. He was approaching the high blue gates of the city by noon.

Chapter 27

"My love, your beard has turned silver!"

Mary rushed to him as he stood blocking the light in the doorway of their throne room. He drew her into his strong arms hugging her for all eternity.

They joined and their bodies melted together like they would never again walk separately. They pulled away a moment, Jesus gazed down into his blond Mary's sweet blue eyes and kissed her deeply, tasting her sweet, open mouth, swirling their lips together and tongues they kissed till the room and the whole world fell away, holding her so tightly, they were one and would always be.

Their kiss lasted almost forever and Jesus filled Mary's open mouth with the sweetness of God's Light, the sweetness he had brought down from the mountain and now poured into her mouth in a kiss, his soul rushing into her and hers into him and the kiss went on and on and they never wanted to stop.

She pulled away out of breath, every part of her wet; she was smiling wide, laughing.

They walked hand in hand into the hall to their thrones. The servants, slaves and dancers were all gone this morning and the prince and Mary were alone to talk freely like two doves on a branch.

"I saw God on the mountain, it was a light that spoke to me."

Mary had known Jesus for years and so knew this was true.

"And what did God tell you?"

"Everything."

Mary's heart was racing and felt weak as a shivering kitten, she dared to ask, "And the journey?"

"Yes, my love, God has spoken and we go on the journey. My children in Rome need me."

Mary smiled into his eyes, her blue eyes fearless and wonderful. She took his great hand, lifted it up and gently kissed it and said, "My love, I will follow you anywhere."

Jesus reached over and pulled her head to his heart.

Chapter 28

"But how can you do this!?"

Demetrius looked over the garden table at Jesus in total disbelief, "How can you walk right into Rome and pinch the emperor's nose?! This is crazy my friend! I have followed you to the ends of the Earth, but this is too much! "

"But you WILL go with me?"

"Of course I will go, I told you the day of the lion-but give me some hope. We are walking into the mouth of doom! Tell me- how can we do this?"

Demetrius stared in silence across the table at the smiling eyes of Jesus. His smile had not melted an inch.

"God knows."

He stared at his friend with the blankness of the Sphinx.

Demetrius closed his eyes and shook his head, sat back up at the garden table and turned to watch the bright blue peacock stroll quietly across the lawn. There was a long silence before he spoke, "And Mary is coming with us?"

"Yes, she insists."

Demetrius looked to the sky, flicked his long hair back, knitted his hands together resting them on the table. He looked over at Jesus who was dressed in his long white linen tunic, sitting back in his chair, his black and silver beard combed perfectly around his broad smile, his bright silver hair rolling down around his shoulders. His brown eyes bright.

He mocked his friend, "Sure of ourselves today, aren't we."

Jesus just smiled wider. Demetrius continued, "When do we leave?" there was a long hesitation then, "Soon."

"And the palace, who will stay here and tend to things?"

"Emmanuel is coming from Alexandria."

Demetrius nodded and just sat there with his hands folded on the table staring at his great friend. Jesus continued, "Fear not, Demetrius, God has spoken to me and I must go to Rome and save my

children who are dying for me. It is my journey, not yours, are you sure you want to come, there will be great danger."

Demetrius sighed, "How can you ask me that? I have followed you to India and on your crazy mission to be crucified, who else will watch out for you, sire? Mary is great but thee will be rough times, besides think of the poem's I'll write."

They smiled and the smiles erupted into to laughter. They grasped each other's forearm in the handshake of heroes.

Demetrius said,

"To Rome."

Jesus nodded and smiled, "To Rome, may God go with us."

"He better."

Chapter 29

The dark blue Persian night had one round, white eye.

Jesus, dressed in his long white robe, walked out of the main gate of the city into the night to pray. The wide, clean desert stretched out before him.

All was deep blue. The moonlight turned the ground chalk-white for clear to the row of mountains.

As he walked out the tall Ishtar Gate, a few dark-robed old men with their hoods pulled over their head walked by him holding onto the ropes to their camel's lumbering slowly behind. Pilgrims and merchants walked past him, bowing slightly to the kingly man in white. One put his fingers to his forehead and then to his lips in reverence.

The main road was washed in silver light. The white moon shined like a perfectly round lamp in the cobalt sky. No stars showed their face, they hid behind whitish blue.

Jesus walked on the moon-white road rising up the hill from the city. This would be one of his last nights in his beloved Babylon. He needed to think, to plan, to seek a vision for the journey.

He arrived at the top of the large hill and gazed out across the endless milk-white expanse of sand and shrub. He felt the warm, desert wind brush his face and fill his nostrils. He breathed in the cool desert, drinking the smell of snow from the Caucasus Mountains ten miles away. He closed his eyes breathing deeply.

He opened his eyes and held his arms out wide, his thin white robe fluttering out like angel's wings. He stood at the top of the hill feeling the wind in his face and beard, and the linen cloth flap lightly on his body.

Jesus, Son of Gods and kings, looked to the Heavens, feeling the warm air, listening deeply to his soul.

The moon glowed turning the sand grayish-white, the wind was clean and sweet and Jesus stood still, a wide smile beneath his closed eyes, he would have stood there all night.

Jesus sent out a thought—

'What now, my Father?'

GO AND FEAR NOT. The words came to his mind instantly 'How shall I travel?'

BY WATER.

'Will all be well?

"YES, MY SON. FEAR NOT. GO SAVE YOUR CHILDREN."

He knew praying was over. He turned and walked back to the city.

Demetrius was praying.

In his bedchamber he was lying inside Starzina's warm valley.

She was a beautiful temple dancer and deep kisses were his offerings.

She was young with long black hair, full red lips that joined his, sharing sweet kisses of swirling tongues. Through the night their bodies deeply joined and her sweet moans answered all his prayers.

Chapter 30

Jesus is a cryptic figure who conceals as much as he reveals.
Harper Collins Study Bible page 1,917

Besides the children, only two others, Mary Magdalene and Demetrius, knew the true story of Jesus.

They knew how Heraclion, a Persian king 57 years before in Galilee had made love to his mother Mary and created Jesus.

How Mary had wed respectable Joseph to save her good name in Nazareth.

His true father, Heraclion was of Alexander the Great's Line, which made Jesus the seventh grandson of a God, Alexander the Great, who was the son of Zeus.

In his youth Jesus ran away with his friend, Demetrius to Babylon to play the role of prince. He was a true prince of Babylon and after living the palace life and after a very bad day in a wrestling arena, where he killed a man, the young Prince Jezep and his friend ran away to find his salvation, he finally found it in faraway India.

Jesus, who they called Issa in their own language, studied Buddha's dream for two years, when he had surpassed the temple master in wisdom he knew he was done.

The new master and his friend the poet returned to Babylon and soon afterwards made one last journey home to the Holy Land.

But the return of a messiah, son of Yahweh was only a myth, a Jewish prophecy. He had taken up the role, acting out the ancient tale of the savior, Every Jew knew the story and Jesus played it well, like he was born to the role.

He had gone to Jerusalem to preach because he truly felt it in his heart but soon he got caught up in the myth. He played at being Christ so perfectly, even riding into Jerusalem during Passover on a donkey as the ancient story foretold.

He lived it right up to the end until it got too real, the prophecy was that he must be crucified and the local priests were ready to oblige. It was too much for a young, hopeful man of 33, so he abandoned his play—acting and escaped.

He returned to his home in Babylon and believed he and his wife would lounge happily into old age.

But from the caravans coming into Babylon he learned how he had inspired a religion called Christianity.

And now perhaps a half million people from Palestine to Rome to the Western Isles followed his teachings and thought him a God.

They called him Jesus Christ.

The people who believed in him called themselves Christians.

This bothered him immensely. Jesus thought his peaceful words would calm the world but instead had enflamed it.

And now because of a cruel Roman emperor, Nero, thousands of his followers were going to their death in the coliseum of Rome for a fire they did not start.

He thought of them dying for him and it made him weep. He was a Buddhist but first a king—and a king must protect his people.

Chapter 31

The late sun hung like a fat orange above the city of Rome. It was three weeks after the great fire and the heart of every Christian and Roman, soldier and slave, was tired and burnt as the sun. Everyone's nerves were twisted ropes.

Whips were lashed, gruff orders shouted and Roman soldiers kicked Christians through the streets of Rome.

The emperor had told the citizens it had been the cursed Christians who had started the fire and they were hated like the plague.

As they were whipped through the streets garbage was heaped upon them and they were stoned to death on every corner.

Enraged citizens would ply through the rubble or dig down into dark hiding places and grab up them up. They would drag followers of Christ wailing into the street and pelt them with chunks of marble, leaving bloody bodies strewn everywhere. It was a good time for the crows and the dogs.

The lucky ones who escaped the harsh stones of the people were whipped into cages by soldiers and hauled away in carts to the jails beneath the coliseum. They were kept there starving, awaiting execution.

Emperor Nero was a raving tyrant and all thought he was quite mad. The Christians suffered every sick whim oozing from his rotting brain.

The fire had been in mid—July. Taking into account the lazy nature of the emperor as well as his interest in gladiators, chariot races and games of a bizarre sexual nature, most everyone calculated the Christians would not be fed to the lions until late August or September.

Making them wait was the worst part of the punishment.

Chapter 32

**With the wine of fornication the inhabitants of Earth
have become drunk.
—Revelations 17:2**

Forty thousand screaming citizens in many colored robes were jumping up and down in the stands. It was noon and they were already drunk.

It was The Festival of Lust, Nero's own invention.

Chubby Nero sat at the far end of the arena on his tall ivory throne. He was in his purple robe trimmed with gold.

He had a round head and black greasy hair combed forward like pigeon wings. His eyes were liquidy and dark with black tint rubbed around them like a woman's. He wore the lipstick rouge of a prostitute. He had a painted mole on his cheek. When he laughed he sounded like a little girl choking with the hiccups.

Loud metal drums started pounding and the drumbeats echoed through the stadium. Black Nubian slaves carrying straw brooms, marched out in a line from the far gate. The crowd roared like a thundering storm.

Three hundred male horses had been up-ended and tied with wide, leather straps around their torsos and set belly facing out around the sides of the arena.

Around the wall, the horse's legs were flailing outwards into the air, their terrified eyes wide and panicking. Loud, pathetic whinnying blared from their mouths. Slaves wearing nothing but plumed Roman helmets marched naked around the arena with long straw brooms and reached in tickling the horses' undersides. The poor, uncomprehending horses screeched kicking wildly, and the crowd seeing 300 long horse members rise up wiggling, while the horses whinnied to the sky made the people wail and laugh to insanity.

The little emperor almost choked at the sight.

Dancing and prancing came one hundred naked, painted prostitutes of every race and color in the empire:

Tall black women from Africa, brown-skinned Egyptian girls, Alabaster white women from Spain, and fat, round Germanic Girls from the black forests of Gaul. There were Greek girls, whores of the virgin temples, and writhing with more gusto than the rest were the dark-haired, buxom Jewish Women. They loved it.

Overly painted Roman courtesans danced among them. Christian Women were dragged by their hair screaming and then whipped along naked, the soldiers loving to defile them in front of Cristus, their God.

The whores were all jiggling and obscenely wiggling their tongues in high trilling sounds like belly dancers, shaking their bodies at the roaring crowd. They twirled around in a wild, bouncing parade.

The painted women shook their painted breasts at the crowd and some fell and rolled in the dirt, jumping up and dancing madly around the arena, arms waving high in the air, wicked smiles on their faces, tongues flicking like cobras, throwing flowers in the air.

The tied-up horses, foaming at the mouth were kicking wildly.

In the center were a thousand people, lying in the grass in the middle of the coliseum, writhing around engaged in a thousand different sexual positions consisting of multiple partners—an acre of wet, squirming bodies.

Most of those in the center on the grass were men with women but a large number of the squishy crowd were men with men and women with women. It did not matter. All the bodies were moving and churning in a sloshing sea of glistening flesh.

Groping fingers rubbing around bodies, fingernails scratching red ribbons into bare backs, teeth biting into shoulders, eyes rolling back in ecstasy and a thousand screams and moans of pleasure were echoed off the high walls.

Naked legs were spread and sticking up like so many V-shaped fence posts, moans of pleasure rising up, loud moans of women and men joined with the sound of pounding kettledrums. The scene could rouse the dead.

Stepping around the writhing couples were half-naked black slave men with long poles where on the end were buckets pouring out warm, olive oil over the moving bodies making them moan louder, and around the mass of people joining, entering, pumping, slaves stepped through with glass jars pouring cold wine into open mouths.

A thousand sex-mad people were glistening in the late afternoon, their moans mixing with the horse's mad whinnying and the frantic pounding of drums.

Nero sat on his ivory throne rocking back and forth, laughing like a girl with hiccups.

Chapter 33

People in the crowd started coupling in the seats. Those without partners were dancing up and down throwing beer and wine from their cups into the air, grabbing and kissing anybody they could find.

After a short time of mass sexual pleasure, wild trumpets sounded in the stands and drums pounded faster upping the speed of the music, inspiring those on the ground to pump faster in time to the drumbeats.

As the tempo of drums quickened the moans and screams grew louder, the sound of drums and trumpets reached a deafening pitch as the dancing girls twirled around the arena in a frenzied parade. The tied-up, helpless horses kicked their legs around madly and ear-piercing horse screeches echoed to the sky, mingling with moans of mad pleasure. Suddenly out of a giant door in the far wall two chariots emerged.

A white chariot swirled with gold ivy-leaf was driven by a tall naked Roman woman, she had copper-colored skin and was whipping her four 'horses' who were four naked men in harnesses, each man a different color.

Prancing beside her in the other chariot of black Onyx and shining silver was a naked man standing up whipping his 'horses' who were four naked women in harnesses, long leather straps over their shoulders and around their breasts and then under their arms with attached feathers inserted near their groin areas.

The men would pull back on the reins, feathers would jiggle between their legs and the girls would howl with greedy pleasure.

The two chariots fell in behind the parade of prostitutes, whipping their naked "chargers" along, each set of four, men and women howling with pleasure as the leather straps were yanked.

Amidst the chaos, Nero waved his fat little arm and at the bottom of the stairway two naked male midgets, painted bright red, wearing devil horns were holding wooden tridents and started poking at the buttocks of a naked fat woman. She squealed and began huffing and puffing up the steps in front of them. She had four teeth and shaggy blond hair ratty as Medusa's.

She was at the bottom of his royal stairs, a hundred feet down from his high throne, and the little red midgets kept prodding and sticking her large, naked ass with their tridents. The gross fat woman wore comical goose feather angel's wings and whenever they jabbed her buttocks she let out a scream and grabbed her butt. Nero giggled and clapped his fat hands together with glee.

Prodded from behind by giggling midgets, she kept performing a lewd, blubbery dance up the stairway, smiling with her red painted mouth, her arms moving around like fat snakes, then she would grasp her huge blubbery watermelon breasts lifting them up offering them up to the little emperor. Her mouth was smeared with rouge and she wore a sickening smile. As she climbed higher, her lustful eyes were stuck on the emperor, all the while flicking her tongue in and out like a cobra.

Nero loosened his robe readying himself for her. The robe fell away and he looked like a fat pink little gnome lying back on his throne. It was a pathetic sight; the soldiers around his throne glanced down and could see he was definitely ready for her.

The mass arena was moving in a mad churning of wet and slimy flesh, the sensual parade of naked men and women and chariots pulled by lashed bodies was going round and round to the sound of lewd screams, moans and pounding drums.

. The fat woman on the stairs was given one final jab and leaped up to the little emperor. In a grand crescendo of wild abandon she threw her fat, sweating body down upon his upright readiness, her eyes rolled back when she felt it, her nails dug into his back and as her head bobbled around she howled louder and louder, Nero squealed like a girl.

Chapter 34

The morning after the orgy two Praetorian guards in red-plumed helmets, silver breastplates and Roman skirts and sandals walked briskly up the steps of the royal palace.

At the top, palace guards pulled back their long spears. They walked quickly across the black marble floor toward the emperor's inner chamber, their boots clacking as they walked. Their faces stern as statues.

Two tall black slaves opened wide the doors to Caesar's throne room and the soldiers looked up at the little man sitting there, his round head leaning sideways on his large marble throne. They boomed out, "Hail, Caesar!"

Nero pinched his sagging red eyes with two fingers, "What is it?" He reached for his goblet and took another swig of wine.

"The coliseum jails are filled with the Christians, when shall we begin, that is, what shall we do with them?"

"Crucify them."

"ALL of them?! There are over two thousand!"

"You heard me, crucify every single one of them, do it inside the coliseum, make them pay for setting the fire, nail them all up—but save a few for me. I have more interesting fates planned for them."

"Yes, sire, when shall we begin?"

"In two days time, ready the arena. Now go."

"Yes, my lord, it shall be done."

The two soldiers put their fists against their breastplates, bowed and turned to go. Their long, trailing red cloaks slid behind them across the floor and the tall doors closed behind them.

The fat king sat back in his throne tightly gripping the arms of the chair. A sinister smirk made its way across his round face as he chuckled slyly to himself.

Chapter 35

Fifty starving lions raced around the arena grounds, terrified and roaring at up the crowd. They were not fed for days.

The scrawny yellow lions ran around in a panic, slamming into the walls, snarling, biting and pawing each other then running around the grounds like crazed horses racing in all directions at once.

The tall coliseum stands were only lightly filled. It was the first day of the executions and most citizens did not have the stomach for it.

Some cheered but most of the white—robed citizens just stared down into the arena grounds because none believed that—Christians would actually be fed to lions.

This had never happened in anyone's lifetime.

Even so, nearly ten thousand citizens had made it out to witness the ghastly scene. They sat in the stands, gulping down huge amounts of wine and beer; vendors wandered the crowd pouring it from pitchers and selling peanuts and almonds as they walked along. The people were wiping their chins, looking with wide disbelieving eyes at the crazy lions running around below.

The starving lions attacked each other, swiping and pawing at each other's furry heads with open claws. Their roars sounded if they were being strangled to death.

High up on the podium under a large purple canopy, pudgy little Nero sat on his high marble throne grinning away, apparently liking this as much as the orgies.

His personal guard of Centurions stood at attention beside him. He waited until the perfect moment and stood up and raised high his arms.

At the far end of the coliseum a door opened and a large group of Christians, about fifty tattered men, women and children crept terrified into the arena. The door slammed behind leaving them trapped facing the lions.

When they saw the yellow beasts they started screaming and running around wildly, vainly trying to scramble up the inner walls, women their eyes wide in terror, crying, and clutching children to their breast, men were trying to hide behind each other, some tearing their own hair out. A few kneeled to pray.

Every single lion suddenly stopped snarling at each other and turned, hesitating only a few seconds and charged.

Many Romans had to turn away and many threw up over the side.

It was all over in a few minutes. When the lions were beaten back into their cages, slaves entered and dragged away the bodies.

Chapter 36

Jesus was praying in the garden felt a sudden pain in his chest. He fell forward but caught himself with his hand to the ground. In his mind he saw lions charging and tears streaming down terrified faces. His head was lowered, his long hair brushing the ground. He did not hear the soft voice calling to him.

"Jesus my love, where are you?"

Beautiful blond Mary entered the garden through the white archway. Jesus hung down facing the earth.

"There you are," she cooed.

She hurried to him beside roses and low, light-green bushes, she was smiling but slowed when she saw him staring in pain. She straightened her white linen robe. He was pitched forward not moving.

She walked to within a few feet of him; His long hair was hanging down hiding his bearded face as he tilted forward. He was on all fours, his brown pilgrim's robe was ruffled around him like a collapsed tent.

He came out of his trance, turned and managed a smile. "Hello, Mary."

She looked at him puzzled saying, "Why are you so sad, my love?"

Her pretty face softened, her long blond-white hair flowing down low and bouncing around her beautiful, thin womanly face and her red lips. Jesus looked at the ground and quietly spoke, "My children in Rome are suffering. I must go and save them."

Mary closed her eyes and cupped her hands together. For years she had to have patience with her prince, she simply said, "My love, how exactly do you plan to save them?"

His intense, haggard brown eyes looked toward the ground and he spoke quietly, "I don't know but God will reveal that to me."

"I believe you, my lover."

Jesus managed a weak smile, to hear this beautiful woman call him 'lover' touched him deeply. His face turned red and then he asked her, "Are you sure you want to come. Rome is so far. Even Demetrius is nervous about it. He thinks we are too old for such a journey."

"You are too old, my love." She giggled.

"Now Mary." He answered playfully, starting to smile.

"But I know you can do anything." she answered.

He hugged her and pulled away, staring into her deep blue eyes and said, "Moses was 400 years old when he made his journey, I am only 57."

"But Moses did not drink as much wine as you do."

Jesus could not hold back a wide smile, squeezing her hand, "True, my love, it is my one weakness."

She kept taunting him, "and Alexander was half your age when he conquered the world."

"True, but you're never too old to save the world."

"I'm with you my love, to the ends of the Earth!"

He pulled her to him and kissed her sweetly.

Chapter 37

A man hath no better thing under the sun than to eat,
drink and be merry.
Ecclesiastes 8:15

The great Babylonian feasting hall was bustling with people. The long white linen table was groaning with food, juices spilling everywhere into the cloth. Throngs of royal friends were seated around it clinking goblets together and laughing loudly.

Demetrius was drinking heavily and leading most of the many toasts to the prince and his lady. Once he burped and proclaimed, "You can toast to me if you want!" They all laughed and toasted him too.

Their robes were many colors, mostly purple filled the hall, the women's long gowns were trimmed with lace, most of them white. Nearly all the men were princes of Babylon and rulers from provinces near and far.

There were some Jews who had arrived in caravans from Jerusalem; there was one rich Roman and his lady from the city of Judea. There were nobles from Egypt and commoners and there were as many great women as men seated at the royal table.

Prince Jezep had always looked on women as equals, as superiors at times, especially in giving advice.

No Christians were at the feast of course, although many were settling further and further east. Their world would collapse if they found out that their savior had escaped the cross.

The guests waited for the prince, the full aroma of the food made waiting unbearable.

The delicious fragrance of many creatively cooked animals wafted through the hall. The silver wine pitchers were set everywhere within easy reach.

Weighting down the table were, sweltering, sugar-spiced pigs on platters swimming in succulent juices, fried peacocks, roasted turkeys slopped with butter, brown-baked ducks steaming with fragrance and a side of beef floating in sweet sauces on a giant silver platter. Chickens, brown and gold, juicy on plates were everywhere down the table.

Wine in ornate golden pitchers with matching goblets were already being clutched by thirsty wine-drinkers and poured into glasses. They could not wait. Unlike the Greeks who mixed their wine with water, in the east they drank it straight—'neat' was the word.

Belying his legend, Jesus was joyful, he grabbed life heartily and welcomed others to do the same. He was jovial. He loved to laugh and as far as food was concerned, he believed it was not what went into your mouth that was bad but the words that came out of it.

By royal decree, any and all animals, cloven hooves or no, were cooked the juicier the better.

The party waited at the table and it extended from the royal throne at one end fifty feet down to a wide performing stage.

The stage was just now empty of bards and dancing girls. The entire feast was awaiting his divine presence, Prince Jezep.

On the end of the table was a throne for the prince and to his right was the seat for his Mary.

His many friends waited at the table and twice that many servants leaned against walls and stood in arched doorways awaiting the noble prince. They were celebrating his journey to Rome, a sadness ran just below the surface for they all knew he would leave and never return.

This was his Last Supper with his friends.

Chapter 38

The people sat down to eat and drink and rose up to play.
—1 Corinthians 10:7

Mary slipped into the hall through the door behind the throne.

"M'Lady!" and "Hail Mary!" echoed around the hall as the guests stood and bowed their head in respect. The white—haired beauty bowed and stood awaiting her prince.

Prince Jesus strode in behind her and the hall roared, "Hail the prince!" "All hail the prince!"

Loud whoops, arms raised in toasts of wine, shouts, thundering applause, fists pounding the table! Every guest was clapping and bowing and smiling.

Prince Jezep was their father and friend, they felt protected in his presence, whenever he let go his broad white smile they felt right with the world.

The clapping and whistling and bowing did not stop until the husky, brown—robed prince with long silver—black hair and beaming bearded smile raised both his hands for silence.

It got quiet and the hall full of friends and servants stood awaiting their prince's words. He joined his hands together, looked down and recited the Lord's Prayer in Aramaic:

"Awoon dwashmaya nithqadash shmakh…"

"Our Father who art in Heaven hallowed be thy name…

"tethey malkuthakh nehwey seweeyanakh…"

"Your kingdom come, your will be done"

"akana dwashmaya ap barah…"

"On Earth as it is in Heaven…"

He ended the old Jewish prayer,

"mitol ddeelakhee malkutha whaila wtishbohta la—alam almeen, Amen."

He raised his head and shouted out joyfully, "My friends, now let's make a dent in this feast!"

All cheered and sat down, talking, grabbing a haunch or wing or a cup and laughed with each other as the hall echoed with light-hearted voices

The food finally dwindled to bones and empty platters and the wine cups were half—full, as they told tales of heroes and men for a full hour before all sat back in their chairs fat as lords.

Lovely Mary was sitting to the prince's right at the table. Her blond-white hair falling free to her shoulders, her green gown revealing just enough soft white beauty. She was eating demurely, taking small sips of wine and smiling at her Lord.

Demetrius sat to his left, the poet smiling, half-shaven, talking away, his jaw a hero's jaw, his green eyes flashing, his head moving back and forth, his dark hair whipping around with each word of a story.

His hair was long and curling, he was 56 and his hair was still pure black. Other men turned silver and gray from their trials but life's problems rolled off Demetrius like raindrops off a goose's back. He wrote and he loved his troubles away. This night he wore the flowing, white robe of a bard, a golden headband around his forehead.

He smiled at his noble friend at the head of the table. After 50 years of facing life and lions together, after hiking, hurting, laughing and traveling down a million trails together it was love and trust they saw. Love and trust.

Jesus looked down the table at his friends sitting back sipping wine and talking, he slammed his fist on the table, a hall full of friends looked up as he shouted to the bard, "How about a poem!"

Cheers and wine sloshed from the cups, "Yes! A poem! A poem!"

Demetrius smiled as wide as the sliver of a moon, stood up and raised his harp above his head, "My friends, I am here to fulfill all your needs!"

Roars filled the hall.

He hopped up onto the table and to wild cheering briskly skipped the length of it, lightly dodging plates, kicking over goblets here and there, to finally reach the end of it and hopped up onto the stage.

He stood up straight and tall, his long, curling black hair rolling down. Standing in his white poet's robe, he smiled his perfect white smile, tilted his head, and strummed his ancient harp. A sweet tingling sound went lilting through the hall as his words turned hearts to honey—

"When kings were men and men were kings
Poets flew on beauty's wings, Ladies lived to love their lord
And Knights defend that love with sword, down the ages ever taught
of riches that cannot be bought,
it's Love that fills our heart at night
and brings the best unto our sight—

If we can lift our life above
trade the falcon for a dove—
Love will forever rise
and Peace once more
will fill our eyes."

It was silent a moment and then thundering applause and up on the stage the poet held his harp to his side and bowed low, drinking in their clapping like the sweet wine of heaven.

"More!" they shouted, "Another!" begged the crowd.

He placed his ivory harp up to his shoulder and lightly strummed the strings sending soft ripples into every heart—

"A friend for every wave that breaks
a sigh upon the shore, a heart will always give and take
then cry again for more

A sun for every single friend
who rises every day, may the memories never end
and never fade away.
And when the sunset takes the sky
and paints it once again, here's to friends who live and die
I'll never see again."

Chapter 39

The great one on the long end of the table stood up and spoke to his friend, "Thank you, Demetrius, once again your poems were wonderful."

The bard set down his harp and turned to everyone,

"As all of you know, I go with the prince and Lady Mary to Rome. It will be a long journey and we will be gone long and will miss our home and friends but we must go."

All turned waiting for what the prince would say. All eyes stared at him; his perfectly combed silvery beard and hair. Deep brown eyes set in a perfectly handsome face. A king above kings. Mary stared at him and beamed like a little girl.

He was like all would imagine Alexander the Great. His shoulders were broad. He appeared like the paintings of the barrel—chested, rebel slave Spartacus and shined like the great Achilles.

His Persian friend, Darius stood up,

"My lord, please tell us—why DO you go to Rome?"

The prince looked directly at his friend and right out in a bold voice, "I GO TO KICK THE EMPEROR NERO IN HIS ROYAL ASS AND TELL HIM TO CHANGE HIS WICKED WAYS!"

A wineglass crashed to the floor.

The silence was loud in the hall. Mary glared up, shocked at her husband and then turned to Demetrius sitting on the far stage. The poet was looking down shaking his head. He had not known what was in his friend's head up till now and for sure he did not know it was tweaking the emperor's nose.

One person started to clap, then another.

And another until the entire hall was a ringing with deafening applause and shouts "Here, here!" "Yes!" and "Down with the Nero!" "You tell him, sire!"

All the guests stood up clapping, the Egyptians, the old Jews and white-robed Essenes stood up, the satraps and fellow princes and their ladies all stood up clapping and whistling at the boldness of this prince. Even the wealthy Romans and their women cheered. Some just held their goblets high waving them around.

Mary stood up admiring her daring husband and Demetrius sat on the stage shaking his head.

Servants were stomping their feet up and down in the doorways and the dogs in the hall were barking, deafening out of control.

Darius shouted, "Yes! Prince Jezep! Go to Rome! Tell the emperor, you TELL off that evil emperor!" The crowd was standing up on chairs and on the table clapping till their hands hurt, cheering till their throats were sore.

Chapter 40

By the time the last guest had left their journey was fully supplied. The rich Jews at the door, vigorously shook the hand of the prince and said, "We will give you camels laden with food and wine, drivers and 2 horse—drawn carts."

"Shalom!" The prince hugged them all and their families.

The kings of the provinces of Bactria walked up, shook the hand of the prince, "Sire, it is four hundred miles of dangerous desert to the coast, for protection we will give you soldiers on horseback."

"Thank you, my friends." Jesus was holding back tears.

Their Roman friend, Actius Vespasian, an important official in Jerusalem, stepped up and before he walked out the door gave the Prince his Imperial Ring engraved with the Roman Eagle.

"Show this to anyone between here and the sea and they will let you pass.

It is the royal seal of Rome."

Prince Tuhtmoses, the Egyptian said, "I will send a ship to carry you to Rome. It will have a full crew and a bold captain, the largest ship in Egypt and it is yours, Prince Jezep. It will be waiting in the harbor of Joppa. Anyone who would curse this emperor is my eternal friend." Then he dropped his head in a bow and Jesus reached to hug him.

"Thank you." He said with tears in his eyes.

A fellow Babylonian Bard stepped forward and gave Demetrius a new gold harp, "Sing many songs with this, poet, inspire your prince on his way!"

"I shall," and he ran his fingers across the strings and then hugged his fellow poet.

The women of the city promised Mary shawls of many colors to keep her and her prince warm on the long journey to Rome.

The hall was soon empty.

The Prince and Mary and Demetrius stood by the door smiling at each other.

Demetrius slapped his friend on the back, " With all these gifts we have to make the journey whether we want to or not."

"True, my friend" they laughed.

Mary looked up at her love with a nervous smile and squeezed his hand. The Demetrius put his new harp to his shoulder; he strummed a long strum, raising his eyes he said, "Here we go again."

CARAVAN TO ROME
Chapter 41

The seaport of Joppa was a bright blue sapphire on the ring finger of the East. It slept on the coast only a few short miles from the ancient city of Jerusalem.

Joppa butted up against the orient facing the whole Mer Romana, the Greeks called it the Mediterranean Sea, the sea at the center of the world.

It was a beautiful port town, easy and free. The Joppa harbor was like an open mouth of a giant two—mile crocodile lying on its side welcoming in ships from many lands. Ships of all sizes and colors were always coming and going.

The legendary King Tut of Egypt had built the port a thousand years before. Other kings had held it but it remained a free—living place through the years.

The port was a mythical and religious.

Jonah had been swallowed by a whale and spat up by the main wharf. A large, black stone marked the spot he was disgorged the shape of a whale.

In recent years, a raving holy man named Peter, had risen a girl from the dead in a house overlooking the waters of Joppa.

Within days the legendary Jesus of Nazareth, with friends, would arrive and sail away on the holiest of missions.

A tall white lighthouse stood on the highest point of land, its beams waved out to sea for twenty miles welcoming Phoenician traders, Roman Merchants and Greek Triremes, anything sailing east.

At sunset the white lighthouse bathed in burnt—red light, turning to rust before night swallowed it up and it beamed its one eye out into the darkness.

On one particularly shimmering red sunset, a long square—rigged ship sailed slowly beneath the lighthouse heading into port. Its red sails melting into the sky's dying colors.

The massive ship was Egyptian, a war ship over 300 feet long with two broad red square sails and many white-clad sailors who sailed it in easily. Rows of oars slapped the water and rose up and down again like long, slowly flapping wings. Jewels dripped from the paddles.

It slid into port; the banks of oars pulled into the ships sides, the huge white ship expertly guided in, lightly spun around until it bumped easily against the wharf, its bow pointing outward toward Rome.

The scurrying sailors tied the massive ship to the old wooden wharf with huge ropes thick as a man's arm. This floating city with its eyes painted on the prow came to rest in the fading light resting in the waters of Joppa.

When they rolled up the sails onto the crossbeams of the main mast it looked like a high cross.

The sailors onboard went about their business quietly. The divine Prince Tuhtmose, had sent them to Joppa to meet a prince from Babylonia.

Obeying their fat captain they were to sail this royal person and his friends to Rome. They were to ask no questions, especially of the prince.

The long, noble Egyptian craft was tied tight and awaited the royal passengers that would soon arrive to sail to the mouth of the Tiber River, the gateway to Rome.

Chapter 42

Make straight in the desert a highway for our Lord.
—Isaiah 40:3

The moon was rising over the blue city of Babylon.

Jesus and Mary in their horse—drawn wagon were to lead the caravan. Demetrius would follow behind them in his own humble cart. The two Essene servants followed in their own wagon. Each of the carts had two horses pulling it.

All three carts were traveling houses.

It was four hundred miles to the coast and thousands by sea to Rome. The carts were lined up in front of the palace awaiting the word to roll.

Jezep, the Prince shook the reins in the night shouting, "Hyahh!" and the colorful entourage of carts lurched forward into the quiet, moon—washed Persian streets.

The horses clopped along and the travelers spoke not a word.

The prince knew they would meet up with an army escort of a hundred men in the morning and later be given camels laden with food and wine.

But tonight they traveled alone in dead silence.

Jesus knew a secret journey would be a safe journey.

Under the half moon an old, bearded Persian man sitting in the sand waved them on as they passed through the great gate.

Three lone carts rattled into the silvery desert night.

Chapter 43

Within days the caravan had swelled to hundreds. As they passed through the towns pilgrims, waifs and even temple whores fell in behind the wagons and joined the caravan.

Villagers along the way looked up at the long row of colorful men and women, mounted soldiers and camels and all marveled at this rattling parade.

Leading the way was a gray wooden cart, a small house tipping along, a silver-haired man and his lovely lady leading the long parade.

A longhaired muscular man clicking his horses forward directly behind drove the next wagon. The long ragged troupe was rough and shabby, no one along the way suspected the carts held a Persian prince carrying a fortune in gold.

Directly behind the cart of the poet was the servants' cart, of Lam and Silvanus, the Essenes and behind them were five camels in a line, laden with food and wine in bulging saddlebags. Colorful Arabian drivers were 'hut hutting' the camels rolling forward down the road behind the old carts.

Behind the camels rode one hundred soldiers on horseback, riding two-by two.

The horsemen were colorful and hailed from three different kingdoms, Babylon, Egypt and Bactria, a Persian Province. Some wore silver and green tunics and turbans, others, the Egyptians, wore short white tunics and light straw vests, the Scythians from Bactria sat loose in the saddle in short loincloths, riding bare—chested with only rough bear wolf skin robes over their shoulder, muscles bulging, they were forever throwing a wine—skin between them slurping the grape and laughing loudly. The Scythians were absolutely fearless, drunken singers and made everyone cheerful.

All soldiers had swords off their belt and held spears and slung bows and arrows over their back—and all were sworn to protect the prince and his family.

Behind the horsemen were ten more camels.

Behind the main body of carts and soldiers were the hangers on, the cast-offs seeking new lives in the next town. As they passed through towns people swelled to the caravan seeking a new life to the west.

And no matter how many joined, always bringing up the rear were the whores in black dresses.

Buyers of fishes or cattle, sellers of various wares or dark women, it did not matter all were welcome. The horses clopping behind the camels and the carts and the clanging of silver goblets and armor could be heard for miles into the desert. The sound scared away lions and robbers.

After eight days riding across the desert not a robber had attacked and no lions were seen.

The caravan shuffled across the Persian tundra, this long, colorful parade of shining carts, flags flying and soldiers marching, a traveling show, a family now numbering in the many hundreds, marching toward the sea.

Chapter 44

It was 3 o'clock in the afternoon and the sky above Rome was burnt orange.

A tall door in the coliseum was thrown open and thirty ragged, terrified people were shoved inside, across the arena fifty lions paced nervously, glaring and hungry. The door closed behind the people and the lions slithered toward them, mouths open wide and blood red.

The tattered Christians clutched each other and cried and the Romans in the stands cheered, clapped and swigged down cups of beer betting on who would be eaten first. High on a platform the emperor was peering downward and clapping, a fat grin across his face.

The drooling lions circled toward the wailing people. The giant cats lunged growling and the screams as human flesh was ripped away was drowned out by the cheering mob.

Chapter 45

Jesus suddenly doubled over gripping his chest.

"What is it, my love?!" Mary yelled frantically, grabbing the reins. He shook his head waving her away.

"I feel something horrible happening to my people, I can feel it."

"You *look* horrible, give me the reins." she took them over, steadying the horses as Jesus slumped sideways in the cart, his head leaning on the upright sideboard of the wagon. His hair was hanging down in wet strings, his hand to his mouth. The desert ahead looked blurry, his head throbbed and he started feeling something was gnawing at his insides.

At that moment in Rome red, fleshy body parts were strewn across the arena floor. Lions were running everywhere dragging bodies in their teeth.

Jesus suddenly put his hand over his eyes and hung his head down and could not move.

Chapter 46

Inside the dank cell beneath Rome's coliseum twenty ragged Christians were lying around on the straw floor.

Miriam the little Christian girl looked up at Mathew with a weak smile, "Will Jesus really come save us?"

Mathew, the old disciple turned to her, "Of course darling, Jesus will save us." He looked at her, his brow sad and wrinkled.

She was sitting down her legs spread on the floor. Her dark—brown tunic was torn and shredded. Miriam, a 13 year—old girl from a rich family was now in rags and no comb or servants to help her.

She brushed her straggly brown hair out of her eyes that were burning red from crying for days.

The soldiers yesterday had terrified her.

Two days before big men in coarse red robes and metal armor had pulled her into an empty cell, torn off her clothes and groped and sucked at her breasts, they'd fingered her private places. One had lain on top of her and entered her. It hurt terribly at first. She had bled yet had felt no knife. It confused her.

She now sat in the cell staring into space; old women stroked her hair comforting her. The others cowering in the jail cell also had drooping, hopeless eyes. They wallowed in their sadness. They were older which blocked their faith, but they dared to listen to Mathew hoping he would fill their hearts this time.

Mathew saw the trembling girl and spoke softly consoling her like an uncle, "Miriam, my dear, Jesus is our savior and he will come, he rose from the dead and promised to return. He will come soon and we will live."

Suddenly screams wailed from the coliseum floor a hundred feet away.

Lions growled, screams of women stabbed into everyone's heart, they heard strangling voices —"NO! NO! O GOD! NO! OHH! MOTHER OF GOD—AAAAAW!" then the cracking of bones, in the stands thousands were cheering. Roars of lions and screams mixed with deafening cheers. It wrenched the hearts of each one in the cell.

Little Miriam fell down onto the floor clamping her hands over her ears crying out loud. She was sitting, swaying back and forth in the dirt sobbing madly, her bare feet kicking out wildly, "O God! I'll be next!" Two of the women moved to comfort her, holding her in their arms.

They looked up at the bars on the window then stared at each other in horror. Every stomach was tight, throats hurting, palms drenching in sweat for each one knew that soon it would be him out there facing lions.

The screams outside trailed off and all was quiet. Every soul in the cell stared at each other terrified.

An old man with a long white beard lying back against the wall cackled, "Jesus better get here soon or *WE* will be the Last Supper."

Chapter 47

"We will not stand this madness another second!" an old Roman man. shook his fist.

In the stands they booed and threw their wool seat cushions down at the reclining lions and smashed their clay beer cups onto the dirt floor of the arena. Some cups hit the lions' in the head and they yowled and tried to leap up the walls into the stands but fell back falling awkwardly. Shouts continued.

"Nero you are sick!" "This is too much!" "Christians do not deserve this!"

They yelled out not caring that the emperor might hear, they shouted at the soldiers down below, some threw their beer cups smashing onto the soldiers' helmets, some bolder ones threw cups smashing against the podium of the emperor.

Romans were leaving the stands, many more after viewing the horrid spectacle were puking over the side. Their white robes smeared in greenish-brown vomit.

Yells grew louder with hatred; "The Christians are not to blame!"

A few yelled right into the faces of the guards standing at attention around the stands. As hundreds filed out after the executions, some stomped on the Roman guards' boots to show their disgust. The guards did not move or draw a sword for they too hated the executions.

Even the older Roman guards knew this was wasn't right.

More than a few were itching to turn their javelins on the Emperor and end this insanity but each guard knew to overthrow the little king would take much more than a few boos in the stands, it would take a great leader with great inspiration.

It was a dream the guards were allowing to slip into their minds. More and more soldiers in the arena were itching to turn their spears on Nero.

Many a guard's thoughts ran to revolution but they each knew the penalty for failure.

If it failed they would all be crucified, so a takeover now was just a rumor in the wind. A frail hope.

Each soldier-guard standing at attention holding his spear in the grandstands knew there were far too many citizens still supporting Nero. More than that, each knew that too many Praetorian Guards were still loyal to the king.

Praetorian guards backed by more than half the citizens would be enough to hold off a charge at the throne.

Nero's personal soldiers cared about as much for the Royal Roman Eagle as a plucked turkey, but they were well—paid and their families were part of Rome, that is why they remained loyal.

But the people had nothing to lose and might stage a formidable riot but the problem was that many citizens still believed the ridiculous idea that the poor Christians had started the fire. Most Romans knew they were a cult of downtrodden fools and would never do something as bold as to burn down the city.

To the average person this idea was crazy but as every soldier knew, the average Citizen's reasoning power was on the level of a pig.

The foot soldiers in the stands watched the carnage each day, heard the boos in the stands, the shouts of overthrow in the streets. Half the army was ready, but the coliseum soldiers continued to stand straight and keep the peace. They bit their lip and closed their eyes while the lions were unleashed. They were sick of it clear up to their chin guards.

The city legions sat in their barracks by the tall, black Pantheon just waiting on the word. They hated the little emperor. He paid three Roman Cestertia per day and fed them slop. Three cents a day buys no loyalty and a lot of hate. He paid for beer but that was hardly enough.

Turning their spears on the emperor would start an even greater fire in Rome, a fire big enough to change the world.

It needed only a spark.

Chapter 48

All could see that Nero had lost his mind. By his imperial order, on three afternoons a week, fifty or a hundred Christians were shoved into the arena and eaten alive by lions. The hungry animals ripped the screaming people apart turning them into scraps.

He knew had to step up the executions because people were starting to blame him for everything and he needed scapegoats. He kept believing the lie that it was the Christians' fault and he'd make them pay with their lives. He started to believe it himself.

But people aren't fools, every day, fewer and fewer citizens were coming to see the slaughter, dwindling to only a few thousand, not fifty thousand that usually filled the stands.

People knew that the little idiot had gone beyond the limits.

Lions were eating women and children and afterwards Nero burned all survivors on crosses in his garden. This was too much.

These atrocities were beginning to sicken even the toughest Roman.

During the first week of the executions people thronged by the thousands to see the Christians killed because they were enflamed with hatred believing this strange Christus Cult was responsible for the fire. But when the people saw Nero building grand temples to himself in the places the fire had burned—they became suspicious.

When a senator made it public that Nero's building plans had been drawn up by the emperor—months before the fire—they knew it was all his evil work.

A month after the fire more than half of Rome and all Italy knew that their own emperor had burned down their city to build temples to himself.

They were enraged and rumors of an overthrow floated everywhere on the wind.

Fists were shaking in the streets. "Down with the emperor!"

Crowds formed outside the coliseum protesting the executions, the cry was, "Crucify Nero!" "Feed Nero to the Lions!"

It was getting harder and harder for the coliseum guards to shove back the crowd.

The louder the cries of overthrow, the faster the king unleashed the lions. It was a sickening deception being played out.

Many still pushed through the yelling crowds and paid the one Roman Cester to enter and see the slaughter. Many still came, bought a clay cup of hot beer and handful of almonds and sat back to watch the lions chomp on the Christians.

He played to his crowd.

The ones who backed him got a grand and bloody show. They always got their penny's worth.

A door in the lower part of the coliseum opened and a cowering group of bedraggled Christians would be shoved into the arena. Romans with long spears prodded them out and locked the door behind them. The whole group would run and hover in the corner clutching each other, then the lions would come.

Seeing the gaping teeth, a few kneeled and prayed but most tried to claw up the walls or break into a run.

Ten or more lions would lunge into the shivering crowd of screaming men, women and children, scrambling around terrified trying to hold off or push back the giant brown animals. The lions would bite into an arm or throat, take hold of the gurgling, screaming person and drag him across the dirt by the neck like a flailing rag-doll.

Naked women eaten alive got the loudest cheers and lions biting into women's' naked breasts drove them absolutely mad.

Huge jaws chomped bodies in half and would eat them right there, ripping human shoulders like they were gazelles in the desert. It was all muscle and teeth ripping away, tails waving as they chewed growling.

The hairy beasts would drag someone away half-alive to a corner and eat on him while the terrified person was still alive. A man vainly clutching at life beat at the lion's furry head with his fists till his screaming wore out and he fell forward in death, his tongue hanging out of his mouth. Blood splattered everywhere.

Romans in the stands cheered and threw beer into the air, with bloodlust danced around like madmen. There were just as many madwomen, eyes full of bloodlust.

But each day the crowds were growing smaller, human beings could not stand this for long.

Every day the stands were peppered with fewer people, only the sickest dregs of the city remained drooling and cheering the carnage.

The bloody drama always continued until nightfall when almost every Christian was reduced to bloody shreds.

The arena looked like a floor strewn with kitchen scraps.

The lions always left a few.

They ate their fill and retired back in the shadow of the wall licking bloody paws and swirling their long tongue around their bloody mouth.

Slave boys came out and gathered up the bloody bones and feet and threw them on mule-drawn carts and hauled the mess away.

At times a lion would charge out and pick off a slave boy for dessert.

There was always a few Christians left.

Roman Soldiers came running out and grabbed them, men, women and even children, dragging them with leather thongs by their feet to crosses around the edge of the arena. They forced them to wear a shirt dowsed in Naphtha, a fire-starter, nailed them up screaming onto wooden crosses and set them on fire.

They were human torches lighting up the night. Their screams echoed though out the arena and across the city.

While they burned, their flaming bodies lighting up the night with crackling flame, half-naked, painted women of the street danced around the arena in the firelight throwing walnuts and almonds into the stands.

When the last human torch flickered out and a black charred body slumped down, black stick hands fell off and it was free beer for everybody.

Chapter 49

Each time he watched the gory show the crotch of Nero's purple robe stood up like a tent pole.

Guards standing near him saw this and turned away shaking their head.

As the last sickening show ended and the last miserable scream died away, the emperor raised his chubby arms above his the laurel wreath of his head and clapped wildly.

His own Praetorian guards, numbering one hundred, stood beside him and stood further up, looking straight ahead and serious, their red plumes fluffing in the night breeze, their silver armor shining brightly in the flickering night.

Their spears held tightly always ready to defend the emperor. Not one showed the least bit of a reaction to the whole ghastly scene.

All the other guards in the arena, standing here and there, numbering about four hundred, tried to remain at attention but were being shoved by angered and disgusted spectators on their way out.

Shouts of "Horrors!" and "Stop this!" echoed in the stands and through the vast killing ground.

The large Roman captain of the guard was disgusted; he turned and left his post. Crowds all around him filed down steps into the street flowing by the hundreds outside the broad walls and into the street. He looked out from a high window down onto the streets. He saw throngs of white—robed citizens milling around, shaking their fists, surging in and pushing at his fellow guards below trying to hold them back.

The lone Roman Captain pondered the scene. Should he go down and stand beside his fellow guards by the wall and push back the crowd or pull off his helmet, throw down his javelin and join the crowd in protest?

The time was not ripe. The last straw had not fallen to break the camel's back.

He saw a sea of people swelling against a crumbling dam but it would take real courage for this shivering flock of sheep to charge a thousand swords.

They needed a leader, a shepherd to lead the sheep.

Chapter 50

**What evil hath he done? I have found no cause of death in him,
therefore...let him go.
—Pilate in Luke 23:22**

The old Roman commander was deep in thought gazing down at the crowd.

He was named Flavius but everyone called him "Mercius", meaning mercy.

He was the leader of the coliseum guard and commanded many soldiers. He was 60 years old, a barrel-chested man with a broad, warm smile but stern as iron.

He had been a guard since the old days in Jerusalem. He had shown his loyalty to Rome and risen quickly up through the ranks.

His one service to Rome that got him his exultant promotion to Captain of the Guard was overseeing the crucifixion of Jesus Christ, the infamous King of the Jews.

At the time it was an everyday crucifixion of a peasant preacher but his legend grew until a mere 25 years later throughout the empire Jesus was worshipped as a God.

Romans knew the name Christ, the troublesome God of these tedious Christians.

Mercius had been the centurion in charge the morning they crucified Jesus 25 years earlier. For that great service to Rome, ridding her of a dangerous rabble rouser, he was promoted to high centurion and transferred to Rome with honors.

His superiors knew he had crucified the so-called 'King of the Jews' but were told he showed mercy by giving Jesus wine to drink on the cross. Because of this 'Mercius' was added to his hereditary name.

From that time on he had always been better off than other soldiers, living in a large villa on the river with his beautiful wife, Drusilla, and his many servants.

No one knew the source of his riches or the secret of that twinkle in his eye, as if he always held some glowing joke within.

Only he and very few others knew the truth.

He had presided over Jesus' crucifixion but had not nailed him on a cross, quite the opposite—he helped him escape.

The captain was paid a fortune by Jesus to do this.

That was the secret of the twinkle in his eye. He was rich because of Jesus. He owed everything to him, his rank, his riches, and his villa.

He had been rewarded for helping pull off the biggest fraud in history.

Mercius had seen no evil in this poor, doomed man and would have helped him escape for nothing, but when he was offered a large sum of money to do it, he gave it his all, arranging everything to the last detail.

He had drugged him on the cross, then when he was still alive—pretended to bury him in a tomb.

He had no idea what ever happened to the handsome devil, he had disappeared from his tomb a few days afterwards and was never heard of again.

As the old Roman gazed down tonight at the rabble rousing in the streets, he thought of Jesus.

He smiled, 'If that Jesus fellow was still around, he'd straighten out this mess, he'd save these people and I'd help him do it, even if I had to crucify that little harp-playing jackass myself'.

Chapter 51

Let us now go unto Bethlehem and see which has come to pass.
—Luke 2:15

On a star-filled night the caravan came to the little town of Bethlehem.

There was a small inn beside the road; it had white mud walls and an oil lamp lighted up the door.

Jesus reined in the horses of the cart and the whole caravan stopped on the road a short way from the inn.

Jesus, in his coarse, brown robe, climbed down from the cart, raised his hand to the servants, the two wagons and the hundreds behind, "We will stay here tonight, make your camp beside the road."

Jesus helped Mary Magdalene down from the cart and hand-in-hand they walked to the little lit-up doorway of the inn.

They knocked on the door and the innkeeper opened the door to greet them.

He was a short, bald Jewish man in a short green tunic to his waist and a long white cotton fluffy cotton pants. His round face was white with reddish spots all over. He was wiping his fat hands on a towel as he opened the door. He laughed out loud when he looked up and saw Jesus and Mary, "Well, well two more pilgrims to see the birthplace of Jesus eh, I must say you two look the part alright. A regular Joseph and Mary you are. Alright, I'm supposed to say, "There's no room at the inn so you can sleep in the stable, it's around back, so there you have it, go on, I have some Motsa boiling, you'll have to excuse me, good evening," He shook his head, "I have to say you two look great, best costumes in a year, Shalom!"

He laughed and closed the door.

The two stared at each other a moment, the prince laughed.

"I guess this is the place."

"After you, my dearest." said she.

They slowly walked around back to the stable and there it stood, the silliest sight they could ever imagine.

There was a stable lit up with candles. Two donkeys stood around outside, A lamb, a cow and five sheep were tied to stakes all staring within at a straw-filled manger.

A newborn baby, a doll made of clay, was placed in the manger. Little clay hands reaching up. On the clay head of the baby Jesus candles were lit glowing like a crude, makeshift halo.

Jesus saw this crazy shrine, closed his eyes, lowered his head and pinched the bridge of his nose very hard; Mary hugged him tight, shaking her head.

He opened his eyes long enough to see the marble shrine and closed his eyes again, he was shuddering not knowing whether to laugh or cry.

There stood a marble plaque, six feet high beside the stable there was a six-foot high marble plaque, Jesus read the words, Manger at Bethlehem, birthplace of Jesus Christ, our savior, in this stable our Lord was born, say a prayer. Smaller words were carved further down, "Donations accepted, Shalom". There was a carved bowl on the ground filled with Roman coins and Jewish Shekels.

The prince looked across the grounds around the stable to see nine or ten campfires glowing in the night with robed pilgrims huddled around each one, some were singing low or chanting, others mumbling and laughing, he knew at once they were all here to worship at the birthplace of their savior.

The prince and lady standing in the dark and turned to each other dumbfounded.

They looked over to see a man inside beside the manger at a table lit by an oil lamp. He sat sipping a cup of wine, when he saw them he gulped down his wine and stood up and walked out to them, He was young, dressed in perfect white silk robes, playing a part. He smiled politely, "Welcome to the birthplace of Jesus of Nazareth, our messiah, you can donate a shekel in that plate over there if you like, one more if you're planning on sleeping here, another if I pray for you."

He pointed to a pile of straw back in the corner of the stable, "You can sleep there."

Jesus stared straight at him, expressionless, blank as a wall. He had been awaiting this moment all his life, the moment he would finally reveal who he was, finally say it out loud. Mary stepped back staring at the boy and back at her man, she felt proud, he straightened his shoulders and spoke, "I am Jesus Christ" He awaited the reaction he believed would be awe and wonder but the boy looked confused, Jesus continued, "And this is my wife, Mary Magdalene, I have finally returned." He felt perfect.

"Wh. Why yes, of course, my Lord, by all means, and this is Mary Magdalene, of course it is, please be my guests, no charge." He put his hand to his mouth stifling a laugh, "Who am I to refuse the messiah and Mary Magdalene." He then burst out laughing and almost fell over backwards, turning red; he managed to point to the corner of the stable.

"Over there, my Lord and would our messiah like breakfast in bed?" He howled and slapped his knee and managed to wobble away into the night. He was holding his stomach waving behind, still laughing, "I'm sorry, my Lord, I really am." He walked away laughing.

They stood and watched him go straight to a circle of Christians sitting around a fire and sit down. He mumbled something and then the whole group laughed loudly and looked back at them standing by the light of the manger.

The prince overheard their words,

"Another one, eh?"

The young host of the manger answered, "Yea, we get about one messiah a month, and this one, get this, is with Mary Magdalene!"

The whole fireside group howled with laughter and a few fell off the log they were sitting on.

"Mary Magdalene?! He really said that?! That is wild. A couple of crazies eh?"

"Yea, I hope they leave without treating me to some raving sermon. They're all crazy."

Soon the entire encampment was chuckling, staring and pointing at the prince and lady in the barn area.

The prince stood by the door frowning at the pilgrims. He heard one of them shout, "Pleasant dreams Jesus!"

Raucous laughter erupted.

It finally died down as the worshippers around the fires resumed their mumbling conversations.

The prince turned and led Mary over to a corner of the stable.

"Fools, they don't believe it's me, or you." They both sat down in the straw, leaning against a wall, she turned and caressed his cheek with her soft hand, she said softly, "Forgive them, for they know not what they do."

He smiled and looked down, his arms resting on his knees.

"I suppose you're right, but this religion I've started weighs heavily upon me, my so-called followers are such fools, they worship rocks and straw and sell my words for shekels. To tell you the truth Mary, the whole thing depresses me."

He hung his head again and then he felt her soft hand rubbing his neck, "They are Jews with a new idea in their head and you know Jews, always joking, come, my love" she cooed, "let us lay down in the straw and forget this crazy religion of yours."

He turned and stared at her moment then kissed her and fell on top of her and kissed his wife again. With his arms around her he raised his head and looked up a moment, "I dread what I've started, look at those fools out there, I feel this new faith will be filled with idiots and emperors and priests like Nero and Caiphus, Mary, I fear the worst."

Mary reached and pushed the hood of his robe back off pulled his head down and kissed him soft and hard warming his body all over. He kept up the kiss, deeper and let his kisses roam all around her neck, she laughed as he kissed her ear and kept kissing her until after a few minutes of playfulness she pushed him away laughing,

"Come my love, let's get some sleep."

He pulled back, "Alright my love, here is my best goodnight kiss."

The prince kissed her and she closed her eyes in the straw of the manger and started to sleep. When she was breathing deeply, the lord prince pulled the hood over his head and sat staring at the glowing manger with a long frown.

A little clay Baby Jesus with chubby brown clay hands reaching up, candles glowing around the manger. There was a collection plate under the manger; it was filled with silver shekels.

After a few minutes staring at the manger of Bethlehem a smile crept onto his face and he had to hold back his laughing with his hand.

He lay down with a broad smile and fell asleep next to his love.

The next morning panels of light sliced through the cracks in the walls of the manger. All the pilgrims were gone, even the young host was nowhere around. Campfires smoldered here and there.

The prince and his lady stood up, picked straw from their hair and brushed off their clothes.

Not far away by the road the caravan was waking.

Soldiers in uniform stood up and fastened their leather breastplates. One hundred horse-mounted men with swords were waking and leaping onto their horses.

A soldier mounted his horse, straightened his helmet and patted his horse's neck. He turned to a fellow soldier,

"Do you think the prince is mad?"

His friend tied his silver helmet under his chin and nodded, "For certain, he's crazy as a hoot owl, and his friends are mad as he is, this insane quest—Curse Nero indeed! Save the Christians, posh! Prince Jezep has lost his mind."

His friend looked over and grinned saying, "Lucky for us we only go as far as Joppa and then the crazy prince is on his own. He can drag others into his madness but not us, thank God."

"Amen to that, my friend."

At the head of the caravan the two mounted soldiers watched the brown-robed prince help his queen into their cart. He raised his arms to Heaven and they heard him shout, "To Joppa!"

Every throat roared, every arm raised high.

He swung up onto his leading cart and the caravan lurched forward behind him. Pots and pans jangling the sides of wagons, colorful flags filling out in the breeze. :

Chapter 52

The caravan had not traveled five miles when a row of men on horseback appeared on the hill ridge to their left. It was a long flat hill stretching a mile beside the road and what looked like an army of men in long white capes, on white horses, were staring down on them. They wore black turbans around their head and this ghostly army stood upon the ridge still as air.

The soldiers protecting the caravan turned to face the men on the hill, drawing their swords, steadying their horses.

Prince Jezep stepped off his cart and met Demetrius beside their wagons. The captain of the soldier guards rode up and spoke from atop his horse.

"They might be robbers, sire, what shall we do?"

"Nothing, I will go talk with them," said Jesus staring coolly up to the ridge.

Just then single arrow came flying from the hill toward them, they ducked and "thunk!" it stuck in the prince's wagon. They turned to the arrow then back up to the men.

"Looks like they mean business," quipped Demetrius.

They looked to the hill and saw the men on horses stretched out above them. There were hundreds of them. All of the horses were white, save one, and the men sitting on them had white and some red turbans around their head with flowing robes behind, the cloth of their robes was waving in the morning breeze and they each had a long curved sword resting on a shoulder or at the side, some held small bows fitted with arrows. More than five golden banners fluttered in the hands of flag bearers. The banners were emblazoned with the Roman Eagle.

"Demerius, let's go and see what they want."

The two walked across the flat desert. The two stopped on the broad plain below the horsemen and waited in silence, silent wind ruffling their robes.

Ivory robes blowing sideways like a thousand birds with white ruffling wings.

The poet saw him first, "Look Issa, the dark one on the black horse."

Jesus strained to see him and knew him instantly, he mumbled, "Judas."

Chapter 53

Off the top of the ridge a huge man in white robes rode down, his horse stepping sideways, clumsily down the sand hill. He reached the bottom and galloped across the flat plain toward the prince and the poet.

His face burnt from the sun came charging up to them. Around his face and head was a white flowing turban, a purple band around his forehead, white robes fluttering behind him as he galloped to meet them, he pulled his horse up in a dust-filled halt before them. A long, curved sword slung at his side.

The prince looked up to the man and spoke, "I will accept your apology." He said in Latin.

The man on the horse was dressed full in white and was wide as a bear, he was obviously a leader with such a nobleness about him, his brown bearded face flashing white teeth as he laughed—

"Apologize for what?!"

"For putting an arrow into my wagon."

The man roared back in a laugh that could be heard up on the hill by his men and as far away as the wagons, "I have three hundred arrows aimed at you and you ask ME to apologize! You are a bold one!"

"Your arrow disturbed my wife." Jesus said calmly.

"Alright, I apologize only because you are bold as a bull. I am Arias, leader of these desert men, we enforce the laws of Veritas Maximus, Roman Proconsul of Jerusalem. He pays us to watch these lands, so tell me, who are you and what are doing here?" His big white horse prancing around.

Demetrius blurted, "He is Prince Jezep of Babylon, great grandson of Alexander and I am Demetrius, the poet, we go to Rome, let us pass!"

Arias reined in his horse, "Another bold one!"

The prince reached over and steadied his friend as he reached for his sword, "My friend, be polite, we seem to be trespassing."

"How can he own the desert?!"

The large Captain spoke loud and clearly, "Rome owns the whole world, and I am Rome."

"And we are Persia and bow to Rome, at least today we do," said the poet in his witty way.

The Captain on horseback atop turned to his men and raised his arm; they lowered their bows.

When he looked back the prince held up his hand showing him the ring that his Roman friend had given him at the feast.

"Do you know this ring?"

Arias, the desert man clicked his horse forward and gazed down at the large gold ring on his finger, he had a look of amazement, "The signet ring of the emperor, that is a powerful ring you have there, prince, If you have Nero's protection I will let your caravan pass."

"Thank you, sir."

The Captain reined in his horse and turned its head to ride away but stopped and walked his horse back up to them. He leaned down, "You say you go to Rome?"

"Yes,"

"I then ask a favor of you. We have two girls from Rome, they are traveling with us, and they are much trouble for it is all I can do to keep my men from having the two little whelps for their pleasure. The girls are disrupting my whole army. Will you take them with you and Zeus help you if you can deliver them to Rome."

"We will take them." Jesus nodded.

With that Arias waved his hand high and then put up two fingers and waved them signaling about the two girls.

Off the hill rode two turbaned warriors, pulling a horse with two girls hanging on its back for dear life. They rode up to them and stopped.

The prince and the poet looked up and smiled at the girls who slid off the colt and walked quickly over to the two standing there. They were beautiful girls, just barely women, but quite beautiful and all smiles. They stood before them happy as two birds freed from a cage. They looked up with little girl smiles.

The muscular poet held out his arms, "Come to me my dears."

They walked to him and they both hugged the poet. Demetrius looked up to his prince, "I like them, I'll take them."

Both Jesus and Arias laughed out loud.

"They are all yours," said Prince Jezep smiling wide.

Arias from his big horse just said, "They're a handful, good luck to you, poet."

The man turned his big white horse, and with his white cape flying behind charged across the plain and up onto the hill and in a moment the row of horsemen pulled away and disappeared.

The two watched them go but saw one dark rider on a black horse remain a moment staring down at them before turning. The poet and the prince both squinted toward the hill, "It is Judas." said Prince Jezep, Demetrius gave him a stern look and they both walked back to the wagons.

The four of them walked back to the caravan, the two men in silence, the two girls jabbering like magpies. They kept reaching for the men's hands and kissing them. When they got to the caravan and were greeted with wild cheers.

The two girls hopped up onto Demetrius' wagon, one on either side of him and giggled. Jesus climbed into his wagon, shook the reins and the horses plodded forward he turned to Mary beside him, his eyes grew dark, "We saw Judas with the soldiers."

Mary put her hand to her mouth staring fearfully into his eyes.

Chapter 54

It was sunset when Jesus pulled back on the reins. He swung down off the old wooden cart and raised his arms high to the caravan, "We will stay here for the night! Set up your tents and blankets."

A cheer went up clear back to the harlots.

Jesus walked back to greet his friend. He was sitting in his wagon seat between the two young dark-skinned maidens his two cute prizes.

Jesus saw his big smile as he slung his long, black hair back.

"Greeting great prince, good to see you this evening." Demetrius jumped down off the wagon and hugged him. The prince playfully grabbed him around the neck in a wrestle hold and joked,

"Well, Master Poet, will you sing us some poems this night?"

"Why certainly and will we have your usual wisdom, good sir?"

"We shall see, we shall see." He looked up at the two girls in the wagon seat, they were giggling, Jesus gave a little bow of his head, "Hello ladies."

"Hello sire" they straightened their hair.

Jesus continued walking back and viewed the parade unraveling along the road behind him. He always walked among them at sunset, joking, encouraging, and asking of their health.

Like a father who loved his children.

He walked back to the camel drivers, they gave him the Hindu greeting of the hand to the forehead to the lips and to the heart.

A turbaned Babylonian stepped up with a smile and bowed, "My prince, it is an honor to travel with you."

He walked far to the back and always ended up his walk greeting the harlots who followed the caravan; he hugged and greeted each one by name.

When he finally returned to his own cart he saw that the servants had gathered firewood.

Jesus knew it would be a great campfire filled with wine, song, and feasting, Perhaps the temple maids would come dance in the firelight.

The sun sank and the rose—colored rays turned the desert hazy pink and the sands turned silver around them.

Chapter 55

Jesus, the Prince, walked over to Mary sitting down leaning against the large wheel of their cart staring into the fire.

Jesus saw the flames reflecting in her blue eyes and she smiled up at him as he sat down beside her. He rubbed his hands together and opened them to the flames before him, "Hello, my love, feeling warm this evening?"

"Now that you are here my love." She leaned in closer to him. The fire raring up before them.

The noble poet sat cross-legged in his bushy sheepskin robe across the fire from Jesus. His harp was in its cloth case beside him and Jesus watched his deep eyes gazing into the fire.

Jesus watched him reach both hands up as his two beautiful young girl friends greeted him from either side; they bowed to the prince as they sat down.

The two young women snuggled next to the handsome poet and as they sat down he kissed one long and deeply and then the other the same way, they both had dreamy satisfied smiles.

Jesus knew they felt protected with his friend, a poet, a wrestler, strong and gentle.

The girls were barely over the age of twenty and Demetrius was 56. He saw the girls were welcome sparks to his heart.

Penelope, about 23, had long thin brown hair, olive skin like a Greek, slim dark eyes with dark Cole rubbed around them. Her ruby lips glistening soft and bright.

Penelope's quick smile could melt stone or start fire. She was thin as a silk curtain and walked like a swaying breeze.

The other girl, Sheba, was darker, like the girls from India, and voluptuous and round, her black hair cupped around her face like tumbling black clouds bouncing when she laughed. Her eyes were bright and playful, not like Penelope's, dark and quiet.

Unlike mysterious Penelope, full-breasted Sheba was a happy, open book. Dark Sheba's full lips were wet and welcoming. Her body was fuller, her breasts like large melons with sweet little points sticking out through her emerald silken robe. To look at her was a pleasure, Penelope even more.

The two girls sitting beside the handsome poet seemed a God-like scene, it reminded the prince of a magical cowherd he had once met long ago in India, one named Krishna.

He blurted across the fire, "Demetrius, you look like our old friend Krishna with his Gopis!"

The poet looked up and smiled wide, "Why thank you sire, I am honored," and he smiled largely and kissed both his Gopis.

Mary turned her head toward her husband and her eyes grew wide, "Krishna?! You mean the Hindu God Krishna?"

"The very one, my love, that ragged adventurer and I met him long ago in India. We smoked some strange herb with him and told tales with him for a week."

"And he had Gopis just like my girls here!" laughed Demetrius pulling them in closer and they both leaned their head on his shoulders and gave out their girlish smiles.

"See, we are Gopis!" laughed Sheba shaking her fluffy black hair and they both giggled. Penelope pulled back, "What is a Gopi? I have to know before I am one."

The poet hugged them both, "Gopis are girl cow-herders."

Mary's then said in amazement,

"You met THE God Krishna?"

"Yes, my darling and he was full of magic and his skin was bright blue!"

"It was." agreed his friend as he kissed his girls long on the mouth, one and then the other.

Mary Magdalene stared at her man who had sat down beside her by the fire.

"So there really are Gods on Earth?" She stared at her husband. He turned serious, "Yes, Mary, there are gods. The last of them are leaving the world."

"My love, you never fail to amaze me, talking to Gods! Demetrius, how about one of your fine poems!"

Chapter 56

The handsome singer of songs pulled his harp out of the cloth and placed it against his shoulder.

He threw his long curls from his eyes and began to strum.

The firelight flamed in his deep eyes, the campfire made his white robe turn bright orange, the girls were smiling nearby, the two servants were leaning against the wagon in the dark and Mary nestled in closer to her prince. All their faces glowed orange in the flames of the campfire as his soothing voice flowed softly,

"When my heart gets heavy thinking
of my problems running wild
I'm saved from all my sinking
by the lightness of a child,
With the lightness of his running
down a lovely Cedar lane
I forget the cunning
of this life and all the pain,
It lifts my heart to Heaven
when I hear the children play, if we could just stay seven
chasing butterflies away.

I lost a whole day's sorrow
turned the day into a smile
and all I did was borrow
a little lightness from a child."

Shouts of "Great!" and "wonderful!" rang through the night.

The poet's girls slid over to him and each kissed him deep and passionately one and then the other. Demetrius pulled them closer and kissed each of them again until everyone around hooted for another poem, The bard broke off from his kiss and strummed again…

Come away, come away
and take hold of my hand, for the world's more full of woe
than you can understand
and we'll sail and we'll sail to a faraway land
and play all the day
in the crystal white sand,
And I'll walk out that door
and I won't know what for
I'll walk and talk to a faraway shore, and the people will grin and
invite me in
and we'll sit and we'll spin
until the dawn staggers in,
And when I travel so far
I'll look in the stars
and wonder in that moment
exactly where you are, I'll look 'cross the sea and
you'll smile back at me
and I'll know by the glow
just where you will be…"

After the words trailed away Jesus spoke, "Thank you, my brother, for your wonderful songs…"

"A pleasure, my friend."

The others standing around the fire drifted away into the night.

The prince and his lady retired to their cart and three hundred souls fell asleep under the speckled blue blanket of the Persian night.

Chapter 57

Their feet are swift to shed blood.
—Romans 3:15

Jesus sat up and clutched Mary's arm, "What is it?" she mumbled "I smell horses."

"Horses?! what do you mean?" She fell back on the bed in their cart.

The prince put on his traveling robe and jumped out of the cart. The morning air on the desert was stinging cold. He stood beside the wagon staring to the hills where the pink fingers of dawn were shooting skyward through orange cotton clouds. The bright and jagged 'bulb star' still hung low in the pink morning sky. The dark hills formed a long black silhouette against the pale sky.

The dank ash smell of last night's fire hit his nostrils but he was staring across the desert but still the faint smell of horses.

He then noticed the top of the hills moving, bristling like thin silver weeds. He squinted, the breeze smelled faintly of a horse stable and dank straw.

Jesus stared even harder into the distance, something was moving over the top of the hills.

The sun's light broke over the hills and the prince saw glistening wheat stalks flashing across the horizon. It hit him with a jolt—

"My God!—those are Spears! WAKE UP! EVERYONE—WAKE UP!" He grabbed his robe from the cart, threw it over his head and tied it and saw his sleepy wife emerging,

"Mary, stay inside! Close the windows and don't come out, no matter what!"

The entire caravan was awakening, shouting, voices echoing down the line, soldiers were pulling on their breeches and armor, fastening their helmets and clasping their swords around their waist, saddling their horses.

Jesus' eyes were glaring at an ocean of soldiers on horseback pouring over the hills, riding straight toward them. The horse smell was growing stronger.

Thousands of men came on horseback with shining lances, and behind them thousands more followed with long, rectangular shields locked together, spears held upward marching steadily toward them, faster and faster.

The prince stared sternly he knew the shields, "Romans." He thought.

Demetrius ran up beside him, sword drawn, staring at the prince, then turning to gape at the approaching army flooding the distant plain.

"Who are they?!"

"Roman Calvary and perhaps a full legion behind them," said the prince coldly.

"That would be over 7,000 men!" Demetrius, the soldier—poet knew.

"Yes," he returned, staring at the mass of men and horses spread out and marching toward them. He glanced back at his cart making sure Mary was hiding. "Why are they attacking us? Such a small caravan."

The prince said, "It must be Judas, he was with that last white horse crew, he must be here for the gold or for me. I'd make quite a prize in Rome."

He walked out toward the approaching army in front of the caravan. He was in his brown robe, the hood down, his strong, bearded face turned to see the caravan behind him fleeing away or dropping down wailing to the sky.

The charging army was a full mile away coming fast, the prince raised his arms to quiet the women and children crying and laying down in the sand.

The Prince turned and faced his trembling people. His soldiers stood calmly beside their horses, trying to hold them, as they were raring up and whinnying. Not one soldier jumped up to ride. They saw the numbers, they heard the hoof beats, the massive Roman army marching toward them. They could hear the fearful clattering of iron on iron, shields clanging together across the desert. The caravan soldiers knew it was futile to resist;

yet they would not run. They awaited their fate, stunned and groggy in the morning desert.

Jesus raised his arms to all and shouted, "FEAR NOT! GOD WILL PROTECT US!"

This had no effect. The people fled and woman wailed, the soldiers stood at attention in silence, children screamed and ran into the desert, the camels were jumping around grunting with the herders trying to calm them, children cried louder and the whores in the far back were sitting down calmly on the road, a black wave would wash over them and afterwards they would be raped, they expected this.

The caravan soldiers, swords drawn, stood beside their horses calmly awaiting the order. The prince knew they would charge if he ordered it.

But it would be foolish, a hundred souls against thousands.

The prince turned his back on the group and faced the marching hordes.

The sun was rising behind the mass of troops, and in the bright morning he saw a row of horsemen stretched out a mile wide galloping toward them, lances pointed forward.

Behind them were rows upon rows of long, square shields marching at them spears down. Legion 7,000 strong, silver helmets of Rome, red plumes, an army closed for battle.

It looked like the entire desert sands were ruffling up and moving toward them, dust clouds floated behind the marching horde. An army enshrouded in smoke marching out of hell.

In front of the rushing army were animals fleeing for their lives, awakened by men, lions, deer, stray camels and wild horses stampeding across the sand ahead of the pounding legions.

The army was coming to slaughter and pillage, coming for the gold and the women and the silk and the glory of killing soldiers in battle. On they charged.

Behind him Jesus heard the shrieks of women, the whinnying of horses and grunting of camels, fear in the hearts of old men in silken robes He turned and saw his soldiers jump to their horses and form up for the clash. The poet was fitting an arrow into his bow.

Chapter 58

The prince stood fast. Not a half-mile away the terrible mounted soldiers were thundering on, men in silver armor and red capes flying behind, each on different-colored horses rushing forward at a gallop, the ground shook, lances lowered for the kill. It would come in moments. The echo of war cries, "oo—rahh! oo—rrahh!" a deafening war chant echoed from the marching legions behind the horsemen.

Jesus stood out front like a massive stone statue, a lone man between the approaching army and his caravan. Armed only with God.

He could see the leader on horseback, a dark figure in a black cape— it had to be Judas charging, grinning, ready to destroy them all.

He saw the wave of cavalry prancing before him, rushing to obliterate them, steal their lives, their women, and their gold! Jesus stood fast.

"Come up with the strength and I will protect you." The words of God on the mountain.

He was sure—More than sure.

Two thousand terrible riders on horses were bearing down, hoof beats were deafening. Jesus suddenly raised up his arms stopping his own soldiers from moving.

"STAY BACK!" He shouted in a deafening voice.

He lifted his arms; they felt heavy with power. He flung out his arms at the charging horsemen, shoving the air, at this horses flipped backwards and the riders fell tumbling in the sand!

Demetrius and the men stared, fear stretched across their faces.

The prince looked across the dust—choked field and saw Judas grinning, sword pointed at him charging, an ocean of soldiers behind him at a full gallop, a quarter-mile away and closing fast.

Jesus stood firm.

Behind him he heard the people of the caravan screaming in horror, running away, spreading out across the sands, running before galloping horses, they would be swept over and killed in minutes, the prince, the soldiers and the poet stood firm, to face their doom, he glanced and saw the strong bard, his bow drawn arrow ready to let fly, his sword on the ground ready to pick up to slash at close range. He stood beside the wagons with the girls inside. His sweet Mary inside the cart.

Jesus, arms raised shouted again to the hordes—

"NO!" he thundered as the hordes were almost upon him.

Then—CRACK!!! A FLASH OF BLINDING LIGHT!!

Jesus grabbed his ears, all went silent, deaf for a moment, the poet and the soldiers were holding their ears and closing their eyes. Faces burning hot.

A hundred horses pitched to their knees, their riders thrown forward into the sand. Hundreds more horses stumbled over them and fell on top of them, the entire cavalry fell in a jumbled mass of tumbling horses and armor and men and spears, churning into massive heaps in front of Jesus and the soldiers.

The lightning cracked again, louder with more wrath.

The legions of shields fell back, but regrouped, gathered and kept marching forward, stumbling over horse bodies and stunned horsemen flailing on the ground, the legions kept coming, they could not stop.

A few bold caravan soldiers charged out to attack, but most held back knowing was complete madness, one hundred against thousands.

Demetrius let fly an arrow, it struck a soldier in the throat and he fell backwards off his horse into the dirt, he notched another and another, two more horsemen gurgled into the dust, their horses dazed.

He threw his bow away, picked up his sword and ran madly toward the wall of the charging army, waving his sword above his head, yelling, defying doom.

"DEMETRIUS!" called the prince, but the poet kept running forward crazy clashing sword against sword, ducking, jumping up to escape a thrust of a broadsword.

One horseman broke through the smoke and galloped toward the lone poet standing with his short sword raised high. The horseman held a long, curved sword above his head ready to slash the poet in half, charging, the poet leaped in the air, almost as high as the mounted rider, he jabbed at his belly and man and horse pitched forward dead.

The dead man lay facedown in the sand the horse ran on. The poet pulled himself up off the ground and fell back, facing the army that had fallen before the lightning, stepping backwards until he stood once again beside the prince, both staring at the burning army groping around in front of them.

The prince looked over and shook his shaggy head, "What were you thinking you wild man?!"

"My blood was up."

They stood breathing hard and staring through the smoke, it was morning but the plain was dark, the morning sun hidden by clouds of black and brown smoke.

The lightning had struck the brush on fire in front of them and shrubs here and there burned like torches and the desert flared up in crimson flame and men were howling as they marched forward the front row was roasting in the desert flames.

The fire blazed higher horseflesh burned and it stunk as men and horses screamed in the desert flames.

Then the flames leaped up into a life of their own, swirling in the wind from the ground upward in a whirlwind of flame spinning skyward in a pillar of fire one hundred feet high off the desert.

A howling column of orange and red flame, scorching and sending burning men back screaming and throwing away their shields running for their lives.

The pillar of fire roared into the mass of men and horses whipping into the hordes with a will of its own. Lashing out, cutting, swallowing. It seemed to laugh as it burned in wide red flames, eating men and horses screaming alive.

A thousand men and their galloping animals halted and burned. On the field between Jesus and the vast army the tower raged higher up into the morning sky, orange and red plume against the light blue, Jesus' face felt hot as he wrapped his hood around his face, as did the soldiers trying to hold onto their raring, screeching horses, Demetrius was kneeling down, his mouth wide open, his arms at his side.

The army fell back like a receding tide.

A thousand swords and shields lay strewn across the ground, those Romans not burned up turned and fled, horses were turned around and in a thundering rush the entire army was straggling back, yelling and running over the hills and in a few minutes was gone.

The swirling pillar kept raging, hissing, garbled words seem to blare from the flames, a language of fire, an ancient babbling language and people standing here and there in the desert fell to their knees in prayer.

As quickly as it had come it fell to earth and disappeared. Silence. Only burning shrubs crackled here and there. There was not an ounce of wind.

The scattered people from the caravan stood at a distance behind, gazing at the fleeing army. Jesus, the poet, and all the soldiers slowly dropped to their knees. No one could look at each other.

Chapter 59

I have seen the affliction of my people, have heard their groaning and am come to deliver them.
—Acts 7:34

Mathew slept on the rancid floor of his coliseum cell and a dream came to him. In this dream he saw Jesus in a shimmering white robe descend from heaven on a beam of light. He had long, shimmering silver hair with a ringing light—blue halo. He saw the lord drift down into the center of the arena alighting amid thousands of lions, all growling and pacing around him biting and snapping at the air. A sea of swirling lions.

He saw the messiah standing among the tawny beasts petting their heads like they were tame kittens, the shaggy lions smiled rubbing up against him, every one tame and smiling.

Mathew saw Jesus smile right at him and speak in a strong voice, "Fear not, Mathew, God sent me to save you and all my people now in chains."

As he spoke the words lions dissolved around him turning into sand at his feet and then to honey, whirl pooling around him. The lions faded back into Earth as he lifted, arms outstretched lifting into heaven.

Mathew blinked awake and did not move. The dream made his heart glow within him. He held the image in his mind and could still see Jesus rising into heaven above.

The stench of the cell hit him as he stared around the floor; his friends were lumps of dark robes sleeping around him. Their hair was straggled and black tangled with straw.

Mathew was awake and knew his lord had visited him and they would all be saved.

Mathew and the others had watched hundreds die horribly in the jaws of the lions but he knew Jesus would save them now.

The lord had appeared in his dream and he knew he was coming soon. He smiled, bunched up some straw from the floor for a pillow and drifted back to sleep.

Chapter 60

Nero burped and wiped his mouth, he grunted, "So how many more of the cursed Christians are left?" his mouth was dripping with strands of beef.

He sat alone at the head of his private table eating dinner in the nude.

He reached for a goblet of wine to wash down his stringy beef. His fat, round head tilted up, and little chunks of red meat slid down his chin.

The plumed Praetorian Guard standing beside him, stared straight ahead and replied, "Does you majesty mean the total number in the city or those now in the jails?"

"I mean, How many in all?"

"There are 5000, with 3000 in the city and 2000 in the coliseum jails."

"Five thousand left you say?" slurping his wine, "How many have been executed?"

"Three hundred have been killed for their crime, sire. The rest are waiting."

"How are the lions? Are they in good spirits?" He laughed gagging on a chunk of beef.

"The lions, sire?"

"Never mind," the little king laughed to himself and spit out a chunk of meat onto his plate.

There was a silence in the room for a long time. The fifty guards standing around here and there always looked straight ahead. To look directly at the emperor could cause any number of horrible things to happen.

He once roasted a guard alive for amusement after dinner and he had a guard run another guard through with his spear simply because the guard laughed when he farted.

Nero always ate his dinner completely naked. He was fat and chubby, looking like a big hairy infant.

All was silent but for the slurping of wine and an occasional belch. He kept eating and the guards in bright red—cloaked uniforms, holding spears by their side stood still as death. Fifty stern guards stood ten paces away from each other around the large marble dining room.

The little emperor sat at the head of a long white marble table. He always ate alone except for a tall black Nubian slave who was his food taster. He stood beside the little man and tasted each dish before he ate it.

The emperor was deathly afraid of being poisoned, a common cause of demise among Roman emperors. He had lost two food tasters in as many months. They had choked and died and fell over on the table right in front of him, victims of ambitious relatives.

The dead food tasters were always pulled away and replaced and the dinner continued.

Nero finished his dripping beef and with his pudgy fingers pushed his silver platter away.

"Guard!"

"Sire?" said the Captain stoically, glancing down at him.

"Are the people pleased with the executions, I mean do they still believe the Christians were to blame for the fire."

"Wh... why yes, sire, it was the Christians, also the people love you."

"And they do not think I had anything to do with it?"

"Of course not, my emperor..."

"You lie!"

"No sire, no!"

"Shall I have Nemius over there run you through for lying? Nemius, come over here and kill Germanicus!"

Germanicus' eyes got wide as silver plates as he backed up, "SIRE, NO! Please!"

Nero cackled with laughter, "I'm kidding. Nemius, stay where you are."

He was chuckling away and prattled on, "I know the rumors about me but step up the executions, the more I kill, the more people will believe the

Christian rats are guilty and I want as many of those vermin punished as possible, and, o yes, add more lions and more naked women to the show, er I mean the executions."

"Yes sire, it shall be done." The Praetorian was shaking and felt warm liquid fill his breechcloth and trickle down his leg.

But he did not move a muscle.

Chapter 61

Christians were rounded up and strung along by ropes through the city but they were no longer beaten. When arresting a child to be eaten by lions, some guards' had to wipe away tears. When the people threw rocks now they bounced off Roman helmets and when they jeered it was not at Christians but at the guards.

"Leave them alone you bastards!" "Go arrest the emperor!" "Crucify Nero!"

The tide was turning, the polluted waters of the peoples' feelings were rotting away the crumbling pier that held up the empire.

Within a short time, over 2000 Christians were crammed into the coliseum jails awaiting their death by lions. Forty and sometimes a hundred a week were killed and dragged away.

The citizens were enflamed.

Huge crowds gathered in the streets railing against Nero, these sometimes turned into riots and ironically—caused buildings to be set on fire and burned down!

The stubborn little dictator countered by paying citizens out of Rome's treasury to support him.

He also doubled the pay of all soldiers in Rome, both inside the palace and downtown in the main barracks. But Six Centares a day, the price of three apples, did not buy much loyalty. But he did pay for soldier's beer, and that saved him.

But the people grew angrier and bolder.

Thousands of citizens, poor and rich, swelled against the coliseum gates and walls shaking their fists, yelling for the executions to stop. The shouts were getting louder, the people angrier, and only the fear of swords kept them back.

The loyalty of the emperor's own guards was crumbling.

Nero's reaction to it all was to bribe more people and burn more and more Christians on crosses each night. Once again, Nero was fiddling while Rome burned.

Chapter 62

A stone of stumbling, and a rock of offense.
—1 Peter 2:8

It was a warm summer night and a million stars were foaming above Jerusalem.

Jesus stood at the top of the Mount of Olives looking down at the sprawling city, sleeping dimly white under the stars.

He looked back at the sleeping caravan in the valley behind him. Fires were smoldering. It had been two days since the attack and the pillar of fire and all the travelers were bone tired.

Most of the campfires were flickering out and the caravan behind him and the wide white city below were cloaked in darkness, only a sliver of a moon lit the city walls and the homes.

Lanterns burned here and there throughout Jerusalem. Public torches were turning the sides of buildings orange but mainly it was dark everywhere, with only flickering shadows of people hurrying home at night.

Jesus had slipped out alone to see where he had been almost crucified years before.

Mary understood and gave no speeches, only, "be careful," he kissed her and slipped into the night.

He stood on the hill above the hazy white city.

The few stars above offered little light but he could see the city was open to the world with no outer walls, houses on top of white houses homes spread into the hills in the distance.

Only the Roman Quarter off to his left had high walls, they had protected the Antonia fortress where Pilate had once lived and walls were needed to hide King Herod's old house from the people, the Romans and the high priest, whoever they were now, were ever hated so they needed walls.

He looked down by the outer walls, strained his eyes and saw it— Golgotha, the place of skulls. A lone torch lit up hundreds of tiny white dots and sticks, skulls and bones.

Golgotha, that horrible place where he had been tied to a cross to make his escape.

He slipped down the hill toward where his cross had been. He was wearing his dark-brown robe with the hood pulled up hiding his face. He had to see the cross or where it had once been.

At the bottom he jumped across the stream below the high walls. Dim torches flickered every hundred feet along the walls and lit up the place of execution. He scrambled up the embankment and edged along the walls to where he remembered his cross had been, in a little canyon area near the city with small steep cliffs rising up around it. The embankments encircled the area like a theater so people across the stream could view the victims to see whom they were praying for.

Under the slim moon he inched around the curving wall and there it was—the place of death—Golgotha, broken crosses were everywhere. Most were just eerie sticks leaning sideways and broken.

Across the stream steep cliffs cupped the death place like an amphitheater.

His heart quickened. Lanterns and candles were burning all around within the little cove and lit up the circle, lighting the rotting crosses and the bones. His nose twitched at the putrid smell.

It looked the same, nothing had changed.

At night there were no crows only the shadows of rats scurrying and here and a few dogs, cracking and gnawing on human bones.

He held his robe up to his nose and slid down the embankment away from the walls, reaching the bottom he hopped the stream and he was surrounded by dark crosses. He stared around the grounds. Crosses pointed up here and there and the high walls were jabbed by the black shadows of crosses.

In a corner he saw one poor soul still hanging limply to a cross. His bearded chin was bent down on his chest. His straggly hair hung down like a black, furry mop. The prince shuddered and pulled his cloak around his face muttering a prayer.

He saw piles of skulls and heard 'crack' as a mangy dog gnawed on leg bone. He heard rats clicking across the bones.

Then he saw it and a jolt shot through him—His cross.

It sent a chill through his body—he saw that his cross was not wooden but made of smooth white marble and shining in candlelight. His eyes opened wide to the realization—it was a shrine! A cheap relic to be worshipped.

A stone lantern burning in front of it showed the slick edges of marble, the crossbeam carved perfectly smooth.

As he walked closer, his stomach got queasy as he saw it was a monument. A place for tourists to leave coins, and worse, a stone idol of worship. At the top the words, 'King of the Jews' were engraved in Latin in the marble, the mocking words of that horrible day carved in stone forever.

Jesus felt empty and betrayed. His own betrayal dug in deepest. The fact he had run away ate into him, a double mockery of all that was sacred. Shame shuddered in his heart.

He walked into the enclosure where the cross was lit up shiny white and perfectly carved, a pillar of slick marble with perfect straight edges.

In front of it he noticed a small black hump, a person kneeling, worshipping this stone thing. The person was bent facedown at the foot of his cross.

He slumped down on a wooden bench twenty feet in front of the cross and the person, he could not take his eyes off of the disturbing scene before him.

Jesus sat out of breath staring up at his cross of stone.

His stomach was churning, he felt sick staring at this blasphemy, the graven idol made in his memory. 'People give their lives to nothing, they pray to a rock' he thought.

To see someone worshipping this sick perversion revealed the lie of all worship, a mockery of all that was sacred. He knew all that was sacred was invisible.

His throat tightened and a tear squeezed out of his eye. He could hardly breathe, as the person in front of him leaned forward, kissed the cross and then stood up and walked toward him on the bench. It was an old woman.

'O God, what now?' he thought. 'What do I say to her?'

The old woman's wrinkled face shined grotesquely from the candle she held in front of her face, but her eyes twinkled like a child's. She walked up to him beaming with a saintly smile.

Jesus looked up into her face, he could hardly breathe. He was shaking to think she was worshipping this stupid cross of stone. Giving her life to nothing, he felt dead as dirt but his heart was crying, 'She just kissed that dead stone cross, O GOD.' He could not move but sat looking up into her smiling eyes as she spoke in an angel's voice, in local Aramaic she said, "Hello Pilgrim, come to worship at the cross of our Lord?"

He sat in silence, but she continued, "I know, the cross has that effect on many, our lord was crucified and suffered here with nails through his hands and feet, and rose again right over there," she pointed in the direction of the tomb he knew so well, "but you already know this, you are a Christian, are you not?"

He had lost the ability to speak. She asked again, "You are a Christian?" She was puzzled at his silence.

Jesus looked past her to the lit-up cross and to the wilted flowers placed around the base of it. He noticed an iron box with a money sign on it attached to the side of the cross begging shekels—to Him not a God but a man, and one who'd run away.

His head was spinning. Around the marble cross were little carved crosses of wood offered for a price. Souvenirs. Cheap crosses sold for silver when he saw the crosses he snapped—

"No, I am not a Christian!"

He pulled back his hood revealing his long white hair, beard and flashing eyes, the words came spitting out—

"I AM Jesus Christ and I'm very much alive, thank God in Heaven, and it makes me sick to see people worship this stone idol and sell these cursed trinkets! Dear woman, go home and believe in yourself and treat others as you would be treated, That is my message, Good night!"

He pulled his hood back up over his head, and walked away leaving the woman standing there dumfounded. She dropped her candle and stood in the dark.

Jesus heard a cock crow two times as he jumped across the tiny stream and headed back to the caravan.

Chapter 63

The day tilted toward evening and the whole sky turned to dull red in front of them. High, thin clouds were the color of brown flour. Thin slices of clouds were dotting the sky from one side of the world to the other. The sun sank and the clouds rippled red and orange turning to dull gray as the sun started dripping into the sea.

The cart of Mary and Jesus reached the top of the hill and there it was spread before them—the dark blue Mediterranean Sea.

"Mary, come look!"

She emerged from the cart and slipped her arm under her husband's and sat next to him on the wagon, they both stared in silence at the wide blue sea.

In all their wanderings they had never seen the ocean.

It spread out before them too large to comprehend. They breathed in deeply, the cold, salt air filling their nostrils.

A vast blue floor spread out before them.

It was silvery blue and the dim red sun resting on the horizon rolled out a bright orange marmalade carpet that ruffled to an end at the shore.

From the hilltop they could see the ocean sliding up against the East. Off to their left like the half-open mouth of a giant crocodile was the harbor of Joppa.

The city huddled in white little cubes beside the harbor. Beyond it on a distant point stood a tall, thin lighthouse. As darkness descended, its bright eye shot a beam of light far out to sea.

Sitting miles away in the dim silver twilight, Jesus could see ships coming and going, their sails puffing out their chest. The masts of the boats at anchor stuck up like thickets of reeds swaying beside the shore.

Joppa was a seaport built two thousand years ago, he knew it had been lived in by kings, and ancient prophets, it lay below them laced along the hills like an ivory necklace. It looked like a white scarf draped around the blue neck of the harbor.

The sun's red forehead still peaked up from the sea as the prince jumped down off his cart and looked behind him to the valley where the caravan had stopped to make camp.

In the light blue twilight the travelers below looked like ants scurrying around. Camels and horses like tiny children's toys. Campfires were flaring up here and there.

Jesus noticed a rider on horseback galloping up the hill toward them. Dust curled up behind horse and rider.

"Who is that?" Asked Mary sitting in the cart.

"You know who it is, only Demetrius would ride half-naked at this hour."

Jesus stroked his beard and pulled his brown robe tighter gazing at his friend growing larger as he approached. Jesus smiled, 'only he would ride without a tunic, Greek style.'

The poet charged up the hill on his white horse and in a wild, eye-stinging cloud of dust, reined in his horse and pulled up next to Jesus.

The prince reached and grabbed the reins by the horse's mouth steadying him, patting the side of the horse's head and looking up at his friend. The famous poet had a strong body, long hair and looked down at the prince from his horse with a smile big as a fat cat, "Hello Issa! Are we there yet?" he swung down giving his friend a quick hug as he rushed past him to watch the last of the rippling red sunset. Jesus followed behind him.

At the front of the cart the poet looked up flashing a smile, "Hello Mary, great to see you, what is this I see before me?!"

He gazed in stunned silence at the broad blue sea and the red and gold sunset.

Only a tip of the glowing orange ball was still showing sending a faint path of gold up to the wide beach below.

"Now THAT is beauty!" The poet stood with his hands on his hips, staring in silence, his back to Jesus and Mary

"Will the poet write a poem about this sunset I wonder?" said Jesus.

"I surely will my friend." Demetrius turned laughing.

He walked back and stepped up taking Mary's hand in greeting. With a twinkle he looked up at her and said, "The sunset is beautiful but can't hold a candle to your beauty, my lady." and kissed her hand.

She smiled. 'I have heard you for years and still believe you."

"Only because it's true."

The poet turned to the prince dropping his smile for serious matters, "Do you think the ship is waiting?"

Jesus looked him and spoke quietly, "I am sure it is, the Egyptian's word is good."

"That is true," he replied, "what shall I tell the caravan?"

Jesus pulled at his silver beard and leaned back against the wagon.

"In the morning tell them to come to the foot of the hill below me, I would like to bid them farewell."

"Talking to the multitudes from the top of a hill, my friend, you've done that before."

I know you will dazzled us all."

The poet leaped up onto his white horse taking the reins in one hand. He gave a quick wave then turned his horse back down the long sloping hill, sagging deeply into the sand of the hill he galloped down to the caravan below

Chapter 64

The flames of the campfire lit up Mary's perfect white face. Her hair was a thick falling mist, her sweet mouth was a bright welcoming cherry. Her eyes disturbed men in such a good way.

Jesus loved her so much he could not stand it. Her love made him feel warm and blessed beyond measure.

He sat beside her with their backs against satin pillows propped up against the large wheels of the cart. His arm was around her and he stared into her deep eyes.

"I love you, Mary, more than I can say." He then looked down.

"I know, my prince, and I love you,"

He saw the flames from the campfire dancing in orange light across her face and it made her blond hair turn reddish orange but her eyes were bright and unwavering looking into his.

He leaned down and kissed her sweetly on her red lips. It felt like sucking on a ripe strawberry.

As he pulled away he looked at her and whispered, "Thank you."

"For what?" she ran her thin fingers through his flowing hair.

"For coming."

"Stay behind in that cold castle while my handsome man rode away, I think not."

She leaned in and kissed him again. His lips felt perfect. He squeezed her hand a little and said to her, "You have braved this journey without a tear and it has been hard, but the hardest is to come, a long sea voyage, we sail on perilous waters to strange lands."

She sat up again and looked right into him, "My dearest, nothing is perilous when I'm with you."

They smiled into each other and then shared a goodnight kiss; they fell back onto pillows and gazed up at a million stars, the sound of the sea singing them to sleep.

Chapter 65

Jesus opened is eyes to the blazing white morning. He ran his fingers through his long, stringy hair and straightened it. He brushed his beard and laced up his white robe. He sat up on the blanket and there past the blinding white sand, stretching out forever was the ocean, dark and blue ruffling in the light wind.

He was sitting on a small hill and the Mediterranean Sea started a mile below its blue carpet stretching wide to the far ends of the Earth. The bright sky was white-blue above. He felt rested.

He sat up cross-legged now not far from the big wood cart and the two horses were nodding their head up and down straining to go anywhere.

Mary came walking from the wagon behind him with two cups of smoking Turkish coffee.

"Here you go, my sleepy one," she cooed, and handed him his morning coffee. He cupped his hands around it and it almost burned them. He took a small sip, "Thank you, dear, very good, and how are you feeling this morning?"

"Quite satisfied, thank you sir." she said laughing sitting down next to him for coffee.

The sky was light blue, a distant white halo of clouds encircled the distant horizon.

Prince Jezep and Mary Magdalene sipped Turkish coffee together gazing out to sea.

They glanced over to the distant town and saw the ships in the harbor, sails of many colors and many more ships with their sails down, their masts sticking up like shafts of wheat.

The thin, white lighthouse sat on the point.

"Is a ship really waiting for us?" Mary asked.

"I am sure of it. The Egyptian promised a large ship with sailors and archers.

"Look, my darling, the others are getting ready."

Down the hill shepherds were gathering sheep, soldiers were mounting up, camels lining up and the poet's cart was in front ready to lead. It looked like a long circus.

Jesus stood up and jumped up on a nearby rock at the top of the hill. He lifted his arms and boomed out, "Good morning my friends!" He echoed for miles.

He heard shouts below and arms raised waving and cheering. A few minutes later the caravan lurched forward on the road, It looked like a long shaggy snake.

He could see it all, and hear the groaning of the goats and bleating of sheep, the coarse deep and course bellows of the camels, dogs barking and nipping at legs, trotting beside the camels, the clanging of pots and pans rattling against the carts. Men shouting, the ringing of finger—cymbals as the women in black danced along the road.

Jesus stood atop a small hill and he looked like Moses.

When he stretched wide his arms two seabirds flew from behind the hill above his head. The whole caravan let out a resounding cheer.

"We have come a long way together and now we must part, know that our way was blessed and your way shall be forever blessed wherever you go!"

Loud cheers echoed in the valley

His arms were still outstretched on the hill, his white robe flowing in the morning wind. He boomed again—

"And now I go to Rome to straighten out this emperor!" and threw his arms straight up high shaking his fists into the sky.

Three hundred voices erupted and bellowed and the entire parade, from soldiers to merchants to harlots danced around madly cheering in the bright valley.

The warm wind ruffled the cloth of three hundred robes and the rippling sound of flags crackled in the morning air.

159

Then they heard their prince shout, "And as we depart I will give each of you a gold coin to send you on your way."

A cheer shook the valley and echoed clear down to Joppa.

The merchants and tradesmen and Persian priests passed by and each and every one received a hug and a gold coin from the prince plucking it from an open chest by his cart.

Each one wept as they passed, the men the women and many hid their wet eyes in their tunic, they would not see their beloved father prince again.

When the harlots finally danced up the road he turned to the women and pointed to the carts with the lazing horses standing before them.

"These carts we give to you ladies for you are neediest of all."

The women all in black let their veils fall from their face and stared back and forth at each other in joyful wonder. They put their hand up to their mouth in total surprise and then all rushed forward to the Master, bowed down and kissed his feet, they also took his hands and kissed them, many girls talking at once, "O thank you, sire! Thank you!"

They walked over to Demetrius and bowed and kissed him.

They swarmed up onto the carts and opened the back doors and peered inside in wonder. They were laughing and walking around inside the carts, picking up things. Clanking the pans together, laughing.

They were women of the street but they knew how to handle a cart.

As the carts lurched forward the women waved and trilled their tongues in high pitched wailings.

The prince and his friends watched them smiling as they rattled down the dusty hill to Joppa by the sea.

Chapter 66

Be not forgetful to entertain strangers, thereby some have entertained angels unawares.
—Hebrews 13:2

Jesus had two servants, Silvanus and Lam, Both were exceedingly tall. Silvanus was white-skinned and pale. His skin was the color of milk. Lam was a bald black man, strong and sinewy as a wrestler. They were Essene holy men from Jerusalem, quiet and mysterious. They had looked a pair as they had appeared before his Persian throne a year ago.

Silvanus, white in a long dark-gray robe and Lam, a black man in a long white robe. They were always soft—spoken and looked after Mary and him and seemed to read their minds providing every need before they even knew they needed it.

They seemed to glide behind Jesus and Mary, always nearby, ever pleasant and ever helpful. They said little and did much and now they stood before Jesus on the hilltop above Joppa.

They both stood calmly before the others awaiting orders from their master. Jesus smiled at them and spoke, "Silvanus? Lam? Are you ready for a voyage? It will be dangerous?"

Soft as morning breeze they answered together, "Yes master, we are with you.'

He might have asked them to pass the salt, they were that quick to answer.

"Fine, it will be a pleasure to have you"

Jesus spoke once more, "Silvanus, Lam, please tend to the horses, they carry everything we own."

He knew that he could trust them both with the one million Persian gold Asters sitting atop one of the horses. That amount could purchase a small town and everyone in it.

The other horse's saddlebags held bread, dried fish, olive oil and cheese as well as wine and water. The servants walked over and held the reins of horses ready to move.

Demetrius stood with thin Penelope under one arm and dark, laughing Sheba under the other. They were both playing with his long black curls, all three giggling.

"Looks like you are ready, my friend."

"I am, my lord, and so are my girls. Ladies, please say hello to Captain Jezep.

They smiled their young girl' smiles and said, "Hello, captain."

Jesus smiled at them, "Have you girls ever been on a boat before?"

Sheba looked up at the prince, straightened her dress and said boldly, "Of course, my lord, our home is on the Tiber River near to Rome, we sailed from there, that's how we got here."

Demetrius stepped backward and stared in amazement at the two girls, "Are you telling me that you two little darlings sailed the high seas from Rome thousands of miles away?!"

"Yes, my love, we did." said quiet Penelope, beaming.

He gazed and blurted, "But, why?"

"To see the world, my lord,"said Sheba, Penelope joining in, "Yes, to see the world girls like adventures too, you know." He looked over and grinned at the prince, "Look, Issa, these little ones need adventure as much as you do."

Thin little Penelope got brave and looked over to the Prince, she gave a little bow of her head,

"My lord, We would be most grateful to sail with you, we miss our home dearly. We can tie ship knots and we don't get seasick."

Jesus reared back and laughed, then reached over and put his hand on each of the girl's head and playfully shook their hair, "Welcome to the voyage ladies, you are my first mates."

They all stood together on the hill beside the sea knowing it was miles of open ocean from this seaport to Rome.

They stood staring silently at the sea as the cool salt wind brushed and danced across their faces. They would sail a thousand miles of wild and Open Ocean together—

A prince, a beautiful woman, a poet, a black servant and white, and two young girls.

In the distance they heard the crack of the crashing surf.

Chapter 67

"May the fires in you soul never grow cold."
—Demetrius, the poet

They started down the hill to the sea.

Jesus walked in front, then Mary, the singer, Sheba, the bigger of the two, then thin Penelope. Following was Silvanus with the money horse then Lam with the provisions. They kicked up dust and when they reached the white sand of the beach, the poet and his ladies broke away like mad ponies and charged crazily across the hot, white sand. They danced and twirled and hooted waving their arms running down to the waves.

Lord and lady and the two servants stood back. They smiled down at the poet and his girls splashing in the surf.

None of them had ever seen a white sand beach before, much less a long beach of it and no one had seen a whole ocean.

Jesus kneeled down and felt pure white sand for the first time, they knew the sand of the desert but it was full of rocks and dirt and it had all been all mud and pebbles by the Galilee Sea and coarse dirt—sand of the desert. But this stuff was soft as an angel's hair and pure, amazing.

He felt the tiny hot granules on his hand then squeezed and as it streamed through his fingers like milk, his eyes gleamed at the magic of it. He looked over at Mary doing the same thing, sand pouring through their hands.

"It is so smooth," showing Mary the stream of sand falling from his fist.

Mary nodded, feeling the smooth sand caressing her palms.

They looked up to see the others dancing and kicking down the beach in the bright afternoon sun. Silvanus and Lam in their white robes stood calmly talking, holding the horses and watching the others let loose.

Eventually lord and lady and the servants wandered down to the crashing sea and felt the cold salty water sting their ankles.

Demetrius, thrashing in the waves, ripped off all his clothes showing his rippling, brown body and his two girls were naked too, their sweet white breasts bouncing and shining in the sea. They were splashing with him in the surf all three naked, laughing, diving, letting the waves wash over them, their young glistening breasts jiggling as he threw each one high landing in the white churning surf, the girls were laughing like they would never stop.

Jesus squinted up at the bright yellow sun then smiled at them playing like children.

Thoughts of the journey returned to him.

He knew each hour and minute Christians were dying in Rome. He waited for a long while and then shouted, "Demetrius! Girls! Come! We must go find the ship!

The bard dipped his head into the water and slung his long hair back and water sprayed high into the air, "Coming, my friend!" He and the two girls, one on each side holding hands, bounded toward the beach, splashing each they managed to put on their clothes.

In a few moments Jesus and Mary and the servants and horses gathered all.

The prince looked in their eyes, "My friends, Rome awaits, let us sail"

THE VOYAGE
Chapter 68

Joppa was so bright they had to squint when they looked at its walls. Every building was of polished marble or white granite. Blazing white. The prince and his friends walked under the high archway and into the city. People swirled around them in a sea of red, blue and dark green turbans, some were sitting beside the road selling everything under the moon or walking to the harbor.

The prince and friends looked up at the light blue sky filled with screeching seagulls.

Jesus breathed the salty air into his nostrils and then raised his arm. He saw it right off.

"That must be our ship!"

They turned to their right and looked down a long pier and there it was—the largest ship they'd ever seen or could ever imagine.

It sat on the water like a high, walled city.

The servants stood still as stones and even jumpy Demetrius stood still gazing at the massive ship. The two girls on each side of him stared at it and clutched the poet tightly. All were silent, dumbfounded.

The prince had seen many wonders in his life but this ship surpassed them all.

Mary broke the silence, "It is larger than my barge in Babylon." and squeezed her lovers hand staring at it with the coolness of royalty.

"Many times larger." replied Jesus his eyes fixed on the floating town.

"Bigger than the Sphinx. It rivals the pyramids." mumbled the poet.

The white ship bumped along the left side of the wharf in deep-dredged harbor, its bow looking out to sea, the only ship on the main wharf. The

Egyptian friend of Prince Jezep had paid the harbormaster well for special arrangements.

The travelers gazed and did not say a thing.

Using the size of a man's foot, as the Arabians were now measuring, the ship was 300 feet long and was painted white with gold and light-blue trim running along the side. It was a long, floating palace.

The hundred—foot mast rising in the middle of it was wider around than a large tree and high as a spire in Babylon. The crossbeam was longer than a large ship. Huge red sails were tied and bunched up along the crossbeam.

The rising stern curling up was the immense, white carved head of a swan, its head rose high off the waterline, the gold and blue eyes of the swan were staring forward, its golden beak pointing the way.

The ivory head of the swan was as large as a wagon and stood smiling atop a smooth tapering neck.

The gunnels or sides of the ship ran 300 feet and the sides were twenty-five feet off the water. It was a high, wide ship and broad-beamed. The long, high sides ran a dizzying length toward the bow that finally jutted out Greek Trireme-style, the lower part a battering ram that was six feet wide at the bow, sticking out many feet, ending in a two-foot-wide man's fist of solid iron painted gold.

At top speed it could stave in a seaside wall or sink any ship afloat.

The long white bow rode up and down by the pier slapping the water with a hollow sound like the palm of the hand. The front was Greek-style sloping up like a high pyramid into a pointed cap that peaked up forty feet off the water.

It took their breath away, an experience to behold.

The white color was blinding in the sun and the bow had bright blue eyes painted on both sides so the ship could see. The eyes were oval, 4 feet long and 2 feet high, within the eyes the bright blue pupils stared out like round shields.

The eyes looked bored and dreamy.

There were holes for oars along the sides, fifty oarsmen a side.

The ship was undermanned for it liked speed and a bigger crew would weight it down. For defense there was a band of archers and a hold filled with Greek Fire bombs that could be slung with catapults and burn down any ship that might threaten.

The sheer size of the ship would scare any pirates away and if encountered by Roman Galleys would be cheered on.

Romans owned the sea and cared not who sailed it as long as they brought wine and goods and paid in gold when they docked.

And this ship could carry enough grain and wine to feed and then get a small city drunk.

The prince and everyone came out of their trance and clumped down the wharf toward the ship.

Chapter 69

Midway down the pier a large gangway plank extended from the side of the ship down onto the wharf. The travelers walked up to it and stopped at the bottom of it and looked up. Not a soul around, a ghost ship.

Jezep stroked his beard, looked at Mary then turned back to the ship and shouted in Aramaic, the common tongue, "Hello! I am Prince Jezep of Babylon, is anyone here!?"

Suddenly at the top of the ship's side a fat, bearded man appeared.

He had long scraggly black hair and big red face, He was an old man but his sunburnt face glowed like an impudent boy. He wore a black sleeveless open tunic showing a chest of silver hair, his shirt was tied with a wide crimson belt, a curved scimitar hung from his belt, it flashed silver in the sun, the blade was chipped from battles past. He saw them and opened his arms wide and bellowed, "Prince Jezep! welcome! It is an honor! I am Captain Barabbas, we have awaited your arrival for a week! Come! " He laughed heartily. "You and your friends come aboard at once! Bring the horses, we have stables below."

He waved his fat arms beckoning them up, all smiles treating them like long-lost friends.

Jesus stared up at the big man and did not move a muscle. He knew this man and the feeling was not good.

"Barabbas, you say?" asked the prince.

"Yes sire, of Jerusalem by way of Egypt, been sailing a long time, come my friends!"

Mary remembered Barabbas and her heart was racing like a trapped dove.

She had been in the crowd the day Jesus was condemned to the cross. It was Barabbas, the robber they released that day, he had jumped into the crowd and ran away leaving Jesus to die. It had been 30 years but she saw it like yesterday.

Demetrius too knew him well. The girls looked up wondering, then Lam, the servant spoke,

"Sire, what is it?"

He turned to them remaining calm and said quietly, "A moment please, my friends."

Jesus looked back up at Barabbas, "We shall be up in a moment."

Barrabas stood at the top of the gangplank and grinned down at them like a drunken pirate, for good reason—he *was* a drunken pirate. He held a wineskin in one hand and it was dripping red drops. He lifted the wine sack, took a long swig and wine spilled down his beard and his belly.

Lord Jezep turned to Demetrius and Mary speaking low, " It is Barabbas?" Dark clouds formed in his eyes.

"It surely is." Said Demetrius frowning with him. "I will never forget that face, that day with Pontius Pilate." Jesus looked up at him pondering in silence. Demetrius spoke, "Life certainly hands you puzzles, eh my friend, do you think he will recognize you?

"Let him, I might throw him overboard."

Jesus held Mary's hand as they walked up the ramp, Demetrius and his girls behind, servants and the horses coming up last.

At the top Barabbas reached his huge hand out to the prince.

Chapter 70

Resist the devil and he will flee from you.
—James 4: 7

The old captain's smile showed jagged teeth.

His nose was flat from being broken in countless tavern brawls, his eyes were dark and liquidy, yet he had a broad smile.

Jesus shook his hand very coolly.

Barabbas looked into Jesus' eyes and blurted, "Wait, I know you," His eyes fixed hard on the prince. Jesus replied, "Perhaps." He stepped calmly onto the deck.

The fat captain loved to the host, "Right this way, my friends!" He stared back at the prince but turned away and ran around like a large, comical monkey leading them across the broad deck.

No one else was on deck, No sailors, no archers, no guards, only the old captain.

Jesus gazed around the open deck it looked like a large town—square made of wood. The wide flat deck had barrels tucked around the inner sides of the ship. There were tall date palms in wooden buckets placed here and there on deck with sand poured around them forming a sand oasis here and there. Chairs were placed beneath the palms.

In the back by the stern was what looked like the front of a house and in the center of it was a large, ornate golden door. There were arched windows with shutters on either side.

Barabbas pointed to the stern, "Them's your quarters, sire, for you and your queen, O hello mom," he said with his broken tooth smile, Mary managed a smile back.

He seemed captivating with a rough charm.

He was a broad fat man with huge arms, his body hairy all over, he was simple and all smiles when he talked and always too loudly, he was full of quick energy but his clumsy manner made him look harmless even childlike in a funny way.

Jesus stared at his new home noticing Barabbas staring at him curiously, "Thank you, that will be fine, and for my friends?"

"Fine quarters below decks. And the horses will be boarded in the stables up front below decks in the foc'sle, we have other horses, plenty of feed, they will be tended to nicely."

All of the travelers looked around in wonder and began to smile seeing the grand accommodations. Truly a floating palace.

Barabbas walked toward the horses and the supplies and the treasure on their backs, and started to untie the sacks on the horses' backs.

"Let me help you unpack your things."

"No," Jesus said abruptly and stepped forward, "that is fine sir, we will unpack our own supplies, come Lam, unload the horses.

Barabbas frowned but quickly lit up again, hopping around, bowing to everyone, even the servants.

Jesus and Mary stood still and gazed around the deck and up to the bow and at the high sides, "Where is the crew?"

"They are below, they are not worthy to greet a prince and his queen. They would have to be on all fours bowing on the deck and it would be a huge bother."

Jesus spoke softly, "We will meet them later, but thank you again Barabbas."

Jesus started to walk but the captain spoke out, "Prince Jezep, forgive me but I know you."

The prince hoped to avoid this.

Barabbas stared up into his face, his red cherub face stretching into a wide grin, he laughed—"Hello, Jesus, King of the Jews."

Chapter 71

Which of these two do you want me to release to you?
And they said" Barabbas!"
—Mathew 27:21

Jesus looked at the grinning, bearded red face of the jovial old captain, "Hello, Barabbas, yes I am Jesus you once knew."

Seagulls were screeking overhead twirling in the pale blue sky.

Barabbas roared back and laughed so hard his whole body jiggled. He caught his breath, "How in Hades can this be!? A crucified messiah come back to life as Persian Prince! How in the world!?"

He shook his head, stepped slowly backward and plopped down on a barrel looking up at the tall bearded man standing in front of him in long a white robe.

"Please, sire, tell me your fantastic story."

Jesus did not smile, feeling five different emotions shudder through him at once.

Penelope and Sheba, the girls, stepped backward, their eyes grew wide open like two long eggs.

They knew the legend of Jesus.

Their mothers had told them the stories since childhood. The birth of baby Jesus in Bethlehem, the bright star above the manger and the three wise men.

Their fathers had told the same stories around campfires. Both girls had heard of Jesus their whole life but never believed there was an actual Jesus Christ who walked on water, and changed water to wine.

The kindly old prince was Jesus Christ!? They both stepped backwards holding each other lest they fall right down on the deck dead with shock.

They were standing a few feet from a God. They dare not speak. If he touched them they might catch fire!

They glared up at Demetrius, Penelope catching her breath, "My love, is this true? Is the prince really Jesus in the stories?"

"Yes, my darlings, that he is." He closed his eyes dreading their next question, "Why did you not tell us?"

He rolled his eyes and shook his head, "Sorry, girls."

The prince turned around looking right at them, speaking softly, "I told him not to, that is why he never told you. The fewer who know of me the better. To the world I am dead and risen. Do not blame Demetrius, he was being a friend. And please, speak of this to no one."

They both shook their heads and looked up at him with his silver hair so kingly. In their hearts they had known it all the time that the kindly old prince was more than he seemed, much more.

Mary walked over to them to pull them into her arms like daughters but they pulled back gazing at her, Penelope with her eyes searching, "And you are Mary Magdalene in the stories?"

"Yes, my dear, I am, please, we are all friends."

They dropped their head in a reverent bow and Sheba said, "Excuse us, please, your majesty, give us a moment to ourselves."

And they both walked back to the stern of the ship holding hands and staring back at Mary and Jesus.

Barabbas chuckled, "Look, sire, you scared them."

"Yes," said Jesus.

"So you ARE Jesus, King of the Jews." The old captain was sitting on the barrel head, with his two gnarled hands he grabbed his knees and leaned forward, puzzlement on his face.

"You know, sire, I always wondered why they let me go that day and crucified you, It did not seem fair. The people loved you, they were yelling at Pilate to release you but somehow they let me go, I always wondered about that."

"Caiphus, the priest paid Pilate crucified me, I was doomed from the start."

"So the whole trial was rigged?"

"That is true, it was all about money, and I paid Pilate to let me go and I escaped. I was a Persian prince long before I was a teacher."

Barabbas slapped his knee so hard they all felt he'd slapped their knees too, "Well I'll be damned!"

The ice melted, a smile crept onto the face of Demetrius and Mary's face lightened. Jesus could look in men's hearts and could see Barabbas was just a man who had been caught up in drama beyond his simple mind, he smiled wide and held out his hand, "It is a long story, can I trust you Barrabas to keep this to yourself?"

"By Neptune, I swear, not a word will pass my lips."

Chapter 72

They sailed that afternoon.

At 3 o'clock sailors hanging over the crossbeam let loose 100 feet of red sailcloth and it rolled down like a blood-red sunset.

Those below on deck made it fast and as the wind kicked up the sail puffed out its bulging red chest and the giant ship lurched forward and began to glide across the water.

Fifty sailors ran around the deck shouting orders, fastening ropes, singing chants and letting go cheers as the massive white ship moved out away from the pier.

The captain held the giant tiller under his arm steering the huge craft away from the pier out into the open ocean.

It was a floating palace and its long, wide hull began chopping easily through the blue waters out of the Bay of Joppa heading west toward the sinking sun.

The two painted eyes looked out, the giant carved swan at the stern was looking ahead smiling, its head bowing up and down as the ship rolled forward plunging onward.

Demetrius and his two girlfriends stood at the rail laughing and pointing at flying fish and each time as the sea spray splashed them they laughed louder.

The two servants, Lam and Silvanus, stood quietly talking at the stern by the cabin of the prince. They were forever calm.

Jesus and his Mary stood on the bow, he held her in front of him his two strong arms encircling her, both gazing forward across the welcoming blue sea. They stared in silence at the golden sun.

Somewhere far beyond that blue line stretching endlessly before them lay the eternal city of Rome.

The ship's deck looked like a wide wooden field.

The deck was made of shiny planks of pine going long-ways for 300 feet and the beam of the ship was forty feet wide. Only the huge three-foot thick mast shooting up like a giant pointed Cedar Tree in the middle of the deck interrupted the flat field of wood. Ropes were everywhere, draped like strands of hair.

The wide deck was clear except for large palm trees with tables under them set in four locations on the broad deck. A servant stood at each oasis beside a table filled with food and wine.

The huge white swan gazed down from behind the massive ship and the deck raced to the bow where the raised V—sides of the Greek walls, where Jesus and Mary stood, cupped the front deck like a stage.

The main deck was kept clear and but for a small crew setting the sail, no one, save the Captain and the prince and his friends, was allowed on deck. A few sailors were allowed on the raised upper level above the deck to steady the sail but the actual deck was for royalty only, only the divine one and his entourage could touch the pine floors of this floating Olympus.

The ship bounded on, a floating town fit for a king.

Barrels of wine and stores were tied against the inner sides of the ship, rounded seats were fixed on the sides here and there with sea—tables in front of them. Pitchers of wine were set in holes in the tables and cups were fixed there too. The prince and his party, when not sitting beneath a palm tree oasis, sat in the chairs along the sides and ate and drank as the ship rolled along.

The sides of the ship were six feet high off the floor the length of the deck with wooden walkways behind barrels and chairs along the sides to stand on to look up over the sides at the blue rolling sea.

At the back end of this long field of wood was the tall front of a house, It had a large square door and two shuttered windows on either side of the door, it was the ocean home of the prince and his Lady Mary.

Inside was a royal bed and the chamber made the Prince of Babylon think he was back home in his palace.

It was laden with fruit, bread and wine, with cushioned chairs to lounge upon, it had couches with wooden legs carved like legs of kneeling camels. Long golden silks were hanging down along the walls and there was even a large black marble bathtub the room had two golden thrones set against the back wall to receive guests.

It was more than a ship—it was a world.

Chapter 73

"A great Leviathan swallowed up Jonah"
—Old Testament

The second morning at sea sailors in tattered loincloths were running around the deck yelling and pointing wildly over the sides.

His friend shouted, "Come Issa! You have to see this!"

The prince ran behind his friend to a foothold by the side and pulled himself up to gaze out at the white-tipped windy waves and there it was—a monster of the Gods. It was rising up and down beside the rolling ship, it had a black shiny back 20 feet wide and this swimming black mountain had a large white eye that peered up at him, the monster's snout was the length of a boat.

The fish thing opened its lower jaw and a hundred teeth glistened like long white daggers dripping bright water.

Suddenly a loud blast of seawater shot out of its huge gray head, sounding like the sneeze of a giant.

The whale rolled along beside the white ship, its huge black body rivaling the size of the ship and as it went under, behind it out of the sea came its wide black tail big as a fishing boat, it slapped the sea and splashed seawater onto the prince and the poet twenty-five feet up. It rose up once more and the prince saw its long black wings flapping up and down as if flying in the sea, It was larger than five elephants!

"What in Heaven is that thing?!" shouted the prince.

"A Leviathan, my friend! It swallowed up Jonah!" and with a laugh he slapped the prince on his back and they both gazed at each other and then out again in amazement to watch the big black beast slap its tail with a loud crack on the surface, then dive down slipping into the deep sea forever.

Chapter 74

Where the corpse is, there the vultures will gather.
—Luke 17:39

The afternoon sun hanging low over the Coliseum was a blood—orange color.

Piercing screams echoed against the high white walls and Romans dotting the stands here and there hid their eyes.

Lions below were criss—crossing around the grounds with people hanging out of their mouth flailing with their last breath.

One lion ran across the field with a man still alive in its teeth, the man's head bobbling across the ground, he was frantically reaching up pounding with his fists at the lion's head as it ran. The lion stopped, coughed the man out onto the ground then lunged and grabbed his head in his mouth for a better grip and kept on running. The man fully naked, was dragged along by his head until he screamed and gurgled and went limp.

In a few minutes as the lion chewed on him the man was unrecognizable as human.

Five Christians, two men and three women, were kneeling in prayer by a wall as three lions bounded across the coliseum grounds and lunged into them with shaggy, shaking heads ripping at them with their red, dripping teeth. They ripped them all apart in one minute; growls joined with bloody screams.

The dying people's eyes were wide, and they howled, clutching at heaven watching themselves being eaten. Seeing this half the Romans in the stands turned away.

One lion, a huge male, with his top fangs hooked the top of the woman's robe and ripped her wool tunic off exposing her large, jiggling white breasts. The beast sank his teeth into her exposed right breast and blood and milk gushed out of it as she screamed madly punching at his hairy head and clutching his mane, this made him close his hairy mouth fully down on her breast, more blood gushed out and her eyes went mad and her mouth opened wide in a silent scream as her fingers clutched the hairy mane of the beast in her throes of death, she pounded with her fists until her arms fell away like dead ropes.

The long yellow lion positioned himself on top of her and pushed down upon her as he gnawed her crimson flowing neck. Her white arms flew out sideways going limp, giving in to the mad, growling lion.

A thousand Romans raised a cheer.

The crowd of togas watched as a lion had another woman by the neck and dragged her across the arena, her arms waving madly at the sky, her screams turning to gurgles as her arms dropped as she bounced along beneath the running lion.

One giant cat pinned a man against the wall standing up chewing away at his shoulder.

The few thousand Romans in the stands gazed down sickly to see the beasts throwing corpses around like rubbish, patches of blood stained the grass, with half—eaten bodies in hideous chunks scattered across the grounds in the afternoon sun.

The sound of the crowd was a low buzz, quieting down, filing out to go home.

As the blood-red sun sank below the wall and the entire coliseum darkened to dusk.

Nero sat up on his arena throne laughing with his chubby arms waving above his head. He lifted high his silver goblet as each Christian was devoured. His personal guards closed their eyes and pinched their eyes in disgust.

Mercius, the head Roman Guard, stood in the grandstands above the bloody mess. His hand was resting on the handle of his short sword, a deep frown was on his face, and he was shaking his head. From time—to time he glanced at his fellow guards who shot him looks of disgust at this bloody drama.

Mercius gazed up and down the stands at the last Romans hanging in the stands gazing drunkenly at this sickening show of lions and blood.

There were only a few thousand spectators left in the entire Coliseum, a place that could easily hold fifty thousand. Nero was losing the battle of favor and he knew it so, Mercius could see, in desperation, he kept ordering more Christians thrown out even as darkness was dropping upon them.

Bodies and ragged parts of bodies filled up the whole arena as lions ran madly around the grounds.

The little emperor knew he must have more blood to prove he was not wrong in blaming the Christians for the fire of Rome. Fewer and fewer were believing him but the ghastly game was on. He would not stop.

More Christians continued to be dragged out, ten more men women and one child were shoved out, more lions were released. The big cats at the earlier supper were lying by the walls calmly licking their paws, stomachs full, swirling around their large tongues.

As more Christians were shoved out to face new lions the screams began again.

Chapter 75

Outside the walls thousands were pushing against the outside gate shouting, "STOP THIS! STOP THIS!"

Mercius left his post to go to the top of the walls to look down into the street. He thought. 'I should open the gate and let them all in, they could stop it with their sheer numbers'.

But his sensible side took over, 'Nero's guards, though no match for my men, would protect the emperor, there would be much slaughter of friends'.

He rubbed his unshaven chin and talked out loud to himself, "Not yet, the time has not come but will come soon, I know it."

The people shouted, cursing the emperor, calling for the killing to stop.

Mercius knew something must be done but a military takeover would be too bloody. He knew Nero's guards personally, the ones he would have to kill. He thought to himself, 'I could give the order but the people must do it.'

'The citizens, not us. They must stand behind us or it cannot be done. They are Rome.'

He heard the shouts outside in the street and the screams behind him down on the grassy floor and at the same time heard his own men calling him, "Sir? What should we do? Should we make our move? This slaughter must end!"

He heard their voices and the shouts. He had the manpower to stop the slaughter but he could not. He was going mad.

Within the heart of the captain of the guards human decency battled against his Roman loyalty. He could not stand this much longer. It was tearing him apart.

The old captain ached to charge the emperor with his men and take over Rome. But if he failed, it would be him down there facing the lions. He could not risk his men, they would die with him screaming on crosses. To a man they were loyal and ready but he would not risk their lives.

So he waited, his palms sweating on his spear.

He knew the Gods not would allow this much longer.

Chapter 76

It was a bright blue morning with no clouds above and men were running across the deck of the massive ship pulling on ropes, securing barrels, shouting orders. The ship rowed on slowly and steadily toward the white city.

The prince did not hear them, he was frowning as he gazed west in the direction of distant Rome, yearning to be there, to do he knew not what.

He only knew he must save his people.

Mary was still asleep in their quarters. A smile crept over his face thinking of Demetrius and his heavy hangover this morning.

Jesus watched the deep blue chop of the sea in front of him. It had been seven days at sea now and, according to Barabbas, ten more days to Rome.

Suddenly beside the ship a dolphin leaped up and as it fell back into the sea looked up at the prince, a look and that eternal smile.

"An omen" he said to himself.

"What was that you said, my dear?"

He turned and there stood his Mary, her long white-blond hair combed straight as silk and her smile beaming.

"I just saw a dolphin jump and he smiled at me."

"They have to smile, it's plastered on their face."

She put both arms around him in a warm hug.

The two hugged a moment then he pulled away looking into her eyes, "I'm so anxious to get there."

She sighed and looked out across the sea as the ship heaved on forward, "I know you are, my love and I pray for you every night, I wonder what great plan God has for you and for us."

The dark brow of the prince hid his eyes, "I must save my people, but I am concerned about all of you, God must have a plan for you and the others."

"I surely hope so, my love."

They both heard a groan from below. They both laughed, Jesus said, "That's our poet, last night I think he drank half the wine on the ship."

They looked up behind them at the gigantic crimson sail puffing its chest forward, they felt the huge ship roll under them and felt the salt spray fly off the churning bow, cold seawater washing their faces.

They saw the crew settling into their places and far to the stern Barabbas was holding the tiller with his huge arms and smiling at the sky.

The morning sun was rising behind them, The ship chopped onward and Jesus and Mary stood entwined at the bow staring into the distance.

Chapter 77

The midmorning sun sent panels of gold into the Roman room. The gnarled old priest Caiphus gazed out through vulture eyes and spoke, "You are absolutely sure it was him?"

The thin, black-robed figure standing before his throne answered, "Yes, Caiphus, I am sure, it is the same Jesus you thought you had crucified years ago."

The Jewish Priest now royal jailer of Rome, clutched the arms of his ivory chair, his bony knuckles like curved twigs. He leaned forward gasping and wheezing, listening to Judas, "The rumors are true, sire, he is alive in the flesh and has turned into a Babylonian Prince?"

The wretched priest looked down at the dark-robed figure before him and continued to listen intently,

"He is called Prince Jezep of Babylonia but it is Jesus, and he is sailing to Rome as we speak."

The old Jew in a cackling voice from his chair, "Judas! I will not pay you one Centare if you are lying or mistaken, this is too much to believe."

"It is true, my lord," Judas, in his long black robe spoke in his hissing voice through pursed lips, his thin greasy beard moving up and down with every word, "I followed the rumors and rode to Babylon, I found him and could not believe it myself but it was him. I met him in his palace using the pretext of informing him of the fire and there he was alive as you or me, He looks similar, still strong but thinner and with a silver beard…"

"How could it be ? He was crucified for God's sake, I was there, I ordered him killed myself." Caiphus clutched the arms of his high chair and glared at the thin man.

Judas looked down at his fingernails, "I never told you but he escaped crucifixion."

"Escaped!? HOW!" Caiphus leaned forward so far he almost fell onto the steps.

Judas knew how, but to save his skin he looked up at the old man and did what he did best—he lied.

"I don't know the details but he escaped to Babylon where he talked his way into being an important prince of Babylonia with a palace and much treasure it seems. He has been living there all these years."

"All these years, but tell me, why does he come to Rome?"

"It's the Christians. When I told him of the poor wretches being punished for the fire he vowed to help them, God knows how but he will try to save them, he is their God after all? "

"One man defy all of Rome?! Go against the emperor and his fifty thousand soldiers?! That is ridiculous but it does not matter, nothing matters except that we have found Jesus ALIVE! Half the world worships him now and so he really IS a threat to Rome. It is exactly as before! And I have him, again!"

"Well, not yet my Lord", Judas interrupted, "he is still free and sailing the sea, he is coming here and he is angry."

"But we will arrest him and crucify him again, the emperor will pay me a fortune for him. This is perfect."

"But, my lord, there are some problems."

"What problems?! When he arrives, arrest him! We arrested him once and crucified him, this time we will make sure he's really dead!"

"He is on a giant ship with friends and much protection and when I saw him set sail in Joppa…"

"You saw him in Joppa?!"

"Yes, but he arrived in Joppa with a small army and a caravan and powerful friends, he is stronger now. I saw him before I sailed, he is a king and travels with Mary Magdalene, with an archer friend and two servants, one white and one black, it will not be easy."

"Hogswattle! Take a company of soldiers and grab him when he arrives in Rome. Do this and I will pay you 3000 pieces of silver!"

"The first time you gave me only 30."

Caiphus looked at Judas snickering, "But now he is a much bigger fish."

Chapter 78
What sort of man is this that even the winds and the sea obey him.
Mathew 8:22—23

One hundred miles off the boot of Italy their large, white ship was under full sail. The sweeping prow rose high on a swell and fell down the other side shuddering onto the sea, rolling ever onward.

The crimson sail was bulging out like the belly of a drunkard and the massive floating palace rolled on.

The ropes lashed back and forth as men easily held them and as the whoosh of the water slapped, the rising and falling hull the deck boards creaked and groaned. The ship sailed smooth as a man sleeping.

Captain Barabbas, and their royal guests relaxed on the deck knowing they would glide into Rome on a peaceful breeze. They were already seeing land birds twirling around the mast.

Demetrius had his arms around Sheba, showing her how to pull back an arrow in a bow. She was aiming at the butt of a wine-barrel. Young Penelope was sitting nearby knitting a sailor's hat.

Lam and Silvanus were sitting on wooden chairs under the palm trees on deck playing chess and in the sleepy afternoon Jesus and Mary slept peacefully in their bed.

Sheba let fly an arrow and it whacked into the wine butt. Demetrius spun her around and kissed her right there, as he pulled away laughing he looked over the bow and something did not look quite right.

The horizon was coming toward them. He yelled out, "ISSA! Come quickly!"

The crew, Barabbas, the prince and Mary were on deck peering across at the sea in disbelief. The entire horizon was lifting up; a black wall of water one hundred miles wide was gliding toward them fast but in eerie silence.

The wave would engulf them in minutes, thrash them to bits.

The ship was a small toy to the wave and all started screaming and throwing themselves onto the deck, their face buried in their hands. Each person clutching a rope, anything, wailing! Cursing! Crying! Horses were screeching madly below deck. Sailors and soldiers started slipping around, running frantically falling, clutching at air.

Mary looked at the black wave rushing toward them a and started to cry shaking her head looking up at Jesus standing beside her by their back cabin, he was watching her tears. Her lips were trembling, her eyes wet, her cheeks shining as she gazed into his eyes.

"Fear not, my darling.," said the prince, "Go into our cabin and hold tight to the wall!"

"My God, I can't do it alone!"

" You must! Be strong my dearest, and fear not, now go." He turned walked across the deck up onto the ship's rocking side by the rising bow.

With only a white sheet hung over his right shoulder, standing on the rail toward the bow, his long body, his brown muscular back, silver hair streaming to his shoulders, he flung his arms outward facing the impossible black wall, now hundreds of feet high rushing toward them. He looked up to Heaven and roared out, "GOD SAVE US!" bellowing louder than any wave.

All eyes were closed, bodies flung face-down on deck awaiting doom, heads lowered, hearts raging, only Demetrius stood on deck near Jesus facing the wave.

Jesus stood leaning over the ship's side, his arms spread wide, eyes serenely closed, his long, white hair dripping seawater down his back.

Suddenly the rolling hill of water was upon them, the ship started rising up the wall of water, the bow tilted up slightly going higher, everything on deck, barrels, chairs, palm trees, sand, masses of tangled bodies started rolling backwards, tumbling, crashing, yelling, falling back onto the stern cabin.

As the long ship started rising up the wave, people fell on people crushing against each other, clutching at the sides, at ropes, anything, horses were shrieking below decks, as the ship rode up the towering wave, higher and higher, halfway up it rode, tilting ever so slightly as it rose up the wave, the dark blue, monster wave blotted out the sun above.

Jesus stood fast, facing the wave arms flung wide he bellowed again, "GOD SAVE US!"

Water poured over the sides and just as the wave was crashing down upon them—the entire wave suddenly parted and two blue hills of ocean fell away and passed by either side of the ship. Huge water curled over the sides but rushed on past.

The ship fell with a deafening shudder onto the sea and slammed down bobbing in the calm water. The tall mast swayed but did not break, the red sails pitched forward like an avalanche onto the deck.

The poet was face down on the wooden floor, his head on his arm. Jesus stood on the rail alone.

The ship rode up and down easily as the mound of water passed out of sight behind them blending into the far horizon.

The prince stumbled back down and lay on his back on the deck breathing hard. In a second he sat up, turned and cried out, "Mary!"

"I am here, my love!" he saw her struggle to her feet up from the gaggle of debris, stepping over ropes and men sprawled everywhere and ran toward him across the deck.

He got to his feet and they met, held each other and could not let go. Her, drenched in her gown wet showing her naked glistening skin beneath, and he, naked but for the cloth over his shoulder.

The ship bobbed to stillness on the calm blue sea. The painted eyes of the ship looked bored.

The crew rose to their feet shaking their head, many fell to their knees, palms in prayer toward the prince. Each knew they had just seen a miracle.

The calm water looked like a wide blue desert, out of sight of land it stretched endlessly in all directions, a flat, blue and gold carpet.

Then everyone on deck and those filing up from below gazed at the prince, who was now sitting on a barrel, Mary stood beside him with her arm around his strong shoulders, He was smiling wide, his beard still dripping.

The crew gathered around him, many on their knees, bowing, Egyptians lived with Gods and this was must be one of them. Demetrius pushed through the crew and rushed to the prince hugging him, "Thank you, Issa, you always amaze me." They smiled at each other and hugged.

Old Barabbas swayed toward them across deck, looking back and forth asking about the crew, how they felt, helping his men up, and then he walked right up to the Prince, "Jesus, king of the Jews, you parted the sea you must be Moses come back to us!" And he let out a laugh, the entire crew laughing with him. "You saved the ship, you saved us all!"

He stepped forward to shake his hand.

The prince shook his hand and then with his wide, white smile opening his arms said, "No, no it was none of my doing, God did all the work, he parts the seas for us."

He opened his arms wide and the crew, a hundred men, all the friends, even Lam and Silvanus laughed and laughed and peeking from behind a barrel in the stern were two young girls, shaking and laughing with them.

Chapter 79

The lighthouse of Alexandria stood 400 feet high and rose like a square gold mountain into the clouds.

Approaching the largest harbor in Egypt, sailors could see the golden wonder shining for miles. Like the city, Alexander the Great built the mountainous lighthouse 300 years before.

The water of the lavish harbor was dark blue turning purple in the afternoon sun, sloshing against marble, the long waters grew narrow leading up to the ivory city that rose like Olympus at the far end of the harbor.

Sailors standing in their triangle, lateen sailing ships or in Greek Biremes gliding through the straits were awestruck at the wonders standing along the shore.

Towering statues of all the Greek Gods stood gleaming atop pillars, lining both sides of the blue sloshing bay. Each one stood one hundred feet off the quay.

The first statue greeting sailors was bearded, muscular Zeus, then next his scowling wife, Hera, then the naked, golden-haired Apollo sat strumming his lyre. Beside Apollo by the wharf stood Athena looking out proudly in her long bronze dress and helmet, her spear and shield leaning beside her.

Her shield at her side was taller than the sail of any ship that passed.

Then came Hermes, the god's messenger, carved thin with winged heels, one winged foot touching the Earth, the other raised behind as if flying, then old Poseidon with his long swirling beard stood, full—chested holding a trident, and even hump—backed, scowling Hades was a statue worthy to be worshipped.

Every towering God was covered in gold leaf and shined like burning gold torches in the blazing sun, sailors had to shield their eyes looking at the Gods at noon.

Finally at the end of the towering procession of Gods stood glorious Aphrodite, the goddess of love's destruction, she was perfectly nude with pure white goat's milk spewing high out of both her nipples streaming down splashing into an enormous pool of milk. A miraculous mechanical fountain flowing with milk day and night, a wonder of the age.

All the golden Gods on top of pillars watched over the bay as sailors and kings gazed in wonder as they glided into the city—Gods standing guard beside the channel leading into the glorious city of Alexander.

Most still believed in them and worshipped them.

The last carved wonder, rearing up at the end of the harbor on a prancing horse, was Alexander the Great, his God—like body in shining white marble, with a ten—foot wide wreath of pure gold circling his curling hair. He was sitting atop Bucephalus, his daring war horse carved in white and gold. The young king's wild hair carved and waving all around, a long spear in his hand raised menacing ready to hurl at the sun.

The Egyptian priests had proclaimed him a God, son of Zeus, so he had placed himself first among his fellow Gods.

Half the western world believed in the Gods, some even worshipped Alexander and many wandering to the city prayed to Jesus, the new messiah.

Voyagers in their ships almost ran aground staring up at the statues and at the lighthouse but most of their awe was for at the ivory city rising like a dream into the clouds.

Some swore they could see the winged horse, Pegasus gliding around the upper temples of Alexandria.

When wanderers or merchants finally docked they threw their ropes up to friendly dock men and were greeted by throngs of fellow sailors in pointed cloth hats or by merchants awaiting their wares. Wharf rats, those human rodents, ran along the long pier while sitting beside walls were bare—breasted women selling flowers.

Some women sold themselves.

Camels and elephants strolled among the people, tall black eunuchs and naked painted women walking al around. There were snake charmers and musicians banging drums and playing flutes. The dank smells of African animals mixed with the pungent smells of mouth-filling incense and with the musky smell of writhing women, and smoke from pigs and beef turning on spits above a fire, this joined in the nostrils with rose petals and the fragrance of a thousand flower stalls selling dazzling flowers, red, purple and brightest yellow to all who passed by.

The market of Alexandria was the largest, most colorful and the loudest in the world, surpassing even Rome herself.

Coins dropped into hands, fluttering hens, colored cloth or beer in clay mugs were handed over. Shops filled with incense sent sweet smoke drifting through the air.

Carts were piled with fruit and vegetables. The meat of every animal hung down ready to chop and sell, stuffed peacocks, burning chicken, beef, rabbits and gazelle. Turtles and fish from the rivers lay out on tables. Some sold camel meat.

The desert men squatted along the streets smoking hookahs filled with Hashish. Boys in colored turbans were leading camels along and flute players and musicians were singing beside bare—breasted women writhing in the streets.

Alexandria was filled with many Gods but all bowed to the most powerful God of all—money.

The giant marble statues were glorious but merchants and street people were too busy swilling down red wine, too busy bouncing naked women on their knee to notice statues.

Alexandra was a shining blue jewel of the Mediterranean along with Athens, Poppa and Rome herself, and in the necklace of cities it was a gem that shined brightest.

It was Olympus itself and on the highest hill of the city—inside a tall, white—pillared palace a plump governor sat on a throne.

His name was Oligarchus Rex, Rome's fat puppet.

He sat all day on his tall marble throne looking like a bag of blubber wrapped in a white toga. His head was completely bald resembling a white gourd and he always wore a golden wreath and held a silver scepter. His eyes, in debauched Greek fashion were painted with black Cole like a woman's.

His hilltop palace was likened to the Gods' and sitting on his throne he insisted that everyone call him 'Zeus'.

This big, comical cherub sat upon his marble seat at the top of a broad marble staircase. He was only a figurehead. The city spread down before him like an ivory dream and Oligarchus Rex, this rotund Zeus sat all day eating grapes and giving out orders, sometimes—outlandish ones.

With all of Rome's power behind him there was no need for a personal show of force, with a hundred Roman Ships in the harbor and three legions nearby he had no need even for palace guards, though he retained two silver-clad soldiers to stand beside his throne for show.

He insisted on being called 'your majesty' and when he drank all had to toast calling him, 'O all-powerful Zeus'.

On his right and left stood garishly-clad Roman soldiers with red bushy plumes rising a high off their helmets.

A royal scribe sat on a golden seat to his far left.

The scribe sat in a smaller throne at the side of the king and held the high station of a poet. This scribe named Emmanuel, was a handsome youth of twenty-eight years, recently from Babylon.

His bronze hard chest was draped with a flowing purple tunic and a gold Roman coin broach fixing it on his left shoulder. He was sitting down most times but when he stood to his regal height he was well over six—feet tall, muscled and thin, his chest well—formed, his narrow waist opening up to broad shoulders' like his father, a great Persian prince. The scribe had rippling stomach muscles. On a leather belt around his waist hung a warrior's sword. He wore the short Greek white skirt with his with high-laced leather sandals; thin leather straps wrapped up to his knees.

The scribe looked like the son of Apollo and when he smiled the sun came out.

Emmanuel was well liked and unlike Governor Zeus, was taken seriously and was sometimes the one addressed when visitors came. This was because he looked royal.

He sat beside the fat ruler writing down the events of the day on curling sheets of yellow Papyrus. He was the court scribe.

The Scribe held the importance of a poet, after the governor and a few other nobles, he could order around most everybody. Royal scribes were honored thus. Writing was considered a form of magic.

The young scribe did more than write he was master of horses, a fine wrestler and knew how to tame lions. At times he would take out the royal ship and sail up the coast.

He would walk along the wharf and flower girls, snake charmers, merchants and soldiers all hailed him as he walked through the marketplace.

Chapter 80

One bright afternoon at the harbor of glorious Alexandria a sailor with a clean-shaven face leaped from a newly docked ship and began weaving through the crowd. He ran all the way up to the golden Palace of Zeus.

The sailor was out of breath when he reached the front steps of the Palace. He spoke to the gate man and the giant bronze doors were opened and he walked inside, papyrus in hand.

He was carrying a message from an important prince and he was to deliver it personally to the scribe of Alexandria.

When he entered the governor's throne room, Emmanuel looked down from his seat by the throne and saw the sailor, a stocky man with shaved head with one large, gold earring. He was in a white sailor shirt open at the neck and short ragged pants. He was barefoot and he smelled of the sea.

Emmanuel motioned for the sailor to walk up the steps. He strode up to him and smiled but did not bow. The bald sailor had that cocky smile of a sailor that mocked men on land, an impish smile that showed that all other men were missing out on life itself—the life at sea. Landsmen were missing out on the great voyages of Odysseus, and Jason and his Argonauts, too bad for them.

Emmanuel smiled down at the sailor and knew his cocky look for he had sailed much in his life. He knew that freedom.

The sailor ran up the steps, placed the rolled up papyrus in the scribe's hand and said, "Here sire, it is from your father." and then flashed a hearty smile.

The barefoot sailor backed down the steps, placed his closed fist to his heart bowing to the scribe and then to the governor, turned around with his back to both of them and hopped quickly and jumped comically through the tall open doors and was gone.

Emmanuel glanced over and saw the puzzled look on the face of Governor Zeus and then peered down at the outstretched paper and began to read, his brow turned dark then his face lightened as he read.

The news was the best and the worst news he could hear.

It was from his father traveling on a ship to Rome. He was on some unbelievable mission to save Christians from lions, Emmanuel's mother was with him and Uncle Demetrius was along too. His father asked him to send a message to his sister Sarah in Gaul.

He did not know how long he would be gone and could Emmanuel please do him a great favor and return to Babylon to take over the palace till they returned.

'Return to Babylon?!' The young scribe frowned, his father had just arranged this prestigious post, the most important job in the Egypt and with a title no less, and now he was asking him to leave it all behind.

He looked up and sighed and smiled weakly at the governor.

He read on and started to smile and he looked up again and fat Zeus looking concerned, smiled with him.

The letter told of the power and riches he would have back in Babylon. A very large treasure box filled with gold and jewels awaited him, buried in a secret place.

It spoke of familiar landmarks in the desert known only to his father where the legendary treasure of Alexander the Great was hidden. He smiled to himself.

The letter told him to go quickly because the servants could not hold back the other rich lords who would soon move into the palace and start drinking the wine and stealing things.

The golden goblets would go first and then the jewel-encrusted thrones. 'Please hurry, my son' his father wrote, 'the servants cannot hold on long'.

His father asked if he would be the new prince with all the power, riches, slaves, dancing girls and retinue befitting a Persian Prince. Emmanuel might consider this.

He smiled so wide his ears lifted.

He finished reading and rolled up the papyrus slowly looking into himself.

He turned to the governor and told him he must resign his post as scribe and return to Babylon. The fat old governor's smile dropped to a frown and then his face turned dark.

"I will miss you, Emmanuel, you are like my son."

"Yes, my lord I shall miss you also."

They would say good-byes and complete the arrangements later away from court.

Emmanuel was told there was a ship waiting in the harbor to carry him north to Joppa and from there a caravan would be waiting with a hundred soldiers to escort him across the desert to Babylon.

The next morning Emmanuel, the new prince of the seventh palace of Babylon climbed into a chariot with two high—stepping, white horses and clopped through the crowded streets down to the docks.

He handled the chariot easily, weaving between the people on the road and in the marketplace, bumping a few, apologizing as he passed.

Upon arriving at dockside by the boats, he pulled to a stop and hopped off and handed the reins to a waiting servant. He threw his traveling bag over his shoulder, straightened his sword belt and fastened his white cape on his shoulder and stepped aboard the small ship waiting for him, heading to Joppa.

The boat was a sleek, forty-foot Egyptian boat, it had triangular, Lateen sails and they were red. He talked to some men beside the ship and after a coin or two were dropped into waiting palms the young man threw his traveling bag over his shoulder, hopped over the gunnels of the ship and strolled up to the bow, his heart pounding.

When the ropes were tossed away, the sail puffed out like a proud man's chest and headed down the long channel to sea, he raised his hand to the statues of the Gods.

The oarsmen pulled, the bright blades of the oars lifted and fell, droplets of diamonds falling from the paddles. The long ship moved out and the bow nodded forward slicing through the light, glassy waters of the bay, it moved beside the quay and the crowds in white and colored robes on the shore cheered as the ship moved on.

200

From the deck Emmanuel looked up at the mighty marble Gods gliding by; prancing Alexander, pink Aphrodite and her spewing breasts, writhing Poseidon and noble Zeus. As he passed the golden lighthouse he turned and gazed back at the bright city gleaming like Olympus in the clouds.

He thought of the fat old governor and his plush life at court, he smiled a moment then turned to face the welcoming ocean, the salt wind felt cool on his face. The young man in a toga grinned at the tossing blue sea. The cool salt wind filled his nose and blew his blond hair back.

He would be in Joppa in a week and then soon to his palace in the desert.

He looked behind to his past slipping into the clouds. The harbor disappeared behind him and the morning mist swallowed the city.

Miles away he looked back and could see he top of the golden lighthouse.

ROME
Chapter 81

The eternal city of Rome floated in the mist.

Jesus the prince shielded his eyes from the morning sun searching ahead, his heart was pounding with the oarsman's drum. They had arrived.

He could barely make out the famous Seven Hills of Rome covered with white buildings.

The great ship beneath his feet had stowed its enormous red sails and was now being rowed up the Tiber River. It was sixteen miles from the open sea to the city. They were now 8 miles up the wide river and the city was appearing in the clouds.

Mud-caked beaches and small white houses lined both banks of the wide river and hundreds of people stood watching and waving at the great ship passing by. To the prince the men and women looked like rows of white doves. Some were rowing out in small boats to the giant ship, some sailing in skiffs, others were trying to swim, everywhere men stood up in the boats waving and cheering at the giant ship floating by like a white cloud passing in the sky.

Prince Jeep stood alone at the bow under the bright morning sky staring up the wide river. Rome was growing larger, white columns peeked out from the hills.

The floating palace rolled up and down very slightly. It was heavy as the world and moved as smoothly through the water.

He could feel the rough, cool wood of the deck on his bare feet. He felt warm in his thick robe; the August morning sun was ablaze.

'We will be there by sunset' he thought, 'and then it will all begin.'

Chapter 82

The red sun was melting behind the hills.

The seaside tavern on the outskirts of the eternal city was so loud roosters on nearby fences crowed day and night.

Mangy dogs maddened by the drunken voices and cups smashing on tavern walls, barked constantly.

The sun was sinking behind the hills of Italy turning them dark blue. As night fell the voices in the tavern grew louder.

The little tavern was filled with citizens in white togas and Roman soldiers in ragged uniforms quaffing down beer in clay and glass mugs. Some drank wine in round-bottomed cups and others drank a green, beverage called Absinthe that made throats burn.

There was a hookah pipe at a corner table burning, and the sweet, dangerous smoke of Opium drifted above the drunkards who lifted their heads off the tables and inhaled it as they swigged down gulps of beer. For one Roman Centare, the price of two beers, anyone could have a puff of the deadly smoke.

Mixed among the tattered dregs lying around drinking or passed out facedown on the tables were twenty Roman soldiers in battle dress, red— capes over their shoulder. Their helmets lay on the floor or on a table as the guards sat drinking, laughing and slapping each other on the back.

The tavern beside the water where the soldiers were getting besotted had a crude wooden sign with a rough painted picture of a naked woman without a head. The tavern's name was "The Silent Woman."

The establishment was reeling on its hinges, big bearded soldiers clacked their cups together in toasts and the cups broke almost every time spilling beer everywhere. Men's heads and tunics were dripping with beer. They laughed at this until they almost choked.

An old bard in a frayed green tunic sat with a lyre on his knee in one corner trying sing. His tin cup clinked with coins throughout the night. He was soaked in beer because whenever they liked or disliked a song they sloshed beer all over him. One soldier liked one song so much he poured a full pitcher of beer over the bard's head.

There was only one woman in the bar; she was a painted Italian whore who danced on the tables. She was young with olive skin and raven hair, dressed in a long red Roman style dress which showed her bulging breasts and her nipples looked like copper coins. She was full-bodied and her bulging assets swirled to the men's delight.

Every time she completed a dance she was grabbed by the arm and dragged into the backroom. It was a bare room with one small bed with a deep, wet sag in the middle.

Every morning she woke up rich as Caesar, but drank it away by nightfall and was ready again.

The soldiers were roaring drunk, the other patrons barely keeping up. Sitting calmly in the far corner was a thin dark figure quietly sipping a tall glass of wine.

On his thin fingers and thumbs were shiny silver and gold rings. He had a bony wrist that daintily lifted the rim of the glass to his thin mouth.

His trimmed black beard came to a point and whenever he sipped, the wine spilled off his thin pursed lips and he had to run the back of his hand across his mustached mouth to wipe off the wine. His eyes were black and small and set in dark pockets like a rat's.

He gazed at the drunks and mumbled, "Rome's finest" and then spat on the floor.

One drunken soldier staggered up and stood in front of him, he was weaving back and forth and belched right in the thin man's face.

The bearded man flung his wine into the man's eyes.

The soldier pulled his hand back to strike him but stopped and dropped his arm. He got a sad, pathetic look in his drooping eyes, "Jupiter be damned Judas!, Why'd you do that?"

"Because, Terminus, you are a pig, and you better get sober and get your men sober before the Jew gets here."

"We will do our duty," he reached up with shaking fingers and pinched the bridge of his nose rubbing his eyes, he slurred his words, "So my lord, I jushh wanted to know when he'll be gettin' here."

"He will be here this evening so you and your men better start drinking water."

"Yessh, my lord, and is it true that this is Jesus they worship as a God! They say he is more powerful than Jupiter himself. Is this true, is this really him?" He almost fell over grabbing the wall to steady himself.

"That is the rumor, now get ready you sot, when we find him tonight we still have to march to the palace of Caiphus in the city, be ready."

"Yes sire, we shall," then *'burp'*.

The drunken captain turned, staggered a few feet and fell face-first flat on the floor, he did not get up, his cheek was lying in dog urine. He began to snore.

The tavern roared with laughter, a soldier nearby kicked him to make sure he was out and they all started pouring beer on him. One drunken soldier pulled up his soldier skirt and peed on his head. A thin yellow stream spattered on his cheek. He didn't stir. The howls were deafening! Metal mugs pounded the tables, clay mugs smashed and drunken hoots shook the windows.

Judas suddenly jumped up, walked to the middle of the room and shouted, "LISTEN UP YOU DRUNKEN DOGS!"

The room grew quiet, heads bobbed and looked up at the head jailer, Judas, his face was screwed up tight as he belted out, "Captain Terminus is passed out drunk, who is next in charge?"

A thick, husky soldier sitting right in front of him burped, wiped his mouth and spoke, "That would be me sire, Second Captain Rectorius Maximus."

"Fine, Captain, I want you and your men sober and ready in five minutes.

A ship is docking this very night that holds the most important Jew in the world, you have heard rumors about him but that is all I will say. Your job is to arrest him and bring him in chains to the royal jailer, Caiphus, Twenty drunken heads nodded slurring, "yes, sire." The new captain said, "Yes sire" and then turned and shouted across the roaring room,

"Barkeep! One more round for me and my men! Arresting a God is rough business." more laughs, and more clanking cups.

A clay cup of beer smashed against the wall spraying beer all over three soldiers at the table and screams of laughter filled the rocking room.

Chapter 83

It was nine at night with no stars above.

Torchlight from the shore lit up the still boats.

A man rowed a small boat through the dark waters. His orders from Barabbas were to row out to the white ship and pick up two men and row them to the far end of the harbor.

The oarsman was a young Christian named Michael and he pulled quietly on the oars, sloshing the dark waters heading out to the ship. Rowing toward the small boat, his back was to the huge ship but when he got close he pulled on his left oar and spun around for a look at the floating monstrosity.

The lights onshore lit up the giant white ship like a palace.

The bay was black as pitch-oil and boats were lit up here and there but all he saw was the bright ivory ship's prow towering above them all. Resting on his oars he could only see the front half of it sleeping on the water like a floating white mountain.

"O my God!" he blurted and dropped an oar out of his hand, it fell out of the oarlock into the black water and he barely caught it as it clanked the side as he pulled it back in.

The ship was enormous, a floating city block stretching into the darkness, it was too big to take in at once. The back of it faded into the darkness. On the black glassy water the shining white battering ram jutted out like a long straight tusk. Sloping up behind it the white bow curved up like a pointed white hat three stories high, the prow was a shining white pyramid resting on the black water.

Up front was a painted eye looking half-asleep.

A floating palace so vast and heavy it did not make a ripple. The water was slick and smooth as glass around it. Michael gazed at the ship and he himself could not move. He was in a trance. The trance broke when he heard a voice booming from the bow on the waterline, "Michael? Is that you? We are over here." The voice sounded like deep, stirring music.

He dipped the oars again and looking over his shoulder he saw two figures standing on the jutting battering ram in front of the ship. They looked small standing below the Greek top hat of the trireme bow. One man had his arms folded at his chest, while the taller man stood with his long arms calmly at his side.

As he rowed closer with the tavern lights hitting the ship on the bow he dared a look over his shoulder and saw they were older men. They looked noble and well traveled, and tough enough for anything.

One was very tall with a thin face, white hair and beard, so white was his hair that it shined at night from within, like a halo. He wore a long white robe typical of rabbis or nobility, the hood fell down behind and something about him made him seem large as the ship in importance. It appeared like he was the center of everything, the night, the water, the ship, the sky, moon and stars, all of it, even of Michael himself. The man stood calm as night and it seemed like he was standing on water. There was a glow about him.

Beside the tall, strong man stood a thinner man of the same noble look, only shorter with less power. His sinewy arms were folded impatiently, Michael detected something gruff about him. He too wore a hooded robe not white like his friend's but of a coarse brown color. Outside his robe by his hip hung a short sword held by a leather belt strapped over his left shoulder.

A small cloth food bag slumped between them. It was a warm September night warm but still as a tomb.

The taller man seemed so powerful, Michael felt a deep well-being, a peacefulness as he rowed nearer the man and the nearer he rowed the more it felt like he was rowing home, like he had known this man all his life.

The thinner man looked lighter, unhindered, like a tall thin boy but hard as stone.

He was thin as a willow's trunk but his arms had muscles coiled like rope.

The sword he wore said he had been around the world more than once.

"Greetings," Michael shouted as he rowed to within twenty feet of the two men on the bow and then pulled the oars back to talk a moment.

"I am Michael, you must be Prince Jezep and Demetrius, greetings sires, let me get in closer."

He slid his boat up to the side of the ship and steadied it with his hands on a rail. The ten foot-long craft was secure resting alongside the wooden battering ram on which they stood.

Michael reached up from his seat in the boat and shook the hand of the Prince, it felt like a pillow filled with iron. The other's handshake was quick and strong. They all smiled at each other.

"Good to see you, Michael.' said the shorter man as he wobbled past him to the bow of the boat.

The Prince, a large muscular man, stepped into the boat in the stern sitting facing him, the other man sat behind him in the front.

He saw the prince's eyes for the first time, calm as midnight and his voice light as laughter. A king. He spoke with a smile, "So you are Michael, the boatman, come to row us ashore?"

"Yes, Sire, I am."

Michael felt a strong hand pat him on a shoulder from behind and then the other man laughed, "I am Demetrius, pleased to meet you Michael, you are to row us to Rome, I've heard."

"Not all the way, just to the tavern, the city is not far, perhaps a mile beyond."

"We are on an adventure, we don't know where we're going!" chuckled the shorter man.

"I know where I'm going, he's lost as usual." said the prince smiling at his friend and then he sat in silence for long minutes as Michael tried to look away, dipping the oars in the black water weaving between the small boats.

Michael was lightening up seeing the prince was not some arrogant, snobbish king, shaking his hand and all, and the poet was friendly, it felt like they were sitting in their kitchen at home.

Michael rowed slowly across the invisible waters. They sat quietly with only the whoosh of the oars dipping into the water and the gurgle brushing the sides. The boat finally bumped against a wood piling of the pier on shore.

"This is where Captain Barabbas said I should bring you, he already paid me and it has been a great honor."

Demetrius climbed up the dark wood ladder beside the pier, he turned and with a quick smile said, "Thank you Michael, I shall write a poem about you, perhaps a song." He climbed quickly up the worn wood ladder and up onto the pier and once at the top peered back and whispered, "All clear and safe, come Issa."

The prince sitting in the back of the boat extended his hand to Michael, it felt like iron, he spoke quietly,

"Thank you, Michael, I hope we meet again, if not, love God and treat people as you would be treated."

Michael smiled and said, "It has been an honor, sire. May Jesus Christ bless your journey"

The prince sat still and stared right through him, Michael felt a jolt inside like he'd said something wrong, perhaps a wrong salutation to nobility, but the man smiled, "Jesus Christ, you say?" he sat there beaming at the boy.

"Yes, sire, I have accepted Jesus Christ in my heart, I am a Christian."

Prince Jesus did not move, he sat in the back of the rowboat and just stared at Michael. His mouth was slightly open as if he wanted to speak but couldn't. A few feet up Demetrius peered down over the top, holding back a laugh.

"My Lord, we must go, no time for a religious discussions," His friend laughed out loud and pulled back out of sight.

"Michael, keep believing in Jesus." the ice broke and melted between them.

"I shall, my Lord."

The prince stepped alongside him and reached to grab the ladder.

Michael held the craft steady with his hand on the piling until the prince's sandal was on the first rung. Michael watched the tall one climb briskly up the pier ladder and swing up onto the wharf above. His white robe disappeared over the top like an angel's wing and was gone.

Michael pushed off with an oar and coasted across the dark water, he had the strangest feeling he rowed into the night.

Chapter 84

"Issa, that was the first time I've ever seen you speechless. He was one of your followers you should have given him some words of wisdom, let go a lightning bolt or something." Demetrius was grinning wide.

"Just keep walking, I haven't gotten used to this religion thing, my followers are mostly fools."

His friend knew when to be quiet.

The lights of Rome threw soft beams into the dark skies. It was like a giant cradle shooting up light.

The two men stopped a moment to stare at the far city and then walked on. They threaded their way across the dark wharf passing by loud taverns and closed-up fishmonger stalls, the air was thick with fish smells. They soon came to an olive grove near the outskirts of the city. All was darkness around them.

. They were out of breath and leaned their arms against either side of an olive tree both staring at the road beside the grove.

"Seems exactly the same, does it not Issa?"

"Same as what?" asked the prince catching his breath.

"As that olive grove years ago when you escaped the tomb and we met those three Jewish policemen."

Jesus answered, "It does, and you talked us out of that one as I recall."

Jesus reached across the tree trunk in darkness to shake his friend's hand and said, "We have been in many tangled groves in this life, eh my friend."

"And many more to come I fear, but look at that city" said the poet, "have you ever seen anything like that from Babylon to India?"

Prince Jezep turned to look at the distant lights and shook his head.

A few miles away seven dark hills peaked up cradling a vast valley filled with massive shining torchlight. It was blazing with a thousand torches and lanterns and lit up the night sky like a bonfire.

They could barely see any stars as if the city shined permanent moonlight upward into the heavens erasing all the stars. In the distance the white temple pillars and high square buildings looked small but glowed dull orange here, white there, and towered high and impressive even from this distance. They were glowing brightly for miles.

Lord Jezep and his friend stared from the grove in stark amazement. Even at night with lanterns lighting the distant city they could see that ten Babylons could fit inside this monstrous city. It made them both feel small and they slid slowly down and sat on the ground leaning against the tree.

"And we are going there? Good luck to us." Demetrius hung his head.

As they stared at the lit-up city to their right up the road they heard loud, grumbling voices, "What the hell are we doing here?!" "Look out for that hole!" "My damn feet hurt!" "Stop, I have to piss." The voices of drunkards stumbling toward them up the road in the darkness, a whole gang of fools.

They were below a small hill out of sight but growing louder by the second. They prattled on in Latin but the phrases were known to Jesus and partly to the poet.

The two men slipped a few trees back away from the road and hid behind a thick olive tree peering out. As the slurring crowd of soldiers came over the rise in front of them they saw something that froze their blood.

Chapter 85

The Philistines be upon thee...
—Delilah, Judges 16:20

His flickering torch lighted his narrow face.

Little rat eyes were darting back and forth searching the night, his thin, greasy beard shining in the torchlight looked like a line of black oil dripping down his chin.

Their hearts stopped when they saw him, it was Judas.

They looked at each other in crazy wonderment and watched him pass by leading the crowd of guards stumbling behind him. His dark billowy cape rolling up like flowing black wings.

They heard a soldier speak, "Where is this famous Jew, my lord,"

Judas' lisping voice growled, "He slipped by us, God dammit, we missed him! and now Caiphus will crucify me instead."

The two adventurers pulled back behind the tree their hearts pounding.

The Roman guards, in red disheveled cloaks, passed by less than twenty feet in front of them on the road trudging along and cursing, a few were holding each other up and one fell face down in the dust, the rest marched on ignoring their him. They could see they were all sloppy drunk.

The gaggle disappeared down the hill behind them and Demetrius whispered frantically, "My God, it was Judas! We travel three thousand miles and here he is in the same olive grove? What does it mean?!"

Jesus fell back against the tree and gazed up into the night sky and sighed, "They are after me, but how did they know I was here?"

Then it hit him; "He's been following us, the army in the desert!"

The poet closed his eyes muttering, "God, you're right."

All grew quiet not even the scratching noise of a cricket.

The stillness was broken by the tinkling sound of urinating. They turned and there was a soldier not ten feet away, swaying back and forth, blindly pissing all over his boot.

"Damn to Jupiter!" he grumbled, "My new boots!" The wobbling soldier looked over and saw the two men. "Hey! Who are you? Wait! You are the Jew we seek!" but before he could tie up his breeches, the poet lunged and threw him to the ground slapping his hand over his mouth but the soldier yanked his hand away and yelled out—"Praetorians! Help! The Jew is here!"

Jesus shouted under his breath, "Demetrius, Run!"

He jumped up and they both turned to flee but the Roman grabbed the poet by the leg and he fell face down in the dirt. The Roman sank his teeth into the poet's ankle and he yelled out pounding at the helmet of the guard with his fist.

"OWWW!" Jesus pulled his friend away, he lifted himself up shouting, "Run Jesus! I'll catch up!"

Torches were bouncing up the road, men were yelling, the Romans were almost upon them.

"Run!" shouted Demetrius, "You can escape, they don't want me! It is you they want—Go, Now!"

"I will not leave you." he stopped and folded his hands in front of his robe awaiting Judas and the guards. His brave friend leaped up and drew his sword facing the crowd of guards running toward them on the road.

"No! Demetrius, put down your sword!"

The Roman on the ground jumped up and grabbed his left arm and Demetrius swung around with his sword slicing off his right ear.

The man howled madly holding the side of his head, blood dribbling through his fingers. His ear was wobbling like a trembling leaf as he tried to stick it to the side of his head. He was howling and jumping around screeching, "O damn! O shit, shit, shit it hurts and look at all the blood!"

Soldiers rushed up, wrestled the sword away from the wild-eyed poet, slugged him in the face and grabbed hold of him and then grabbed Jesus.

As the last soldier ran up in the scuffle, following him was the dark figure of Judas.

Jesus shook the men off and gesturing to the hurt Roman let out a booming, "STOP! This man is bleeding!"

The four soldiers who were holding Jesus' suddenly let go. A spell had been cast. The soldiers pulled back forming a circle around the tall one as the bleeding guard was hopping around howling and holding the side of his head.

Jesus walked over to the man, put one hand on his shoulder to calm him and put his other hand up to his bleeding ear hanging off his head. Jesus cupped the ear with his strong hand, pushing it against his head and held his hand upon it a moment and closed his eyes whispering something into the night sky. The ear joined back onto the man's head and the bleeding stopped.

Jesus rubbed his hands together and in the torchlight they saw the blood disappear on his hands, the man felt his ear wiggling it back and forth like nothing.

The soldiers grew silent and in the wavering orange torchlight gazed in awe at this tall silver-bearded man. They looked back and forth at each other, their haggard, unshaven faces peering out of their helmets, their eyes wide and mouths open.

Every single one became completely sober.

Twenty Roman guards backed away from this tall Jew in a widening circle, not one said a word as they stared at their friend squeezing his ear and chuckling, "Look! My ear is fine! Can you believe it?!" wiggling it again and again. All continued to stare in awe at this strange white—robed man with a silver beard standing calm as a statue smiling in the torchlight.

Chapter 86

The ear man sank to his knees, looking up at the prince's face. The kneeling Roman was speechless looking from calm Jesus to the smaller defiant the one who had sliced him. The crime was forgotten with the miracle.

Judas suddenly charged into the quiet circle, glaring at Jesus, spitting out, "Up to your old tricks again, eh master!"

Jesus was smiling as if he were standing in a field of flowers. The Roman Guards glared at Judas roughing up their new hero. One man spoke up, "Sire, this man cut off Galliuses' ear and the tall one stuck it back on his head, it was a miracle."

"It was a trick, this man is a magician!" Judas barked, he was unmoved and sneered at his old master, "Old friend, tricks or no tricks, you are caught tonight and there is no escaping this time. And once again, I am delivering you to Caiphus. Sound familiar?" he let out with a cackling laugh and looked to see Jesus' face.

Jesus opened his mouth in amazement, "Caiphus, here?! In Rome? He must be a hundred years old."

"Close, but he is here and more powerful than ever. When he sees you he might even slice your ear off or maybe your head like your cousin John the Baptist, he will be most glad to see you again."

The eyes of the prince grew cold, "The feeling is not mutual."

Judas smiled putridly then turned to Demetrius, "You come along too, poet, striking a Roman guard is a serious crime."

"Curse you, Judas!" and he spat on Judas' boots. Judas reached out and slapped him across the face. Blood flew from his nose.

"I won't be turning *my* other cheek, you rotten snake!" barked the poet.

Judas turned to the captain of the guard, "Chain them up!"

Roman guards moved in clumsily and respectfully attaching leg chains to the legs of the taller man, then they chained them together.

Judas shouted, "Move it you mangy dogs! Get these two criminals to Caiphus, now march!"

And standing silently among the group, the man with the miracle ear whispered to the tall Jew, "Thank you, sire with all my heart, I am forever in your debt."

He reached down and took his hand in both his hands and shook it vigorously.

Jesus knew every word he'd spoken, he knew Latin and smiled and replied, "It is fine, no need for that, does it hurt?"

"No sire, thank you."

Jesus and the poet shuffled forward in silence surrounded by soldiers in front and behind. The dark, figure of Judas leading the way to Rome.

Chapter 87

**My Lord, I am a woman of sorrowful spirit
—Hannah, 1 Samuel 1:15**

It was midnight and Mary stood by the bow of the huge ship gazing across the lit-up harbor. The shining black water was dancing with a million white candles from the torchlights on the wharf. Ships at anchor were bobbing all around with slick sides.

"Do you think they are alright, Barabbas?" her eyes did not leave the distant glowing city.

He was sitting behind her on a big barrel.

"Of course, my dear, Jesus is immortal is he not?" She turned to see his big fat grin.

"Not hardly, he lives on luck."

"But he is a God, he parted the sea, I saw."

"O quiet, Barabbas, I don't know what that was. He is only a man and a sensitive one at that."

"Don't worry, he will be fine," The captain sounded sure.

She turned to see fat, hairy Barabbas sitting on a barrel leaning back with his hands laced behind his head. He was grinning showing off his five teeth, he sat back up and reached for a round red fruit on a sea table beside him, "Pomegranate, my lady?" and his big hands cracked open the fruit the tiny juicing seeds like tiny rubies. He offered her a half.

"Thank you," she took it and bit into it boldly, red juice streaming down her chin. She crunched the sweet cold seeds in her teeth.

The ship's deck was like a quiet city street, the whole town of the ship was asleep.

Mary bit into the seeds and Barabbas looked up her, she almost liked him now after the long voyage. Her two hands cupped the fruit to her mouth.

The old guy continued invading her thoughts, "My queen, will you go to him? After two thousand sea miles don't you want to see Rome? It is dazzling beyond anything you have seen in the deserts."

She stopped chewing and smiled down at him slightly, "I have seen a lot of things, my friend, Babylon is beautiful also."

"Yes, mom, I do not doubt it, but what I really mean is, will you follow Jesus into the lion's den? Be there at his big moment, whatever that is?"

She was annoyed at a slobby captain questioning her about her personal feelings.

"You ask many questions, Barabbas, but yes, I will meet him when the time comes, when God directs me."

She placed the empty husk of the fruit on the small table and said quietly, "Thank you for the Pomegranate." And then she turned back to her vigil at the bow staring across the dark water, past the bobbing, clinking boats to the lit-up wharf and far beyond to the city.

Cradled in the hills at night it looked like a glowing fire pit "Goodnight, my queen", and he stood up and walked to a portal in the deck and disappeared below.

"Goodnight, Captain Barabbas," she said absentmindedly

Just then out of the darkness a bright white owl flew above the ship winging toward the city.

Her eyes followed it until it was swallowed up in darkness. She looked back down and pulled her shawl closer around her head and shook with tears.

Chapter 88

The towering white columns of the city made Jesus forget his chains. He and Demetrius shuffled along surrounded by Romans following Judas.

It was nearing midnight and the street torches revealed the splendor of the city. The columns of the many temples shot up high into heaven and seemed to hold up the night sky above.

He turned around to his friend and they both gawked at the shining city of Rome unveiling herself before them.

The shining marble stairways leading down from even the smallest buildings spreading out like hundred foot wide gowns, each one dwarfed any stairway in Babylon, it took their breath.

If there *had* been a fire, it was somewhere far from here. The city appeared newly built and shined brightly even at night.

The buildings went on forever in a hundred shapes and carvings and tall statues of strange Gods and naked women were everywhere.

The sights made them dizzy.

Rome was Olympus and they gazed around them in awe. They were still gawking as the troop of Romans led by Judas led them up the wide steps into the dark house of the Royal Jailer, Caiphus.

Jesus' heart turned to ice.

He would meet Caiphus now after thirty years and all secrets would be out and he would be naked once more before that rat. A rancid taste filled his mouth.

Chapter 89

Across town Christian prisoners were pretending to sleep. Night gave no relief. The floors of their coliseum jail cells were hard green mulch mixed with straw. This was the only bed of the Christian prisoners, the smell mixed with fear kept them awake all night.

The jailers sometimes tossed in buckets of dust and salt to make it bearable. Their food was also served in buckets.

In cell XXXI there were twenty condemned Christians turning in uneasy sleep. They were fairly evenly divided with seven men, seven women and six children, one girl was thirteen.

This was one of their last nights on earth.

All were condemned and counting the dreadful days before the lions would pounce, before the unthinkable would happen to them. Their days were filled with thoughts of sharp teeth biting into their neck or their arms and legs.

At night blood spilled through their tossing dreams.

The morning light soon streamed through the window of the cell and the Christians stirred awake around Mathew. The women were sitting up combing straw and fleas out of their hair with their fingers. Men were grunting and coughing as they woke.

Mathew pulled his husky body up, ran his hands through his shabby brown hair and spoke to the others, "I had the dream again, the one about Jesus. He was standing in the middle of the lions and they were purring."

"Praise the Lord!" said one, "Is he coming to save us?"

"Yes, he looked at me and said he would save us all."

A few dared a smile, a young one in the back, Samuel, said quietly, "I believe your dream."

The dream gave them tiny hope, a candle in a hurricane, a flicker against the dark wind of fear. A warm breeze to their souls.

But as the sun rose up the sky the knot returned to their stomachs, the dread returned to their chest.

For soon the screaming would begin, the growls and thundering shouts of the coliseum. The stench of burning flesh as friends were lit like torches on crosses in the yard.

The dream of Jesus was fading for each one knew in a matter of days it would be them out there being chewed by lions.

Chapter 90

Caiphus sat on his small throne, he was wrinkled from head to toe. He wore a white tunic and looked like a large gray prune dressed in loose clothing.

Judas stepped into the old priests' small chamber and when he saw the little old man on his stone seat he dropped his head in respectful greeting, he looked up and saw he was snoring.

His gray, infant-like bald head was slumped down, his chin resting on his chest, he was drooling on himself. A thin string of spit hung from the corner of his mouth.

Caiphus was impossibly thin and his drooping head was bald, thin blue veins showing through the crown, streaked around his white head like a map of roads.

He wore the High Jailer's crown, gold and jagged at the top, of enamel and cheap jewels, it looked comical leaning off his head, which itself looked to be but the size of a grapefruit.

His bony arms hung over the arms of his chair and his fingers were long claws draping over the front of the chair like two dangling spiders. His thin legs hung out of his white toga over the seat and did not touch the floor. His bony feet in sandals dangled like puppet's feet.

He was 75 years old and frail but he had been appointed jailer many years before by Tiberius, the emperor at the time of Jesus, and though the little troll could barely walk he would live out his last miserable days as head jailer.

His current job was finding and executing Christians, he and Judas did it all. Every Christian devoured, impaled, stabbed and burnt was entirely by their hand.

Caiphus had once condemned Jesus to the cross, condemning people was his life's work. Soon after the crucifixion Judas had arranged to be his faithful partner—Judas always chased the money.

Caiphus awoke with a start and lifted his head wiping off the drool with his cloaked arm, he rubbed it on his robe and swayed in his seat in a daze. Two tall, gaudily attired Centurions, fluffed with high red plumes and gold armor, stood on either side of his chair looking sternly straight ahead, long silver spears in hand.

Caiphus managed a pained smile and cackled, "So Judas, did you find that devil Jesus of Nazareth?"

"Yes, sire, he is right outside."

It looked like all the lights coming on in a large city.

The wrinkled old man leaned forward in his seat; his talons gripped the arms of his chair and a smile as wide as the Nile cracked across his ancient face.

Chapter 91

"He's here?!"

"Yes, Caiphus, he is right outside in chains, along with Demetrius if you remember him."

The old jailer-priest sat back and his fingers dug into the stone arms and scratched at them like claws.

The large, red-plumed guards both looked down at Caiphus, as did the other guards in the room. They lowered their spears and looked back and forth at each other. They had heard the legend of Jesus, King of Jews, and their eyes grew wide.

The guard by the seat dared to speak, "Sire, is this the famous Jew known as Jesus, the one who rose from the dead? That Jesus? He still lives?!"

Caiphus glanced up, looking pained, "Yes, you fool, the same! He almost destroyed me in Jerusalem and when he disappeared they thought he rose from the dead like a damn god, I hate him, with all my soul I hate him—Judas bring him in, I will finally have my revenge."

The weak old man rocked back and forth in his high seat, his tongue working around in his slobbering mouth.

The Roman guards in the room left their posts and gathered by the large chair behind the jailer preparing to see a legend, a God.

"Yes, sire, you can have your revenge, right now if you like." said Judas.

Judas let a grin creep over his mouth, he bowed and turned back to the door, his dark cape rustling across the marble floor.

Caiphus allowed the guards to stand where they wanted, knowing this would be an event they would never forget.

Judas stepped outside and remained with Demetrius and the Guards.

The door swung wide and Jesus the Christ, Royal Prince Jezep of Persia stepped into the room. He stood there alone, sunlight from the open-air ceiling pouring down upon him like a shaft from Heaven. The door slammed behind.

All ten Roman guards in the room bowed their heads. Ten Romans bowed to a Jew and then stared up wondering at themselves.

From the open ceiling a beam of dusty light shone down brightly around him.

He looked to be 7 feet tall, long shining white hair. A faint light seemed to shine around his head. He had a regal silver beard down around his thin handsome face, his eyes were shining like two blazing suns at noon. He stood in a dirty white robe that draped to the floor.

He was calm as a morning pool. The Romans glanced at his chains and they seemed out of place on such a noble person, like chains on a king.

He stood glaring at Caiphus. His eyes burning the air, drilling into the old priest, who had once condemned him to die.

Jesus was silent His eyes glared. The guards grew very still looking straight ahead.

Every Roman knew the stories of Homer, Achilles, Ulysses, Hector, the Gods. In the stories the Gods sometimes made the heroes stand taller and shine more brightly, that tallness and light now shined from this man, wondrous to behold.

They had their own gods but all had heard the story of the Jewish God that walked on water, changed water to wine, and rose from the dead. They squinted from their helmets, was this him? He appeared like Jupiter come down to Earth.

All eyes fixed upon him. Two guards stepped backwards.

The fear in Caiphuses' throat was gagging him but he swallowed and managed a quivering grin. From a high seat in the room, Caiphus, the withered old apple, still had to look up to Jesus standing broad and tall four steps beneath his chair.

Like a tiny squirrel confronting an eagle, his voice cracked, "Come closer, Jew."

"I will stand here."

"Come forward!" His shrill voice creaked.

He did not move.

The old priest looked around at the guards and flicked his withered hand for them to do something. They shook their heads. He turned back to the tall prince and snapped, " You are still a thorn in my side."

"If the truth hurts you, so be it." said the prince coldly.

Caiphus jumped to his feet and staring at Jesus shouted at the head guard, "Arsius! bring the prisoner to me!"

The guard standing to his right pulled back, "But sire, he is a God, I cannot ..."

"Do it or I will have you killed!"

The red-plumed soldier slowly moved down the steps in from of the royal chair, he came up to Jesus who glared down at him but seeing the man terrified, nodded to him and walked by himself and stopped in front of where Caiphus was standing in front of his large chair, the soldier returned to his place looking sternly forward, sweating.

Chapter 92

**Jesus entered the synagogue and a man was there
who had a withered hand.
—Mark 3:1**

Caiphus, withered and old, stared head to head with Jesus. He grimaced, the eyes of the prince were burning darkly.

The old man slowly stood up and slapped Jesus hard on his cheek. It echoed through the room and the guards turned away.

Jesus did not move but a broad smile slipped across his lips, "I have another cheek, if you care to strike again." He did just that, the second slap was harder echoing through the marble chamber and the guards stepped back in fear.

Jesus remained calm, smiling with reddened cheeks. A small trickle of blood dribbled from his lip. Then Caiphus sat back down and grinned up at the regal one.

"Still defiant after all these years. Tell me how did you escape the cross? All saw you crucified."

Jesus stood in silence staring straight ahead his hands folded in front of him.

"Talk to me, you dog!" shouted Caiphus.

Jesus stood in silence, searching out an escape, his great mind wandering the room, the palace, the universe.

"Judas tells me you are a king of Babylon"

"I am only a prince."

"Ever humble I see, but Jesus, this time you will not escape. This is glorious Rome not that pigsty Jerusalem. I have you this time. You will be crucified again—for real."

Suddenly Caiphus yelped in pain, he reached for his right hand clutching it tightly, the hand that had slapped Jesus.

"What's this?!" He cried, "O GOD! My hand is burning!" He started rubbing it frantically.

The Romans turned to him frowning, then gazed at each other. His shrill voice echoed throughout the chamber, "God, it hurts!" rubbing and rubbing.

Jesus stared at him in silence, his eyes wide.

As the guards and servants gazed on, they saw the right hand of Caiphus start turning red then slowly turn black and the fingers begin to shrivel like burnt, curling twigs! His shrinking hand disappeared up into his sleeve. He was screaming, and writhing in his chair, pulling up his sleeve to watch his hand turn ghastly black and twisted.

Before everyone's shocked eyes all the fingers on his right hand began withering curling up like the legs of a grotesque spider until, with the horrible putrid smell of burnt flesh—his hand was completely eaten up and burnt away, only a bizarre nub remained.

"OHHHH GOD IT HURTS!"

His hand was burnt off to the wrist, no blood just a knob of blackened flesh.

It had dissolved completely and everyone nearby turned away holding their nose for there was a putrid burnt smell coming from the little man's nub. Everyone was calling out and yelling in horror, shrinking backwards, Jesus himself glaring astonished at the sight.

Caiphus lay back in his chair with only an empty sleeve hanging by his side. His eyes were glaring frantically and he was trembling madly, clutching his stump. Everyone in the room enduring the deafening screams of this gnarly little man flailing around in his big chair.

Jesus stared at the spectacle. He had not done this. He kept shaking his head, frowning.

The large door banged open and Judas ran in followed by five guards, behind them two more guards were pulling Demetrius in chains.

"What is it?!" yelled Judas, "I heard screaming!"

He flashed a look up at Caiphus seeing him twisting around on his chair holding his sleeve and screaming. His crown had fallen off and his face was a sick red in pain.

"His hand has burnt off!" yelled a guard pointing, all the guards stepped backwards with only one clumsily stepping up to help.

Judas watched in horror at the wrinkled old priest flopping around on the throne, "God! My hand! He has taken my hand the cursed Jewish dog! O GOD! It is burning! Take him away, kill him! Take him to Nero! Away you fools—out of my sight!"

He sat squirming and wriggling in pain, kicking his spindly legs, with his good arm he was madly rubbing through his sleeve at only a nub.

Romans ran to him, baffled and dumbstruck, placing their cloaks on him, one threw a pitcher of wine on the nub of a hand and he screeched even louder.

The guards, with Judas rushed Jesus from the room, along with Demetrius. At the door the tall one stopped and turned to the little man booming out, "You old sinning priest, God is dealing with you."

"Damn you, Jesus! Damn you to hell!" He cackled out his curse and turned away crying miserably in his high chair.

Judas grabbed Jesus' shoulder turned him around, looking coldly into this eyes, "The emperor is going to love this." He shoved him and kicked him along.

They could still hear the screams as they walked down the steps of the building out into the cool night air of Rome.

They were led to the dark steps of a small house, it was two in the morning an ice-cold breeze cut across the faces of the prisoners. Judas himself shoved Jesus and Demetrius down, and placed his boot on the chest of the prince pressing him against the cold marble steps. Judas cackled, "These steps are your pillow and your blanket is the night, sleep well my old friends." and he laughed, turned to soldiers around him, "Guard these dogs. In the morning we will pay a visit to the emperor."

He gave them both a sneering smile, wrapped his cloak around himself and disappeared into the night.

Chapter 93

It was September, 54 AD and over 2,500 Christian prisoners were in their cells awaiting death by lions. So many that more animals had to be brought in to keep up with the killing. Wolves, jackals, and spotted leopards were added to the arena cages along with some Hippopotamuses and a strange beast from Africa big as a wine cart. Its skin was like thick leather and it had long pointed horns on his snout. They called it a Dino Beast—'terrible beast'. The Greeks called it Rhinoceros.

To see all these animals let loose to devour, trample and skewer human beings was absolutely gut wrenching.

But as the truth crept out through Rome and the empire that Nero himself had set the fire, the sympathy for the innocent Christians grew more and more.

People were fed up.

And instead of doing the humane and politically expedient thing of releasing the innocent Christians with some face-saving, royal decree, people were disgusted to see that Nero decided to do the opposite.

He made it a blood bath.

As with every power-mad emperor, he had too much pride. He believed himself divine and the killing of the followers of a false God, especially those he had divinely decreed to be at fault, was the only path.

He was a God and this was his godly wrath and revenge and anyone who even whispered against it found himself down in the death-pit with them. Some Romans had been shoved into the arena along with the Christians. A lesson not lost on anyone who would question the emperor.

He knew of the citizen's sympathy for Christians and this made him even more resentful. He sat day and night upon his throne, his head hung down thinking, 'How dare they side with them and not their beloved emperor. I will show them Divine power.' At times he would weep and then break out in eerie laughter.

The guards nearest him witnessed a dark change in the little fool. They watched the evil cherub binge on wine for a week, they heard his mad ravings nightly, cursing the Christians and the sympathizers screeching— "I will kill them all!"

One night Nero got roaring drunk and ran naked through the palace waving a sword, as he wailed to the moon he stabbed an innocent Greek servant boy to death screaming out he was a Christian spy.

His personal guards were itching to end his reign with a swing of a sword.

Chapter 94

And the wild asses did stand in the high places.
Jeremiah 14:6

The next morning was muggy hot, the emperor was sitting on his throne picking his nose, driving the guards out of their mind.

Gold morning light sliced in the windows and the drifting blue-white smoke of the hookah pipes drifted through the panels of it.

Fat lords sat around sucking on long hoses, bubbles flared up in the glass then they blew out the smoke, the sweet clouds of Hashish floated on the air.

The throne room was filled with bare—breasted, painted women lounging on couches.

Parrots flew from wall to wall trying to hang on but clacked cackling to the floor all day long driving everyone crazy. A black leopard sat in a corner held by a gold chain around his neck hissing and coughing up hairballs.

Naked jugglers and Egyptian belly dancers swirled around the room clinking finger cymbals and black and yellow snakes curled around the marble floor.

The guards were disheveled, their red cloaks falling off a shoulder and each man was a tiny bit drunk leaning on a spear.

Suddenly the tall doors slammed opened and Judas Iscariot blew in like a black wind. He walked up and stood in front of the emperor and slapped his thin fist against his chest, Nero stopped picking his nose and looked up,

"Ahh Judas, what do you have for me this morning, more Christians?"

Like the eyes of the asp that bit Cleopatra, Judas' eyes grew thin and the tip of his tongue licked the sides of his mouth, " Sire, I have brought you the prize of a lifetime, outside in the hall I have Jesus of Nazareth, the messiah of these Christian swine."

233

"So he is here—The real Jesus Christ, by the gods what do you mean? They say he was crucified!?"

"No, your majesty, he is right outside. It is Jesus himself, I know him well, I was once his disciple."

"Yes, we know the story how you betrayed him and look, you're doing it again."

The guards and servants in the hall laughed nervously.

Nero glanced over his shoulder at the head centurion then back,

"I have heard he is a God, what is he doing walking around the city with the likes of you and what's this I hear of old Caiphus and his hand, did this Jesus do this?"

" Yes, your majesty, most unfortunate, he is a clever magician but he is no God, he is a common criminal, he ran off back then, it was all a hoax."

"I see…" said Nero nodded his head, smiling so wide two layers of wrinkles hiked up his face, "So all these Christians we are burning believe he is a God that rose into Heaven when he is just some cheap magician who escaped and it was all a big trick!"

"Yes, your majesty."

Nero laughed so hard his head flew back and his gold wreath fell off and clanked across the floor. The entire hall, down to the belly dancers, laughed till the walls smiled.

He wiped his eyes and blurted out, "So this Jesus is just some charlatan?"

"That is true, Sire."

The emperor laughed again but soon composed himself and straightened his purple robe, "So let us see this Jewish jester!"

The whole hall was laughing up to the moment the prince walked in.

When they saw him they stopped laughing.

The tall prince of men enchained in his wrinkled white robes strode in gallantly and stopped in the center of the room. He did not wait, in perfect Latin he boomed out, "Nero, I have journeyed far to tell you that you are wicked, it is *you* who burned down Rome. I demand that you stop punishing my people or face my wrath, which is the wrath of God!"

All fell silent and heard a tiny mouse scurrying across the palace floor. Guards, dancers, and the emperor himself were stunned. In a moment all the snakes were gone from the hall.

Three plumed guards started down the throne steps, their spears pointing at Jesus.

"NO, Stop! I will deal with him!"

They stepped back and returned to their post.

The little bald emperor with a red-splotched, alcoholic face, leaned forward and spoke calmly, "Wicked am I? That may be but I am also imaginative, especially in my punishment of fools like you."

"It is you who are a fool and a traitor to mankind!" blurted Jesus.

"Well, if you truly *are* the Jesus of legend, I see your tongue is still as sharp as the first time you were condemned."

"The truth is sharp and cuts through lies."

"Quiet, you beggar! I am God! I rule beside Jupiter himself! I cannot lie, you ragged fool, you will die a horrible death with your foolish followers."

The little king sat back in his throne in silence stroking his chin when suddenly a wide grin snuck across his face and he began to speak slowly, " I just got the most interesting idea. Tomorrow in the coliseum you shall relive your pathetic little drama. We will place a crown of thorns on your head, you will again carry your cross and be whipped and then crucified. I will play the role of Pontius Pilate and wash my hands of the affair, we will act it out for the people, the crowds will get quite the show and with the real Jesus himself, how grand." He clapped his chubby hands and smiled around the room.

Everyone in the marble throneroom laughed at the prince. Guards relaxed their stance and laughed, as did belly dancers, servants, fat lords and eunuchs.

Laughter rang around the room as the King of Men stood calmly with his head bowed and then quick as a fox he looked up and glared into the emperor's eyes saying, " No, son of Satan—YOU will fall."

The emperor looked around in absolute shock and turned with fire in his eyes and looked down at him and bellowed,

"Listen, my deranged Jew, tomorrow you and thousands of your followers will die in a painful, pathetic spectacle. You are no God but a miserable beggar."

He turned to his guards, "Take him to Captain Mercius, he will arrange our little drama tomorrow, alert the Christians that their messiah has returned and will take every last one of them down to Hades with him! Now Go!"

Judas led them out.

The giant doors slammed loudly behind them leaving the throne room guards and circus players of the court looking at each other in disbelief. Snakes returned and started slithering around the emperor's feet.

Chapter 95

At noon, a young man with cropped hair, dressed in a white tunic stepped into the throne room and bowed.

Nero sat on his throne with his two guards beside him. All the others were gone; this Jesus devil needed all his attention.

He trotted up the steps to the throne, a plumed guard handed him the latest orders of Nero. They were written on a scroll, he stepped back from the throne and read it and then looked at the emperor with horror on his face, "All of them, Sire? You want to kill ALL the Christians in ONE day!"

"You can read, boy! Tomorrow at 3 o'clock, every last one of those Christian devils will be fed to the lions, this is IT!"

The messenger in white tunic stood staring at plump king who was twisting his hair with his chubby finger. The messenger's hands were trembling but this crazy, unimaginable decree made him brave enough to speak, "You mean the city prisoners as well? That is over 5,000 Christians eaten and burned in one day!?" He would have added "are you mad?!" but knew where that would land him. He would have also told him there were not enough crosses ready, not enough lions to pounce but that would confuse the little idiot and probably get him killed.

"Is there a problem with that?" mused the round-headed madman, saying it as casually as asking to pass the grapes.

"Sire, this is too much, the people will not have it, they might riot."

"Damn the people! And if you say one more word against this order or if it gets to Centurion Mercius one minute late—you will be thrown to the lions with them! Do you understand?!"

"Yes, your majesty" bending low on one knee staring at the floor.

"And messenger, there is something else."

"Sire?" he dared to look up.

"Did you know we actually have their precious messiah, Jesus Christ, here in jail right now?"

The young messenger managing a faint smile, " Sire, what are you saying?"

"I am saying Christus, leader of these Christians, has returned and will be thrown in the coliseum first."

"Yes your majesty, that sounds like a good idea."

The messenger lowered his head concealing his mocking eyes that said, ' The emperor has finally lost his mind.'

He stood straight up, snapped his fist to his chest, turned and walked down the steps.

He sprinted down the wide, outer stairway of the palace carrying the death sentence for 5,000 innocent men, women and children and one Messiah.

Chapter 96

As Jesus was pulled along through the city in chains he looked around and saw white, shimmering temples and columns rising into the clouds. Demetrius was even more dazzled.

He saw bright cobblestone streets, cleanly-dressed, happy, long-robed people walking around him, some smiling, some turning away from the all-too-frequent sight of yet two more Christians marching to the lions.

Many people paused and stared at the two men being dragged along the city streets.

His Roman captors called him 'Sire' and acted respectfully toward him. They were still in awe at the healing of the ear the night before, they let his friend walk beside him and gave them both food and drink whenever they were hungry.

As they walked along the prince noticed his friend getting a little down in the face. The prince reached and put his arm around the poet's shoulder, they looked at each other and smiled, he finally blurted, "We *will* get out of this one, Issa, tell me it's true."

"It is true, my friend, this will all be a poem someday.'

He slapped him on his back, they laughed and kept walking, the Romans glanced over at the tall Jew and his friend, one grunted, "They are going to their death and they are laughing?' now that is heroic."

Chapter 97

And God said, Let there be Light.
—Genesis

They walked on rough stone streets but inside the mind of the Wise One he walked in green meadows in the bright sunlight. His mind was with angels in the clouds above. Celestial music was playing and he saw the angels surrounding him as he stood in sweet, swaying meadows in his mind.

The honey air of Heaven swirled around him and God, always white and bright, was filling him with the light and strength of Heaven.

Jesus walked, lost in thought.

He knew he had seen God on the mountain so there was no need for faith because he knew God was real. Having faith means you are unsure. Who needs faith to see the earth and sky? Who needs faith to smell the sea? Is God any less real than the ground beneath your feet?

Having faith means you are not sure, faith is doubt.

Faith is hoping there is a God, not knowing.

Having hope is even more sacrilegious because hope is what you cling to when you are in deepest darkness. It is further proof you don't trust there is a God watching. Therefore despair and darkness are insults to God, running further away from him.

Hope and faith are weak emotions, people should not bother with faith or hope—they should just know.

You came from Heaven and will return there, that's all you need to know.

All religions are founded on the weakness of faith, the exploitation of hope, when God spoke he did not say, 'have faith" he said "'I am that I am!"

The devil rubs his hands with glee when he sees people blindly clinging to faith for that is a signal that they are blind. That's when he reaps new souls for the fire.

God is the only light. It is where all the little lights come from.

Churchmen and the devil do the same thing, they manipulate the darkness.

Those who know God, do not fear Satan, the devil fears them.

Those who know there is a God have no need for that rickety house called religion.

They leave that shack to stand outside in the light.

To those who know there is a God—the whole world is their church and they are free.

The prince smiled for he had seen God. The stones of this world hurt his feet but that was the worst the world could do.

Chapter 98

The people which sat in darkness saw a great light...
—Mathew 4:16

Judas led them to the coliseum, the walls rose beyond the sky, the sun sat glowing down behind the walls.

He clanged open a door and Jesus and the poet peered down a long corridor. Arms were sticking out from the cement jail cells, fists flailing at the air. When the door creaked open prisoners started yelling,

"It is Judas!" "Judas, you dog!" "Look, he has two more of us!" "Curse you, Judas, betrayer! Rotten pig of a man!"

The voices screeched from the cells, fingers clutching at the air like hawk talons. Jesus held his nose, it smelled like a horse stable filled with dead, rotting horses.

Judas and the Romans led the prince and the poet down the straw-filled hallway between the cells. Faint light paneled into the long hall from the outside cell windows.

Withered arms reached out at them, deafening curses echoed in the hall. The chains of the two prisoners scraped across the flat rock floor and the sound of clanking chains brought more curses from the condemned Christians.

Bony arms reached out of each barred window, hundreds of them down the line, flailing at Judas.

Pure hate was spitting out at him from the cells.

Each one knew it was Judas who had betrayed their Lord years ago.

In the center of the long hall Judas stopped, the chains stopped scraping and the guards snapped to attention, spears straight up.

"Curse you, Betrayer!" "Dirty dog!" "God will punish you!" a hundred fists were still flailing up and down from out of the windows.

"Silence you Christian Dogs!" Judas yelled loudly

"I have a very special prisoner with me today." Judas hesitated a moment to get their attention, "Jesus Christ himself, your very own messiah. He is standing right here next to me."

Jesus boomed out in a voice that echoed through the halls, "God Bless you all, I have come to save you."

Silence, then a voice yelled out, "Blasphemy!"

A storming sea of voices began again and the Romans ran up and down banging the butt-end of their spears against the jail doors. It soon grew quiet again and Jesus and Demetrius, the Romans and Judas stood in the hallway.

One man looked out from his jail cell window and from the side saw a tall, muscular, man with long, rolling whitish hair and light silver beard. He wore a white robe and was standing still looking forward, his brow was dark and menacing. He had a perfect and strong nose and his square jaw was clenched. 'He looks so regal' thought the man, 'Could this be our savior?' He dared to believe.

Standing beside the tall one was a shorter, thinner man dressed the same, only in a brown robe. He had long, dark hair and a square, beardless chin. Roman guards stood around them blocking them a bit from sight but he saw that the regal one stood a head above all the others. There was a light in him, something divine, his bearing so great it seemed like he was the leader of the Romans, or of Rome itself! The soldiers looked so small and shabby beside to him. There seemed to be a faint light around his head.

Judas broke the silence, "Speak, Jesus, tell them it is you."

The prince spoke out loud enough for all to hear, "I will reveal myself soon enough."

Judas, then chided him, "Come, Savior man, there is one here who knows you, our old friend Mathew, you remember Mathew."

The man looking out the cell window saw the regal one give up a broad smile.

Judas cackled, "He is just down the hall, let's pay him a visit."

The prisoner watched the man walk on out of sight of the window, his friend with him, he heard their chains jangle on the cement floor as the Roman guards trudged by his cell window and were gone down the hall.

243

Chapter 99

Mathew, a large man two months before, now resembled an empty wine sack. Worry had whittled him down.

He had a wispy white beard. His neck like a turkey and his skin draped over his bones like a thin sheet. He was standing in the middle of the cell clutching a dirt-glazed blanket wrapped around him.

He and the others in the shit-filled cell would die the next day but he was smiling. He had heard the name, 'Jesus' in the hallway and had heard him speak, it was HIM—his dream was true!

Mathew heard a key turn in the lock. His heart pounded.

The door swung open.

There stood Judas in the doorway, he was in his gray jailer's robe pulled tight with a black leather belt around his skinny waist, his thin, greasy beard was dripping with sweat, his rat-eyes glared into the cell.

He looked at Mathew and his stare felt cold.

Judas spoke sneeringly, "Mathew, our old Master is here and wants to say hello." His insolent tone tore into the old man's stomach. Then Judas stepped to one side.

There was Lord Jesus smiling like the sun.

His arms opened wide, "Hello Mathew, my old friend."

Mathew's heart fluttered like a thousand birds rising into the sky. His dull eyes shined.

He raised his shaking arms, his old eyes brimming with tears. He joined his shaking hands in prayer then raised them to his forehead and dropped to his knees before his master.

Shaking like a child he began to cry, "My Lord, it IS you!" he touched his forehead down onto his Lord's sandals.

Judas stood back letting the guards see they had the real Jesus.

The Christians in the cell had never seen the Christ, they barely believed he was actually real. But the heavenly Lord, their God in Heaven this old man in a mud-specked robe standing in their cell? How could this be? Was this the ruler of Heaven and Earth?

Their eyes were bulging like startled frogs. A few sank down slowly.

He was just a longhaired, bearded man in a wrinkled robe, noble, yes, but their GOD? They stared at him then looked back and forth at each other.

A white-haired man, strong with lines of life etched in his cheeks, a tall, royal-looking man, but he felt strong with a glowing innocence around him, one by one they found themselves falling with Mathew kneeling down before him.

A few did not move, stepping backwards, glaring around skeptically.

The Roman guards looked at each other like they really needed a drink.

Jesus stepped into the cell, when he got to the middle of the small, rock-walled room he outstretched his arms and as Mathew rose up he hugged him reaching out for the others to join him.

'Why not', they thought, they would die tomorrow anyway and here was a small bit of love glowing in their dark cell.

"My friends, This is the Lord!" Cried Mathew, "our Jesus—I swear it is Him!" tears were streaming down his cheeks.

"And look" Mathew turned back to the door. "Here is Demetrius! Come my friend, join us!" he turned to the others, "This is the poet I always spoke of!"

He stepped through the open door and fell into the group hugging them all.

The prince stepped back smiling at the prisoners. Demetrius kept hugging them, the women, the children, the old men, shaking hands vigorously like it was a party back in Judea. The poet stepped back a few paces and stood beside the prince amazed again.

For a few minutes the bedraggled prisoners forgot they were in a dirty cell in Rome, this fatherly man made them feel safe and free as if this was a Sunday picnic on a sunny hill somewhere that would go on forever.

245

Chapter 100

The prince reached and took the hands of Mathew in his, looked in his eyes, "Fear not, my friend, no one will die tomorrow—I have come to save you."

"Ha!" laughed Judas from the door, his voice clawed into their hearts like a nail. He spat, "Jesus, you fool, stop giving them false hope! They will all die tomorrow along with you and the poet. O messiah, I will now take you to your apartment where tonight you will have your REAL Last Supper."

Jesus turned to Judas with words calm as a morning pool, "Very well, Judas, lead the way."

Jesus and Demetrius backed out of the cell awkwardly in chains, hugging each person. As they stepped outside, the door banged shut. Jesus put his hands together in prayer and shouted for the whole jail to hear—

"Fear not, you all will live!"

Mathew and the others stared at the closed door and then looked at each other in silent wonder.

Was this He? Every soul dared to believe it.

Whispers spread like brushfire through all the cells of the Coliseum. By nightfall in the two hundred catacomb cells deathly silence hung over the entire prison. Giving hope this late was a thin a branch to hang onto yet all dared to reach and hold tight.

The messiah had returned, they dared to believe

The sun went down and in the cells wet, cold darkness closed in. Bare skin against cold hard stone.

Beneath burning torches on the prison walls Roman guards prattled on in rough Latin. Some were sitting on the ground throwing dice, some drank wine from goatskin bags. The walls were dark and brown, lit up orange in the torchlight.

They cared not a fig for Christians or their stupid messiah, 'Jesus? Who in Hades was Jesus? These peoples' king? Some magician?" and then they'd laugh and throw their dice and shout and laugh and curse.

Two thousand Christians sitting in their dark jail cells were stunned and confused, their souls grinding like mill wheels about this messiah.

They'd seen no heavenly light, no angels, no blaring trumpets, the sky did not open. It was just a bearded man in a dirty white robe trudging barefoot on cement, and to make it worse he let himself be pushed around by Judas, the Rat.

One prisoner shouted, " Jesus, here in the cells, enchained by scrappy Romans and ordered around by that pig Judas? It couldn't be Him. We should give our life to a mere man hanging around with a poet? What is this?!"

Yet all had heard Mathew, the disciple, swear this was the Lord? He was shouting it out! He'd known him in Jerusalem, he'd walked with him for years, saw his miracles, saw him die at the cross and rise again.

It must be Him.

And Simon Jacob from his cell swore he'd seen a halo around his head! Souls cried out to believe. Aching to believe.

They heard the lions growling in the night, elephants trumpeting, the huge Dino beasts knocking against fences snorting loudly with a deep snorting sound that chilled their bones. Wood cages cracked in the night.

No one could see the stars, only blank walls. Each tiny voice inside whispered, "It is him,

He will save us."

The Romans and their two prisoners walked down the hall, Judas stopped at a jail cell and opened wide the creaking door. It smelled like an animal cage, heavy with must and shit. Judas turned to Jesus pointing into to the stinking room.

"Here is your heavenly palace enjoy your last night on Earth, messiah man." He chortled.

The Roman guard whose ear had been healed by the prince leaned in, "I hope it is to your liking, Sire."

"O shut up you fool!" Judas shouted pushing the guard back, "Get in there Jesus, and Demetrius go with him, tomorrow is your last day on Earth."

Jesus shuffled into the cell followed by the poet. He turned and spoke in a low, sure voice—

"No Judas, tomorrow is your last day."

"Jesus, you are a fool. Your Last Supper is on the way, bread and water, enjoy it."

It killed Judas to see the prince smiling as he closed the door.

He turned and led the guards down the hall and out of the underground jail. He pulled his cape around him, with an upturned arm he dismissed the troop of thirsty Roman guards and disappeared into the dark.

Twenty guards checked their spears and swords into the coliseum armory put their helmets on the shelf and walked quickly to the nearest tavern and stayed there drinking all afternoon and late into the night.

Chapter 101

Every man at the beginning doth set forth the good wine…
—John 2:10

That night Flavius Octavius Mercius, Captain of the guard, sat in his chair drinking strong Italian Wine.

He swigged down a gulp of the red juice from his silver goblet, wiped his beard with the back of his big hairy forearm then clanked the empty cup down on the table.

The barrel-chested old Captain was dressed as a common soldier, brown woolen shirt, a leather belt crossways over his chest.

He was wearing the same sword belt he wore at the escape of Jesus many years before. His sword had a name, 'Vivias', meaning life.

Holding the silver cup in his huge hand he poured wine into it from a silver pitcher. He sat at an old wooden table gulping down wine. A lantern lit up his red face and dark red beard.

He was in his Coliseum chamber where he stayed during the executions. It was small room carved out of the rock. He had a large villa by the river with servants and gardens of flowing fish pools but on nights before executions, as his stomach cringed and his conscience ate him up, he stayed here in this rock-walled room. He hunched over the table staring at a crumpled piece of papyrus in front of him.

Mercius took another long drink then read the emperor's message for the third time running his fat fingers through his shabby hair, "Five thousand people executed in a single day! God help us! and Jesus, the real Jesus is here in this jail?! Has the emperor gone totally mad!?"

He read it one more time. He leaned back and gazed at the lantern light and shadows dancing on the ceiling. He shook his head mumbling to himself, "The crazy little emperor wants Jesus to carry his cross in the coliseum and wear a crown of thorns and be crucified just like in the legend, the little twit has lost his mind."

He sat back in his chair and folded his arms across his wide chest, "Was this really Jesus? Here in my jail?" It suddenly hit him and he beamed bright as the lamp, "He has come to fix things, I know it that's why he came."

He banged his huge fist on the table and gazed into the flickering lamp. His eyes twinkled inside his whiskered face, and through his broken teeth he laughed, "I think I'll pay my old friend a visit."

The moment Judas had slammed the jail door Demetrius ran to the little window looking out into the arena.

It was too dark to see but the musty smell of animals hung heavy choking the air. He heard lions growling and the spine-chilling growls of other beasts yowling and yapping in the night. An elephant trumpeted. Large animals were snorting or banging against wooden cages, cracking wooden gates.

The poet gazing out the dark window exhaling the words, "I hope you have a plan, O Great one, otherwise we are lunch for lions."

The prince in his dirty robe standing in the center of the room turned around smiling, "Ye of little faith."

"Don't give me that right now, Issa—we are in big trouble, I don't relish being supper for some lion tomorrow and you can't tame a hundred of them at once, you're great but not that great."

"Demetrius," The prince held up his hands as light and friendly as if they were standing in the garden back home. He walked to the window and leaned on the sill turning to his friend, "God has brought us this far, do you not believe he has a plan for us and all these people?"

"Truthfully…no, I don't. Those animals out there are real, can't you smell them! And in case you failed to notice we are in a jail cell surrounded by ten thousand Roman soldiers who, except for one whose ear you fixed, don't happen to like you or me."

He felt for him. Jesus walked over and put his hands on his shoulders and looked right at him, "Demetrius, we have been to India and back, faced lions, elephants and armies together, and a wave the size of a mountain, it won't end here, my friend, I promise you."

He hugged him and pulled backwards.

His friend managed a smile and looked up at his friend and said, "Back in Babylon you wanted an adventure, well, I hope you're happy."

Chapter 102

Let us eat and drink; for tomorrow we die.
I Corinthians, 15:30

A key creaked in the lock. The jail door swung open and there stood a large, bearded Roman Soldier smiling like a silly pumpkin.

His broad smile full of bad teeth showed he was harmless. He stood in the cell doorway swaying back and forth. He had a thick neck, was dressed in a leather vest and soldier's skirt, his mussed hair showed that he was fairly drunk.

In one hand he held a large silver pitcher, red wine sloshing out the top, in the other hand he held two silver goblets, He burped and said, "Hello my friends, excuse me but I have brought only two goblets and there are three of us, hell, I'll drink from pitcher."

Jesus and the poet looked at each, smiles broke like white waves and they gestured for him to enter.

An hour later Mercius stood up and hugged them both, when the laughs trailed off, the old Roman stepped back and all three got quiet. The old captain spoke, "Jesus, my friend, I hope you have it in you."

"We shall see, my friend." The prince looked straight at him, eyes like iron.

"And good luck to you, Master Poet."

The jovial Captain gave them a wink and walked out the door. It closed behind.

The two were still frowning.

"We shall see," said the poet, "I hope you still have it, my friend."

"And I too."

Outside the cell the old Roman staggered down the dark stone hallway.

Guards stood up as he walked by and he blindly waved as he stumbled along the dark corridors.

Tomorrow in the coliseum might be hard to face but he had found out one thing—this Jesus fellow was here to save those poor devils and by Hercules, there might not be any killing after all, that made him smile as he opened the door to his room. He stopped in thought a moment, "We shall see what this Jesus is made of." And then he fell face first onto his bed.

In a few moments he was snoring.

Chapter 103

If thou be king of the Jews save thyself.
—Luke 23:37

Jesus and his best friend were just falling off to sleep when their cell door opened again but this time it was not a jovial drunken Roman. It was Judas and ten big guards.

They stepped into the cell and Judas barked out, "Grab the other one and hold him fast." Three soldiers grabbed Demetrius and dragged him to the back of the cell and held him by his arms against the wall.

Jesus stood up slowly like a bullfighter facing the bull.

"Judas, what are you up to?" His arms were folded tight.

The evil one snickered, "We are going to make your crucifixion real, just like before only the whipping will be real this time, grab him!"

Jesus let the men take ropes and bind him facing the wall, the ropes through two iron rings held his arms fast. The Romans stripped him bare and he stood naked in the lamplight of the dark room.

NOOO! You Roman dogs! Leave him alone!" screamed Demetrius. A guard slugged his chin with the butt of his short sword, Demetrius fell to the floor shaking his head, blood dripping from his nose.

He looked up to see two Roman guards take out a Flagia, a foot-long wooden handle of a whip with short strips of leather.

An arm lifted up and slashed the whip across Jesus' bare buttocks. He turned sideways at the guard and with a fearless smile and quipped, "I have another cheek, if you'd like to smite that one too."

The Roman's didn't get the joke and raised the whip again.

"ISSA! NO!" screamed Demetrius from the floor as Jesus was whipped again and again on his backside. The poet kneeled down staring death at Judas, watching his best friend being ripped by the leather.

He saw that during the entire flogging Jesus uttered only a few short grunts.

The flogging finally stopped. His back was laced with red ribbons. He lay on all fours, and before they left they kicked him in the face before they closed the door. Judas turned, "Now they will believe you are Jesus, sleep well." he cackled and closed and locked the door.

Chapter 104

A million little stars were twinkling above the harbor. The painted eyes on the bow of the ship seemed drowsy resting on the water.

Old Barabbas was walking the decks looking everywhere for Mary. He peered into rooms off the deck, into the windows of her large chamber but she was gone.

For the past two nights he had stood with her on the bow looking toward Rome, constantly talking of her husband the prince, wringing her hands, confiding in him, even crying and now she was nowhere to be found. The white-haired angel had disappeared.

The crew was asleep below, along with all the archers. Barabbas walked to the bow and stared out to the distant wharf. Beyond the other ships anchored in the night harbor he could see the taverns aglow, the windows bright with laughter, drunken shouting and joking rising and falling across the water.

He started to turn away but something caught his eye and he turned back glaring toward shore.

He saw a rowboat pull up to a distant wharf and a thin figure climb up a ladder. In the lights from the tavern he could see it was a woman and saw the glint of silver hair.

He smiled, "Good luck my dear, but a beautiful woman traveling alone…" he shook his head and watched her disappear out of sight.

He walked alone across the immense deck of the ship. It was bathed in faint starlight. He gazed up into the dark, spangled heavens. He shook his dull head, 'Jesus gone, Demetrius, and now Mary and I have not seen those two slaves of theirs for three days now, only those two girls are left on board."

As he drifted to sleep in his loft he heard rowboat oars clunking below and splashing. He heard the giggles of two girls. He lifted his head then fell back asleep.

In the morning Barabbas awoke, splashed water in his face from a silver bowl. He stepped outside onto the deck shouted to the crew. Soon the entire crew was assembled before him on deck.

A hundred sailors stood around like straggling pirates hanging around the inner walls of the top deck. Some lounged on top of barrels, some stood up, arms around each other's shoulder.

The fifty archers in white tunics stood at attention on deck, their bows against their shoulders. The old captain spoke loud, "Men, our mission is done, we have delivered the prince to Rome, now get to those oars, drop the sails, we head home to Egypt!"

Men ran across decks, oars were shoved outward and dropped to the water, the wide red sails tumbled down and filled out full like the fat belly of the wine god.

Old Barabbas held the tiller, the ivory ship swung around majestically and one hundred oars on each side dipped and then lifted, dipped and lifted, into the waters of the Tiber River and as a thousand people waved from the shore the floating palace moved easily down the river soon turning into a red speck far out on the open sea.

Chapter 105

a son, and they shall call his name Emmanuel
Mathew 1:23

A handsome, blond-haired young man was sitting on a high, marble throne, a wreath of Persian gold and rubies encircled his head.

The blue, winged God of Babylon was painted on the ceiling above his head. Zarathustra, the bearded eagle with square wings.

The young ruler had a square chin with a natural smile that beamed around the room like a small lighthouse. His long, blond curls splashed onto his shoulders. He was 'cute' as the young girls say, and he had deep brown eyes like his father, Prince Jezep.

He sat regally on his father's throne, resting his goblet of wine on the arm of the throne. His wide, muscular chest was bare and sunburnt, over his muscled shoulders was a white cape trimmed in purple, he wore the royal white skirt of Babylon, the garments of a prince. His sandals were laced up to his knees with thin strings of gold.

He ruled with a look and his eyes were instantly obeyed.

He sat gazing across his throne room at the dancing girls, wearing nothing but thin scarves, their white, succulent breasts jiggling as they danced.

Lithe ladies were skipping and twirling around the shiny black floor, red and gold scarves were flowing from their hands like tiny winds, when they danced together facing the throne they smiled up at the prince and his consort and wiggled their sweet naked breasts around in perfect, rubbery circles.

They leaned backwards, swirling their hips to the flute, the harp and drums, and as their arms drifted to the sound of Persian melodies, all the men in the room were rising to the occasion.

The handsome prince smiled down at the dancers. A sensual, red—haired woman sat entwined between his knees, her head resting back on his manhood.

Tall black Nubian eunuchs stood on either side of his throne; they wore leopard-skin cloaks, and waved wide ostrich fans above the young nobleman and his woman.

Prince Emmanuel lifted his jewel-encrusted, golden cup, his voice like deep water, "A toast to my father, the prince, God bless him! and my mother wherever they are, and God bless Demetrius!!"

A roar went up in the hall, nobles, dressed regally, attendants and friends were lounging around the room on long velvet couches, some sat on the steps and some out in the courtyard, all were cheering their faraway prince.

Salome, his lover sat between his knees.

She was a young, red-haired woman with large bare breasts, swaying upwards, Nipples like strawberries. She gazed dreamily up at her prince, rubbing her cheek against her long pillow, her ruby lips parted, "Kiss me, my love?"

Emmanuel drank down his wine from his silver cup, set it down and smiled at her, he pulled her up onto his lap, and with his right hand cupping her bare left breast, he kissed her long and deep, laughs and mocking cheers rising in the hall.

The handsome prince pulled his mouth away and let her slide back down to the floor to sit languidly between his legs, her crimson lips were smeared, her eyes lost in a dreamy smile.

With a large smile he raised his goblet high as the hall rang with cheers.

FREEDOM
Chapter 106

The coliseum's dirt floor shined brightly in the morning sun. Hot raindrops slanted out of a clear sky whapping the dry earth of the arena like darts. Sunlight turned the sparkling raindrops red and they fell like a billion drops of blood.

The crowd was gazing at the sky in fear at the mad raindrops falling from a clear sky, Nervousness filled the air like a billion bees.

Five thousand Christians would die horribly this day, chomped to death by hungry beasts.

A line of silver trumpets lifted and blew.

The terrible show was beginning.

The seats rippled with thousands of Roman citizens dressed in colored togas, red, blue and vastly white and the roar of the fifty thousand drunkards was heard clear to the sea.

Word was that Christus, the God of the Christians, had actually returned and was here.

He would be crucified again just like the legend. Half the city poured out to see it, thousands were cheering madly drunk on wine and beer.

It was the circus of the century; a God crucified in the arena!

The people in wide rivers flooded through the gates, some paying one thousand Cestercia, the cost of a new chariot, for a seat by the rail. The cheap seats higher up were filled at twenty Centares, a month's wage for a commoner. By Imperial Proclamation, this day was jokingly proclaimed King of the Jews Day, businesses closed and slaves were to be given only the lightest duties.

Even to the Romans the return of Christ was big.

Romans, Jews, Christians, black men from Africa, Egyptians, even visiting Britons and Gauls all knew the legend of the savior born in Bethlehem. They knew of his miracles, his crucifixion, and now this God of legend would be standing before them—they were thrilled out of their minds.

The mass of people were inside in the stone seats sitting on rented cushions cheering for death to Christians or outside the gates screaming to save the life of Jesus! Many were yelling for the overthrow of Nero.

Even the old ones eating grapes in the cafenions inside the gates agreed it was the biggest thing to hit Rome since Cleopatra.

Their grandfathers had actually seen her enter the city and told how she had rolled into Rome atop a golden pyramid with five thousand naked black men and women and herds of tigers and elephants.

They all agreed this Jesus pageant was bigger than that.

For the grand show the arena workers had brought out the lions in open pens around the edge of the coliseum for all to see. Roars shivered the skin. They had constructed large, open-air enclosures for the other beasts to roam around so the people could see all the exotic animals before they ran out and chewed everyone to pieces.

Citizens drunk on beer and wild expectations looked down and saw the mad zoo that would be unleashed to devour the Christians.

Pacing back and forth in open-air cages were hundreds of lions, big maned males and sleek yellow-brown female lions growling and jumping madly against the metal bars of the cages, their claws ready to slice and hold down their gruesome lunch. They had not been fed for two days. They were down to eating grass and chewing on the wood gates, when unleashed they would rip people to shreds in seconds.

Hyenas from Africa, hundreds of them were racing around yapping and growling in an open pen, flaring their bloody teeth, hungry for human blood. There were wolves from Germania, tigers from India and leopards from Africa. A river of furry animals was rushing around ready to kill and eat anything.

In a strong wood paddock African elephants were lumbering around, with big, long white tusks and could toss people high in the air and then stomp their heads like melons.

There were the Rhinoceroses big as wagons, with gray, armored sides and giant pointed horns curving 2 feet up from their snout.

Handlers used long poles to whack their genitals making them meaner. The gray monsters stood in the dusty pen bobbing their head up and down, their horns stabbing the air. Their huge sides twitched as little black birds flitted around their back pecking at bugs in the folds of their skin.

There was a herd of Hippopotamuses milling around a large paddock. They would be stampeded into the men, woman and children crushing their screams to silence.

To certain the destruction of the prisoners, in a corral at the far end one hundred black bulls with sharpened horns ripped around the yard. Their under—nuts had been tied to their tails to give them pain and they were whacking their horns against the gates, ready to rush out and gore everyone in sight.

A bull had already killed one guard, his horn had jabbed under the guard's chin and tossed him screaming and flailing in the air. After writhing in the dust he lay still, two litter bearers carried his body away.

An elephant had stomped another guard to death. The crowd was howling, throwing clay cups. Vultures twirled like black slivers in the sky.

Chapter 107

All knew it would be a quick slaughter. Thousands of Romans were secretly itching to watch but at the same time wanted to run away. They were repulsed by slaughter but there was rumor of the emperor's overthrow and they wouldn't miss that for the world.

A dangerous feeling rippled through each citizen. As Romans they distrusted Christians and loved a gory spectacle, but as human beings they could not stomach all the death.

Women and children didn't start the fire, yet they were being killed. Half the multitude cheered and half booed. Fifty thousand people were drunk on beer, here for the madness and blood, however it came.

Every seat in this cheering round world was filled, not one square inch to spare. People sat on each other's laps, the aisles were filled with people standing and cheering. It was brimming over with togas and a third of the crowd were women dressed in long, many-colored dresses, red, green and bright orange.

When the lions growled the people yelled out, when a bull slammed against a wooden wall they howled with laughter, some threw clay beer cups down onto the backs of the Rhinoceros called 'Dino beasts'. Guards ran into the crowd slapping drunkards around, dragging them away.

At the far end of the stadium sat Nero high on his royal stage.

The royal rat was under a purple ruffling canopy sitting on his throne, a dark shadow sitting as calmly as if he were having tea and biscuits.

His colorful royal guards stood around him at attention, their spears leaning forward. One hundred men stood near him and a row of red—caped, white-plumed Praetorians stood along the stairways on the walls leading down from either side of the raised royal canopy. Their breastplates shined golden in the morning sun.

The coliseum guards stood throughout the stadium—each one with an eye on their captain, Big Mercius. He had made mention of something quite insane that might happen today. The nervous speech he gave revealed little, but ended with "Be ready, men."

Across from the emperor he stood, Captain Mercius, husky leader of the guard. He was the ringmaster and would direct the entire show. He would start this Drama of Christ and at the end unleash the animals. His hands sweating rivers. His heart pounding like a war drum.

He was reading the people. His old warrior hands trembled.

He stood alone on a raised platform overlooking the arena and the mad zoo of animals, he was low enough to direct the production yet high enough to be safe from the beasts.

He looked like a square brick house dressed in dark-brown leather armor.

He was wearing his plain iron battle helmet with the short, black horse-hair ridge over the top. He wore a short sword as well as a dagger, dressed for battle. He stood straight, his fisted hands at his sides, his large head looking up to his right and then his left carefully eyeing his soldiers in the stands.

The multitude of drunken Romans were cheering, some were sloshing beer from the stands, throwing cushions, clay pitchers, flowers, Mercius stood still as a rock.

In the midst of the deafening throng he nodded to his men on the left side of the coliseum, they motioned with their spears, then up to the right he made eye contact with other soldiers and they motioned the same way and nodded nervously.

Mercius looked down at the men by the cages, at his order they would release the animals to rush out and eat everyone in sight. His job was to give them the word to open the cage doors unleashing lions, tigers, leopards, hyenas, wolves, bulls, elephants, and the giant, horned Dino beasts. There were also fifty, large hungry Baboons screeching away.

The men in charge of opening the gates looked up at him, waiting nervously. Hopping out of the way would be a problem.

Mercius stood firm, his hands were sweating. Would he have the guts? He knew that when the animals came out the slaughter would be on his head. That tortured him inside but he was a Roman officer and following orders was bred into his bones.

Through the tossed cups and flying seat cushions, he looked at the emperor sitting 300 feet across from him, awaiting the order to begin the show.

Christians would enter and the grand play would begin. There would be blood, so much blood. And sorrow.

He saw the emperor rise from his seat and raise his hand.

Chapter 108

brought as a lamb to the slaughter.
—Isaiah 53:7

Fifty silver drums pounded loudly shaking the walls, the drunken populace was waving scarves and sloshing beer cups.

Trumpets blared and echoed and Mercius lifted his right arm and signaled the Christian prisoners to be released, a thousand ragged Christians trudged out of the main gate behind him, all gazing up in fear. A minute later a thousand more ragged souls poured forth from the arched opening behind them. Then two thousand more stumbled into the sun of the arena. They rolled out in waves of dirt and cloth.

Like the Exodus of Moses they poured forth.

Mercius saw they were downtrodden, hope-lost men and women, crying or tearing their hair. They dragged along their wide-eyed children crying beside them. Women wept with their heads down, some raised their hands to heaven in prayer, and many walked with their head held high, making their God proud.

Character is a funny thing, it will reveal itself as a husk of dry papyrus that crumples or remain smiling like uncaring iron. No one knows his own true character until death snarls with bloody teeth in your face.

A few fell to the ground and then crawled slowly along hoping to somehow hold off their horrific death.

Finally the entire ocean of doomed prisoners flooded into the coliseum and filled it with dirty robes and cries of sorrow. Arms lifted to the heavens, men fell facedown praying, clutching at hope. Some men stood with chins raised high defying the lions to do their worst. The wailing of the women and children as they fell down and tore at the grass pierced every heart.

Lions caught the stench of thousands of unwashed bodies and growled louder, as they did screams of horror wailed through the walking crowd.

Bulls kicked the gates trying to charge out to trample and gore. Wolves howled at the sun, and hundreds of crazed, starving animals slammed against the flimsy boards pawing and scratching to get at the crying Christians walking but a few feet away.

A few made their God proud standing nobly facing death.

Baboons screeched sending shivers through a hundred hearts and caused more of the women to scream. Mothers covered their children's eyes and ears in their woolen robes yet still the children screamed and fell in the dirt. A few kids broke and ran across the arena.

Through slats in the fences the Christians could see the yellow eyes of the wolves and the blanks eyes of lions and the sharp, pointed horns of ghastly animals jabbing the air, and a hundred furry monsters moving around kicking and snorting to come out and kill them.

The old leader of Romans looked down from his platform, an old battle scar on his leg was throbbing.

In minutes he had to order the gates to open for wild animals to rip bodies apart, rivers of blood would flow and spatter everywhere.

He remembered a battle years before when an entire grass hill was piled with slain men and turned the whole hill red with blood. He clenched his eyes tight and shook his head.

The entire crowd in the coliseum grew silent watching the sobbing of women, the screaming children and the roaring of animals.

In the blazing hot arena mothers were clutching their crying children who were looking frantically back and forth screaming hysterically, uncontrollably, one boy started running across the field, he tried climbing the walls and fell back down. A huge black hunting hound broke loose and chased the boy down. Its jaws chomped the boy's neck and shook it till he wiggled no more. The people in the stands cheered and sobbed.

Near the Christian hordes, not ten feet away, were the cages of growling lions and the other mad, hungry animals, all slamming to get out

Mercius had been given orders to leave a walkway between the Christians and the cages the full length of the grounds. It was part of the Passion Play, Christ's walk to be crucified, The emperor's big show.

267

The bloodbath was minutes away but first would be The Return of the Messiah.

The air was thick with excitement as well as fear and dread, every palm was sweating.

Before the release of deadly lions Jesus would stagger with his cross.

It would be the event of a lifetime for the Christians, before they died they would see their savior. Most Christians could care less as they screamed for mercy.

The air was charged with invisible lightning.

Chapter 109

Love thy neighbor and hate thine enemy.
—Mathew 5:43

Silver Trumpets blared and Mercius pointed to Nero shouting his opening line, "Behold, Pontius Pilate, washing his hands of the whole affair,"

All knew the Jesus Story.

Nero walked out from under his dark canopy into the sun and a servant stepped forward holding a silver bowl filled with water. He washed his hands and raised them dripping up to the crowd.

Nervous laughter and applause rippled through the stands.

Then the little emperor gestured across the area to Mercius and shouted. "Bring out the prisoner Jesus, King of the Jews!"

Every head turned, eighty thousand Romans, a thousand guards and throngs of shivering Christians, even infants—grew quiet.

Under the far archway he appeared. He stood in his robe like a tall, white oak tree.

His silvery, bearded head was raised upward with the bearing of a king. His face was smooth, not a scratch. Healed completely from last night's beating. His robe was clean.

Over his right shoulder he was dragging a long, wooden cross.

He stood under the fifty-foot high archway staring defiantly at the emperor.

His wavy hair and curling beard were shining silver and when he stepped out of the gate into the sunshine—a bolt of lightning cracked across a clear blue sky.

All started screaming. Romans looked up, back and forth, as cracking thunder blew out their ears. It could not be! The sun was shining bright, fear rippled through the crowd turning legs and hearts to jelly.

They timidly peered down at Jesus standing in the archway.

He was wide as a bull, a Hercules. His stern, silver-bearded face glaring upward. Eyes stern and blazing mad.

He reached for the crown of thorns on his head, threw it down and stomped it in the dirt with his bare foot, then kicked it away.

Lightning cracked again from a clear sky, pealing long and deafening.

The people screamed, looked to the sky and pulled at their hair.

Throngs of Christians dropped down to their knees and folded their hands in prayer, every mouth opened watching him walk toward them across the open field.

Animals were screeching and snorting. The thunder had made them crazy, kicking at walls, biting the other animals.

Jesus walked toward Nero and did not speak or look to his right at the Christians or up to the stands, he stared only at the dictator at the far end. Driven. He walked between the people and the cages dragging his cross behind him.

Thunder rolled again and the Roman started shouting and yelling and the women in the stands were crying frantically, pulling at their hair, gazing at the heavens.

Citizens were drawing backwards high into the high seats, tumbling back over masses of people to hide from this strange thunder.

Hailstones started shooting like a million arrows out of a clear blue sky and bounced like a million white stones on the grass, clacking on the marble stands. Many hailstones hit Romans, but not one hailstone fell on the Christians cowering on the grass.

Nero in his purple robe and round head crowned by a gold wreath stood up and walked to the edge of the royal platform, he was unmoved and staring down at Jesus walking steadily toward him. Dragging the cross behind him, it dug a long line in the dirt behind him, the prince stopped and glared up at the emperor.

The hail stopped with him. All grew quiet.

The cries died down, buzzing voices stilled to silence. The only sound was the flapping of the large white and blue flags crackling in the morning breeze, whapping loudly in the quiet.

Suddenly Jesus threw his heavy cross into the dirt, the crowds gasped.

He glared up at Nero, pointed his finger and through cracked lips, boomed out in perfect Latin, "Nero, You are evil! I proclaim that your time is over, no more killing my people!"

The Roman throngs sat stunned in their seats awaiting the arrows that would fly and this Jesus drop dead pierced by a hundred bloody shafts.

But no soldier fitted an arrow or moved a muscle. They were gazing warily at the sky, some at this Jesus.

Chapter 110

The applause started as a trickle. Growing louder and louder, rising up drowning out the roaring of lions and the screeching beasts below.

The applause and shouts could be heard for miles and did not stop. Tears streamed down a sea of faces.

One by one, the Christians stood up and stared in amazement at this silver-haired savior and then looked up stunned at pagan Rome clapping, standing and cheering this brave man in ragged white robes.

The doomed ones got to their feet staring up at the citizens, some dared to clap but most stared terrified at the animal gates ten feet away. They knew the cheers would soon quiet down and lions would charge. For them the show was coming to a close.

The animals were growling, slamming against the boards ready to bust out and kill them all.

The little emperor was looking frantically to his right and left, as the applause rose up louder his soldiers stared back and forth at each other. Where was the pendulum swinging?

All saw that Jesus, this bedraggled God, had defied the emperor. What now?

The little king gathered himself and screamed back, "No, beggar! It is you who will fall! Mercius! Open the gates! Let loose the animals!"

Christians turned in horror to the gate men whose trembling hands were holding the lock pens reaching to unleash hell.

Applause died, all stopped breathing dreading what had to come next.

The prince looked up to Mercius, as did thousands of terrified Christians, sixty thousand people in the stands were gasping.

The guards by the cages stared at Mercius awaiting the order to fling wide the doors.

Screeches, growls and bellowing ripped the air, wooden gates snapping from animals throwing their bulk against them. One board of a gate broke, a horn jabbed out and people screamed.

Mercius gazed up at the stands and then looked down grimly to give the order. He drew his sword and leveled the blade down at the gatekeepers below, he was surprised at his own bellowing voice, "Do NOT open those gates!"

Across the stadium Nero fell back in disbelief, like a wounded eagle he squealed out, "Guards, open those gates or I will have your heads!"

"Don't touch them!" Shouted Mercius, his teeth grinding, his eyes glaring down like pinched ice.

Jesus was standing near the gates; he wheeled around to the guards by the pens and said calmly, "Follow your heart, boys and don't open those gates!"

The gate men, mesmerized by this brave, bearded man, looked at each other and one by one, nodded up to Mercius, then slowly stepped away from the cages and dropped their arms to their sides.

Not one gate was opened.

The animals were slamming the fences, growling and roaring in the cages.

The Roman mob looked back toward the canopy where Nero was standing, he was waving his arms around frantically screaming across the arena, "Guards, arrest Jesus! Arrest Mercius! Crucify them all!"

Chapter 111

Pride goeth before destruction, and a haughty spirit before a fall
Proverbs 16:18

The chant started high in the stands.

One by one, they got to their feet yelling, "NO! NO! NO! NO! "

Then another refrain—"JESUS! JE—SUS! JE—SUS! JE—SUS!!!!"It was deafening, pagan Romans chanting the name of a Jew unknown to them but they had just seen courage in the arena below, courage worthy of the Gods.

Thousands of fists were shaking and a thousand curses were hurled at the emperor. They were throwing clay cups and seat cushions at the emperor's platform, the floor of the coliseum was strewn with broken cups, cushions and hundreds of sandals.

A thousand clay cups crashed against the emperor's podium, pillows pelted his velvet canopy, daggers and even small swords were thrown and stuck in the wood platform and in the ground all around until with a long 'screek' the canopy tent fell over in a heap. The little man was left standing on his stage in the blaring sun. His bald head shining like a top.

He grabbed the sides of his bald head looking small and pitiful.

The spark of revolt was lit and burning.

Nero's rat-eyes darted around in panic, his personal guards did not move a muscle. He started running around frantically on the open platform, screeching at his guards, pushing them, cursing them but they stood still and stern.

They knew what was coming and they were smiling.

Jesus along with five thousand faces looked up as the emperor on his platform screeched out, frantically, "Mercius! I command you to bring order! Have your men stop this outrage, silence these people at once!!" The little man was shaking his fist.

Mercius saw the spark was lit, the wall of power was crumbling. The shepherd had come for his flock.

He looked up to his men and gave the signal to one thousand of them here and there in the stands. Every one of his faithful guards in iron helmets and leather armor turned their spears in the direction of the emperor.

The crowds saw and a cheer went up and sixty thousand thumbs jabbed toward their necks, the signal of death, the roar was deafening—

"KILL NERO! KILL NERO! KILL NERO! ! !"

The little emperor saw thumbs jabbing at necks like a million daggers calling for his death.

He tried to run down the steps behind the stage but his own soldiers grabbed him and pushed him back up onto the podium.

The Praetorian guards emboldened by the crowd, grabbed his arms and marched him like a crumpled puppet to the front of the podium. Two large soldiers lifted him up like a squirming rat and presented him to the entire coliseum.

Thundering applause shook the sky!

He stood at the edge of the high stage his bald head hanging down, he was sobbing like an old woman. His arms went limp and he collapsed in a purple heap. One guard reached down and picked up his gold crown where it had fallen on the stage. He waved it high in the air then comically placed it on his own head—the crowd laughed, then he flung it onto the earthy arena below. A boy running forward picked it up off the ground and placed it on his own head laughing. His friends wrestled him for it, a plaything now.

The guards dragged Nero like a crumpled bag of rocks down the royal steps behind the stage.

It was over.

The people leaped out of the stands onto the arena grounds, dancing, hugging, running. They let go their pent up hatred of the dictator.

Joy threw its hands in the air and thousands cheered till they could not speak.

The one thousand guards loyal to Mercius Flavius were pointing their spears in the direction of the emperor, who was now a purple, crumpled mass being dragged away.

The Christians on the grounds of the arena started dancing around in a mad spree, joining arms, hugging each other, mothers hugging children, doomed families gathering together for the first time in fearful months, they all hugged and wept.

Everyone turned to Jesus who was standing not far away on the grass, his perfect, bearded face beaming in a smile.

He walked toward his people and they ran and washed over him in an ocean of love.

Mercius had done his work and was gazing out at the chaotic drama unfolding below.

The dumb animals below him in the pens were pacing around in a daze; the gate men stood by the gates at attention. Zoos across the empire would be filled, elephants would be put to work.

No more Christians fed to the lions.

The emperor was hauled away from the platform, his own guards walked him down the steps under house arrest.

Mercius knew they would not execute him.

The dragon of Rome needs a head, a leaderless empire would appear weak to her enemies. Nero would remain alive—in prison. If the little idiot had an ounce of honor he'd fall on a sword.

It was a military take-over, some ambitious soldier would rule, a Praetorian or a General. Perhaps he'd be offered the job, but he would refuse. His work was done and besides he loved his villa by the river. 'Let some young hothead rule, I like my wine at sunset too much'.

Chapter 112

Almost thou persuadest me to be a Christian.
—Acts 26:28

He looked down from his platform at Jesus surrounded by his ragged, grateful people—he had been the spark—the long-awaited flame.

Mercius knew he could not have acted without the support of the people and Jesus had sparked them and then freed them.

The prince had lit the spark, it was up to Mercius and others to keep it burning.

As Jesus walked toward the grand archway leading out to the city he looked up from the arena raised his arm up to him and smiled. The old Roman did the same. He watched as the great man's followers closed in around him, hugging him, kissing the hem of his robe, dancing madly around him.

Jesus stood in the center of a circling swarm, love went out in waves. The citizen crowds in the stands kept up the applause and took flowers from their hair and tossed them down to the people below as they walked by, ivy wreaths were strewn everywhere across the ground. Some Christians put them on their head and waved.

Roman Citizens reached out with open arms over the rail to the newly-saved people and to this tall, silver-haired man standing in the center of it all.

A legend come to life right in front of them.

To the Romans, he seemed like Apollo or even Jupiter, certainly far beyond a Caesar. Seeing him stroll so majestically saving his people—they were yelling themselves hoarse.

In the stands the guards stood fast, spears still pointed in the direction of the empty canopy on the far end of the arena.

The overthrow was complete.

Mercius looked down from his high post and saw what he had waited so long to see and what the enslaved Christians had prayed for every waking moment of their lives—Their Jesus to return.

Amid deafening cheers and falling flowers and brightly colored scarves fluttering down around him, the tall, silver—haired man in a tattered white robe walked with head held high. He strolled across the arena surrounded by his flock of thousands streaming behind him. They were dancing and skipping and walking behind the prince out the high gate to return to their homes.

A golden sun still hung high over the walls and misty drizzle like a cool blessing floated down out of a clear sky. The ragged crowd of Christians raised their faces to heaven and drank in the cool falling drops drenching them with happiness, every face was streaming with tears of joy. They were alive! Thanks to this Jesus, they were alive!

Tall as a God, Jesus the prince raised his arms up once to the raving crowds and as he passed the platform he smiled up at the Captain of Guards, gave him a nod and then walked on.

They poured out the gates into the city and were greeted by throngs of Roman citizens, rich and poor, offering them bread and fruit, cheese and wine, new clothes and blankets and even invitations to their homes.

Christians in all the jails were set free and as they joined their brothers and sisters in the city square, over five thousand joyous souls dancing in the streets beginning their lives anew.

The wide plaza outside the coliseum was filled with Roman families, men and women and their children waiting for them with an offering. Tables were set everywhere filled with food and wine.

A feast of kindness began and lasted far into the night.

Chapter 113

Woe is me! for I am undone.
—Isaiah 6:5

Jesus walked out of the coliseum beaming with love, people came to him their arms outstretched with fruit and bread and the finest wine. He was happier than he'd ever been in his life.

A block away Judas was waiting to kill him.

Hiding behind a pillar with dagger in hand he was ready to stab the messiah.

Judas' heart was frozen with hate. He had followed the master long ago but too much dirty water had washed under the bridge. The bilge had stopped up his heart.

Too much of the wretched goodness of Jesus had washed away his life.

Years ago in Jerusalem when Judas yearned to be the one loved and worshipped, Jesus had taken that away and he was thrown into the heap of nowhere.

Now once again this 'so—called messiah' had stolen his world, destroyed Caiphus and in one day overthrown the emperor who was eyeing him, Judas Iscariot, as the successor to Caiphus. He would have been a powerful man in Rome.

But Jesus had ruined it, again.

He would have been respected, given a palace, a company of guards, it was days within his grasp and now Jesus had knocked the emperor off his roost

His world was gone.

And on top of this the damned savior had burned off the hand of Caiphus and driven him mad, another piece of wood thrown on the fire of his hatred.

So he waited outside the gates to kill him.

'No sleeping potion and secret cave this time, my lord.' He kept slipping his long dagger in and out of the black and gold scabbard staring down at the shiny steel point He had killed before, it would be easy.

After the celebration Judas knew he would walk this way, the road to the harbor. Judas leaned against a wall behind a pillar his lizard—eyes darting back and forth.

The prince appeared down the street like a tall, white angel.

Judas slid back into the shadows he unsheathed his ten-inch blade throwing away the scabbard.

Jesus was two blocks away striding between the tall buildings. He was smiling.

Judas felt cold then hot, his black-silk robe was splotched with sweat and his hand felt clammy around the hilt of the dagger. 'Could he do it?' 'O yes!' was the reply.

The prince was getting closer, he looked and saw him smiling as he strolled along, he was humming a song. He was getting closer and Judas could see his face and it was completely healed from last night's beating and shining like it always was. 'Amazing', thought Judas, 'Those scars could not be healed overnight, so he is special, no matter.'

The dark one slinked in the shadows clutching the dagger, raising the blade to strike.

In seconds Jesus would turn the corner, his sandals were slapping the stones, humming a bright tune, he saw his hands, his white robe, he was here.

From the darkness the clammy soul bleared out of watery eyes watching the tall prince pass in front of him, he walked a few paces more, Judas clutched the dagger in his bony fingers and stepped out of the shadows raising his dagger, Jesus was right in front of him, he eyed his back, the evil one lurched forward, jabbing the blade downward—when suddenly Judas himself screamed in agony.

He looked down with such pain and saw the point of a sword sticking out of his chest, blood was pouring down the front of his robe. He screamed again in ghastly pain as the sword was yanked out of him from behind.

He stood swaying a moment, surprised full of pain, holding back the blood with his spidery fingers as it poured out like warm olive oil. He looked up in a blur to see Jesus gazing at him in horror. He felt a foot kick his back slamming his face onto the cobblestones in a painful crack, the pain was bad but the awful gushing of blood made him see his own horrible death, its cold shadow now covering the edges of his eyes.

"DEMETRIUS! STOP! NO MORE!" Jesus was shouting.

'Demetrius? How could it be?' Judas pondered, face down, sloshing in his own blood, his face wet with it, for a moment he was terrified and then he felt cold and then everything slowly went dark. The last thing he saw was the white cobblestones in front of his eyes. Then all was black, forever.

Demetrius wiped his sword back and forth on the black cloak of Judas who was lying facedown in the street between them. The poet looked up at Jesus, who was stammering and shaking, "See his dagger in his hand?! He was going to kill you!" shouted the poet.

The prince did not move, he froze staring down at Judas lying on the ground and then at Demetrius in questioning horror. He was shaking his head as his friend kept talking, "See the dagger in his hand? I saw him and followed him, aren't you glad I did?"

"Glad? Am I glad? Thank you, but no I am not glad, a man has died." the lord was shaking his head.

He stared dumbfounded at Demetrius then at Judas lying face down at his feet. The Man of Life and Peace knelt down and gently turned Judas over.

Even in death Judas had a scowl, his face had turned white and looked like a skull with a thin beard. His mouth hung open like a sagging actor's mask.

The prince reached down and felt his heart—nothing, still as wood.

"Perhaps I could. . ." Jesus put his hand on the heart of Judas, he closed his eyes and turned to the sky. His friend looked away shaking his head, nervously staring behind him checking the long empty street for soldiers.

The Lord held his hand to the dead heart, praying and beseeching heaven.

Demetrius looked down at his friend and quietly said, "Issa, it is no use, he is dead."

"But I could save him, I have before…"

"My friend, some things are meant to be,"

Jesus was kneeling by the body looked up and saw a block away a crowd of Roman soldiers pointing and running toward them.

"Romans! You must run!'

"But you too!"

"No, I have friends here now, I can get out of this but not you, run, go to the docks, wait for me there!"

Demetrius stepped over Judas' body and sprinted around the corner of a building and was gone.

Seven big Roman guards rushed up to Jesus standing there calmly waiting. The leader demanded, "What is this? WHO is this?!" pointing with his short sword at Judas laying face—up on the street, gangly legs sprawled sideways, his wet robe stuck to his chest with blood.

"It is Judas Iscariot, a jailer of Rome, he would have killed me but someone saved me."

The old Roman frowned, "Someone! Who is that someone?"

The other soldiers gathered around the dead man and Jesus, staring, shaking their heads, mumbling to each other.

"A friend."

"Does this friend have a name?"

"Yes, he is called, the poet"

Suddenly the captain grinned blurting, "Wait! I know you; you are the Jew who saved the Christians! You got the emperor arrested, by Jupiter and all the Gods—*it is YOU!*"

The others looked up amazed, "It's him!" They all forgot about the body on the ground and stared at this tall light-bearded man with the scratched up face.

"Let us get Judas out of the street."

"Yes, yes," said the leader coming back to his job, "guards, lift him." they pulled the body to the side and placed him face up in the shade of a building. Jesus reached down and straightened the legs and arms of Judas and covered his face with his black robe, then stood back up facing the leader of the guards.

The leader turned to the prince, musing, "What shall I do? A murder and you know the murderer, that too is a crime but you are the hero of Rome. I am stuck, I will take you to Captain Mercius, he will decide your fate."

"Very well." said the prince hiding a smile, "Let's go see Captain Mercius."

"But you will forgive me if my men guard you and walk you back to the guard post. You two, tend to the body, I will return soon.

Down the stone street, five red-cloaked Romans walked beside and to the back and in front of the prince who stood a head taller than all of them.

In the next street over they heard loud cheering, the celebration was still on.

As the five Romans and the Lord turned a corner onto another street, it was full of people, and when they saw Jesus they cheered, all eyes upon the one who had saved Rome.

Heads were turning, arms were raising, people in robes blue, brown and rust-colored started walking toward them, hands were reaching out to touch the savior of Rome, suddenly the guards looked beside them, helmets turning this way and that, the tall man was gone. He had not been an arm's length from any of them, one soldier even held him by the arm, Five Romans drew their swords, peering into shops but—the tall Jew had vanished, as if by magic.

Chapter 114

"Yeee Haa!" came the happy cries.

In the plaza outside the coliseum the festival was clinking cups and singing off-key drinking songs.

The shrinking sun was turning the white buildings dark gray and in the pale blue twilight the first faint star appeared.

None of revelers saw it, there was no sky above only faces around them.

A thousand Christians along with a thousand of their wives and sons and daughters were this evening being treated like royalty by Romans. A citizen would dip into a wine-barrel, fill up three cups and balance them spilling through the crowd and then hand them to the religious ones and the citizens and everyone laughed together.

There were slaps on the back and bad jokes. They spoke different languages but the wine joined their hearts as one. The festival spilled out for a mile into the city. People were standing and sitting between marble and wooden buildings.

Outside the arena where the Christians had emerged long tables were set out with

Roast chickens, ducks and swans, platters of grapes, mounds of cheese and hills of bread piled high. And of course more wine than could be drunk. Servants served food, as dogs barked, and the children, both Roman and Jew, ran in and out between grown-ups playing.

Men and women were hugging each other, men with their arms around shoulders, all laughing and drinking and for one night lightness rang through the city of Rome, and Romans and Christians were almost equals.

Chapter 115

It was a bright sunrise.

Mary stood by the harbor watching the dawn sky turn to pink then shimmering gold. She was standing at the end of the pier gazing across the water at the boats bobbing in the harbor.

Jesus appeared at the head of the pier behind her and stood watching his love, her long white-blond hair spilling down her brown cloak.

She felt him and turned and his heart held its breath. Her smile sent shivers through his heart. Her eyes laughing with pure light.

"My love!" she shouted and ran up the wooden pier, he walked toward his wonderful love.

Their full hug warmed all of heaven, tears stung their eyes. Her hair smelled like an ocean breeze. She looked up into his eyes, they were windows to a clear sky, her light hair in a white mist surrounding her perfect face.

He pulled her mouth to his. His lips felt her sweet warm mouth open and in a swirl of sweetness and wonder, his mind spun off into nowhere.

They engulfed each other, her fingers dug into his robe and they were lost in each other's mouth, tongues and love and pressing lips becoming one.

He forgot he was on a pier, forgot the boats, the world was completely lost in their warm kiss. After forever, he pulled away, put his hands around her waist lifting her up twirling her around the pier, he set her down again and cupped her face in his large hands and kissed her again, they hugged and came back to Earth settling into their perfect love.

They turned and walked arm in arm back to where the pier met the shore.

Mary spoke like playfully, "I have heard that a great messiah saved his people yesterday."

The great one turned with a wide smile, "You heard that did you?"

"Yes, I did."

"And what else did you hear?"

"I have heard he kicked the emperor right off his throne."

"No, I don't believe it."

She stopped and turned to him, squeezed his arm tight and looked up into his deep dark eyes saying, "I am so proud of you, my Love. The whole world is proud of you."

"Pride will get you in trouble, but thank you, darling, I did what I came to do, what God wanted me to do, that is all."

She hugged him and then they kept walking lazily up onto the shore.

They saw a man in a short white tunic walking toward them up the beach.

A white headband was around his forehead, his long black, curling hair trailing behind, he was smiling like the sun at noon—

"Demetrius! by Zeus!" Jesus shouted, then smiled at Mary, then ran to his friend and they met on the beach with a long hug.

Jesus stepped back and looked at the poet, "Great to see you, I'm glad you got away."

The poet frowned, "It was no easy task, my friend, soldiers were everywhere, but you are here, how is that?"

"Let us say I escaped but tell me a tale, my friend, and where are your two girls?"

"They went back to their families, the little darlings, they live near here. I'll miss them dearly."

Chapter 116

Mary walked up and hugged Demetrius, "Great to see you, my friend, you have had quite an adventure, I imagine."

"Yes, Mary, much has happened in the last two days. Sire Jezep here is quite the hero now."

"Yes, I've heard."

The three walked together along the beach in the direction of the harbor houses and the taverns, the bay to their left it was filled with a hundred boats, all different shapes and sizes.

Demetrius stopped and turned to the two, "Let us sit for a moment, much has happened since yesterday and you must know of it."

They sat down in the sand and gazed in silence out at the bay. It was the wide slow moving Tiber River, so wide and slow it was still and dark blue like a bay. It was over a mile wide and on the far shore brown hills blended into the horizon.

The bay before them was filled with boats, large bulky triremes with painted eyes, sleek Egyptian scows with triangular Lateen sails, and smaller rowboats were everywhere, round-sided fishing boats with nets hanging over the sides.

The three sat in the sand gazing out, the prince tossed a pebble out into the water. They sat in silence.

Demetrius broke the silence, "You know the ship is gone, Barabbas sailed this morning."

The prince stared at him in disbelief.

"But what of the money! Did he sail away with the gold? There were many Talents of gold coins in those bags!"

"No, no, everything is fine."

"OH? Please tell me."

Demetrius picked up a shell and sailed it across the smooth water and then began, "You remember when Judas put us in that cell?"

"A bad night for sure."

He continued, "They took you and left me in that rotten cell. I sat in the jail and watched your big drama from the window, it was absolutely grand, Mary, you should have seen him shout down the emperor. I sat in the cell all that day and feared they'd forgotten poor Demetrius and I would rot down there forever, that's when the cell door opened and Lam and Silvanus were standing there, they had somehow opened the door and came right into the cell.

It was a miracle how mere servants could get past all the guards, through all those doors and open my cell."

"I believe they were much more than servants." said Jesus but he asked, "But does this have anything to do with the gold?"

"Yes, they had all three bags filled with the gold coins, they had brought them from the ship, they kept two of them and handed me one of the sacks filled with many Talents of gold and, as you can see." Demetrius reached into his cloak and pulled out a large bag of gold coins and jingled it, "It is heavy to lug around, enough to keep us alive for a long time."

Jesus and Mary leaned over and dug their fingers into the sack of gold trickling golden coins through their fingers like bright metal raindrops. Jesus through his silver beard asked, "And what of the other two sacks with more than 2000 Talents of pure gold, a fortune."

"They told me they would give it to the Christians. They left and went around in the streets handing it out to the poor, but they gave me this bag, one third of the coins—all we have is this but believe me, it is enough."

A smile spread like dawn across the silver—bearded face of Jesus. He stood up, raised his arms high and shouted,

"Halleluia!"

He stood up and ran to the water up to his waist and turned back at them raising his hands started shouting, "That's wonderful! We saved them and then took care of them! It's perfect!"

The two sitting on the sand turned to look at each other then back at

Jesus. He walked out of the water and stood in front of them smiling as the morning sun rose behind him, Demetrius looked up at his friend and spoke his mind,

"So Issa, the mission is done, let's go home."

Chapter 117

The prince got quiet and looked at Mary, "So my love, what do you say?"

"I go where you go, my darling." A soft breeze whipped her blond hair sideways brushing her uplifted smile.

The prince smiled, "That is what I knew you'd say, my love."

He then turned to the poet, "Home, you say?"

"Issa! It has been a long journey and we are tired to the bone, Let us return to Babylon and our palaces and feather beds."

The prince was gazing down at the sand and said, "Our easy life? Is that what you want? Servants and wine and waiting for the end?"

"You say it so badly."

The prince looked down at his friend, "I miss Babylon too but haven't these last months been the most thrilling of our life, We've been more alive than we have ever been?"

"That's true," said the poet gazing at the boats, the prince kept talking, "Do you remember back in the palace yearning for this—to see the world before we die!?"

"So what are you saying, you mad prophet, we should go on? But where?" he stared up at his friend's laughing, boyish eyes.

The prince lifted up his arms to the sky and laughed, "Anywhere! Everywhere! To the West, to Gaul, to the Pillars of Hercules, to Britain, or to Egypt and see the pyramids! Africa! Greece! The world calls to us!"

Mary said not a word, she only looked down at a tiny scurrying crab and smiled.

Demetrius could feel home slipping away.

He could never hold out long against his friend. He had followed him on a life to the stars. The poet knew in his heart that if he had not met Jesus many years ago in a street in Nazareth and not been swept up by this tall man's dreams, he would have lived a very dull life sitting on the muddy shores of Galilee.

This wild prophet had given him adventures beyond his wildest dreams, had made him a prince of Babylon, let him travel the Silk Road to India, see dazzling sights, drive chariots, chase lions and love beautiful women, he had shown him the wide world, its heights and its depths, and here he was again spinning his web around him once more.

Jesus stared down at him with a broad smile, "Well?"

He finally crumbled and let loose those three magic words that had opened the gates of life before him, "Alright, let's go!"

Mary and Jesus clapped and at that very moment they looked up and saw a flock of white birds flying west.

Chapter 118

While Jesus and Mary had breakfast in a nearby tavern Demetrius went out and found a boat.

He went back and found his two friends and talked their ears off all the way to the pier, when they arrived at the top he pointed down to a ship and crew by the pier.

"There she is, ready to sail, and she's all ours." The poet smiling wide as a sail.

. To say the Prince was pleased would be to say that angels liked playing harps in Heaven.

He slapped his friend on the back. Mary kissed him on the cheek.

The ship rested beside the pier like a long smile—a 70-foot Egyptian sailing ship sleek as a seagull sitting on the water.

It had a cedar mast that rose up forty feet in the center with a straight crossbeam and a square white sail tucked in the length of it.

When they walked up the crew stood and waved.

Demetrius put his hands on his hips and said to Jesus, "All you need do, my friend, is sit in the bow, give orders and dream of distant shores!" The prince replied, "Poet, you amazed me. Lead the way."

The grand boat was facing outward at the end of the dock, rocking up and down ready to sail.

The bright yellow sun was straight above as the three proudly paraded down the pier and stood beside their ship beaming away.

Demetrius shouted to the bustling crew on the deck and to the young captain standing by the tiller, "Look, here is Jesus, Hero of Rome, ready to sail!"

The sailors shouted a cheer and rushed forward.

"And this is his royal queen, Mary!"

Every one of the men bowed their head then threw their arms up and let out a hoorah!

The prince dramatically lifted his lady up in his arms and set her lightly onto the ship, burly sailors helped her down onto the deck. The prince jumped into the ship and many hands slapped his back and more cheers went up. Demetrius climbed in and as they settled in, the lines were tossed away and the noble ship let go of the chains of the land and began to drift.

Long oars on each side slid out and on the open deck bare—chested men began rowing, The wild poet stood high on the bow shouting out a song, "Away! Away, we sail to lands, to lands so far away"

The loud booming voices of the rowers answered back a chorus, "Sail to lands far away!" and in a happy cadence pulled on the oars.

The ship bounded out into the middle of the bay and the bow rode up and down like a wooden horse, its huge head dipping and rising in the sea.

As the ship headed to sea, Demetrius looked far behind and saw two young ladies on shore, Penelope and Sheba, they were waving goodbye.

He stood up and waved back to them. They jumped up waving wildly to him and then they settled down holding each other sitting on the beach. He pinched a tear from his eyes and knew they felt same tear drifting down their face as he sailed away.

They had warmed him across deserts and oceans and he missed their sweet kisses on his cheek.

Demetrius, sitting forward felt the sea spray splash over his back and smelled the free ocean air. He looked over at Jesus and Mary sitting beside him in the bow both smiling, their arms around each other. He looked back down the ship and saw the brown sweating backs of the men pulling on the oars, they were singing his song—"*Away, Away, we sail away…*"he shouted back carrying the song —"*To Persia, Egypt and old Cathay, to oceans west we leave the nest, we sail the sea our hearts so free, away, away we sail…*"

He looked back to the stern and saw the young, dark—haired captain gripping the tiller, he raised his hand in a greeting as the long ship headed out into broad blue sea.

The rising spray of the sea splashed over the bow behind him over his head, cold sea spray shocking his bare neck and hair. He laughed with the prince and Mary, they laughed and shivered.

Demetrius was sitting across from Mary and Jesus in the bow, they leaned against plush pillows and watched the backs of the oarsmen pulling the oars.

Demetrius glanced up at the mast rising up with the high crossbeam going straight across near the top. The sails were lashed tight to the crossbeams. 'The mast and beam look like the cross' came a thought, then quickly passed.

The poet smiled over at his friends, and in the whoosh of the sea splashing over them they smiled back. The wind whipped their long hair into their faces as they all watched the shining white city of Rome slip behind into the sea mist.

The sun was bright at noon charging through the choppy blue water.

Their hearts were light as spinning gulls.

Demetrius glanced up at the tall mast and noticed wooden pegs sticking out of either side, a ladder leading up the high mast to a small flat board sticking out below the crossbeam, it was called the 'crow's nest'. It was a short board that stuck out where a sailor could stand and hold onto the crossbeam and search ahead for miles.

He turned and saw that Jesus had noticed this peg ladder up the mast.

The prince got that twinkle and gave him a wink and a big broad smile. He then kissed Mary on the cheek, jumped up and put one foot on a peg and then another and another, higher and higher to the top.

The prince wore only a white cloth wrapped closely around his waist, sailor-fashion, as he climbed steadily to the top of the mast. Bare legs and chest, he reached the small, flat board sticking out and then turned around standing on the perch, facing the open sea ahead.

The poet saw what he was up to, it gave him a chill.

Mary was looking up, smiling and shaking her head.

By the top of the mast, Jesus stood straight up against the mast and stretched his arms out on the crossbeams.

The bright, shining sun circled his head.

With his arms outstretched, Jesus smiled down at them and turned his bearded face to the heavens and laughed and laughed as the proud ship bounded on.

Epilog

The old scribe with a long white beard looked around the dark, candle-lit scriptorium.

His fellow scribes were copying holy words that would be rolled into scrolls and then sent out across the world. Yellow papyrus was curled everywhere on the tables.

It was the words of their Prince Jezep, rumored in the west to be the Christ.

They also copied the Gospel of Demetrius, recounting Prince Jezep's travels to India and back.

The old scribe pushed out from his seat, "Let's take a break."

"Here, here!" shouted a scribe.

"Good idea" said another, dropping his stylus.

Ten young scribblers in white robes walked out of the cold room into the sunlight and sat on stone seats around a marble table. The green garden encircled them, the open sky made them feel free.

They threw back their hoods. The old one reached for the pitcher of red wine on the table and filled the goblets of the others.

One of the young men took a sip and asked everyone, "Where are they now?"

Another answered, "No one has heard from the prince and Demetrius since they left for Rome last summer, who knows where they are?"

The scribes looked down and then took quiet sips of wine.

Silence reigned for a long time then Darius, a young longhaired scribbler, turned to the Old Scribe sitting alone and boldly inquired, "Sir, have you finished the last Gospel?"

"I have."

Darius, dared to ask the question, "You have seen the Ten Laws?"

"Yes, and they are finished, before he left the Master ordered the Ten Laws to be carved in white marble, the prince wants to be the next Moses, I think."

"Can we read them?"

"Of course, fill your cups, boys and prepare yourselves." And he walked back into the darkened room.

The scribes were sitting around the table in the morning sunlight sipping wine.

Darius finished a sip, wiped his mouth and turned to scribe Xenophon, " Xeno, Do you believe our prince is the Christian messiah they talk of?"

Xenophon turned with a quick smile, "Of course he is, someone as great as the prince would be talked about from here to Rome and his words are wise as the old ones, if there was ever one worthy of legend it's him."

The others took sips and nodded.

Xenophon lifted his cup, "To the prince!" all together yelled out, "To the prince!"

Just then the old man emerged from the dark door holding two marble tablets, one on each arm. He sat down at the head of the table, stroked his white beard and smiled, "Behold the words of Prince Jezep."

He placed the two thick tablets upright side by side on the table before them. They all put down their wine cups and read in silence.

THE TEN LAWS OF PERFECTION

I   There could not be an urge to get better if it were not possible to be the best.

II   Every race has a finish line, no one would run if halfway was as far as he could get.

III   Human improvement implies Human Perfection—we will all be perfect someday.

IV   Humility comes from the word humble, similar to human. Humility is the state of being human.

V   God is not in the tomb of religion, God is alive within you.

VI   Humans evolve toward perfection by instinct.

VII A caterpillar does not turn itself into a butterfly, it happens naturally. We are becoming perfect naturally.

VIII Life is death and rebirth for the sole purpose of improvement toward perfection.

IX   Mankind and God exist side by side. Does not God want you to be stronger, strongest.

X   Religion muddies the Holy Water.

The young men slowly looked around at each other, some took quick sips. The old scribe pulled the tablets into his arms, stood up and walked back into the dark door. The young scribes nodded at each other, clinked their cups together lightly and said, "Amen."

NOTES:

I have always been fascinated with Jesus.

If he *were* real he would have to have been large and loud, wise and gentle, a real hero.

There were many spiritual leaders at the time of Jesus—but he stood out above them all and was remembered.

Jesus could not have been a quiet preacher, people don't go home and talk of quiet little people and little sermons, they talk of booming, bold heroes who thunder in their heart, who make them nervous by breaking the rules, by being loud. That's who is remembered.

Jesus was no mere humble holy man wandering the countryside. Jews are not a quiet people, to be heard he would have had to be the loudest of the loud.

He had to have stood heads above everyone else in everything he did. The bible tells he was "tall and robust."

He had to have had the charisma and power of a king.

He raved, preached and healed within a small geographical area for three long years disrupting the whole region before anyone had the guts to stop him.

And when they finally did stop him they could only do so with the help of the high priest, King Herod and a powerful governor of Rome, Pontius Pilate, even they feared to condemn him.

Would great kings fear a small, meek person?

A lesser person the head Hebrews and a Roman Governor would have crucified without a blink, tossed into prison without a second thought—but with Jesus they were impressed, in awe.

They must have seen a man with the power of a Hercules, Apollo, Achilles, or Alexander standing before them, perhaps a Moses, why else would they make a big production of him when they met him? Powerful Romans and Jewish Kings would not be impressed by a ragged, homeless person, to be so fearfully respected by these rulers he would have to have the bearing of a king.

LEGENDS AND LIONS

If Jesus did escape the cross and live on, what would he want to do afterwards as he sat around getting old?

He would probably want to help somebody, especially Christians.

It just so happens that not too many years after the date of the crucifixion at about the time the escaped Jesus would be middle age, Christians did need saving—from the lions.

And just my luck, Christians being thrown to the lions is an event that just about everybody in the world has heard about, and—it really happened at that very time, about 30 years after the cross.

The perfect plot.

Here is where historical fact and fiction join and get very interesting, almost mind-boggling.

I did not discover these coincidental, historical facts until after I had come up on my own with the fantastical story of Jesus going to Rome cursing the emperor and saving the Christians from the lions.

I thought my story was totally original but to my dumfounded surprise I found that someone actually did these things I wrote about—these events actually happened at that same time in history.

A holy man, Apollonius of Tyrna (in modern Turkey) lived at the same time as Jesus Christ, performed similar miracles and acts as Jesus and preached the same messages as Jesus. It has even been suggested that the Jesus of Christianity never actually lived and his life and the religion are based on the life of Apollonius.

He was born at the same time as Jesus but (like my story) lived on past the time of cross. He lived into his 60s (also like my story).

299

His writings and teachings are similar to the Bible and were documented during the same time period, so Apollonius, is believed by scholars to be the Apostle Paul (A 'Paul' onius) who wrote much of the New Testament.

Some believe Jesus himself is a later fictionalized person based on Apollonius.

This sounds outlandish but the theory is that Apollonius, who lived a much purer life than Jesus, would set higher more unrealistic standards for everyday living than the meat-eating, wine-drinking Jesus. Apollonius also preached sexual abstinence, clearly an impossible requirement for the average person to follow.

They had to 'water down' the real messiah to make him more human.

It is believed that at the Council of Nicea around 300 A.D where churchmen chose the books of the Bible and standardized it, to make it more palatable they "morphed" Apollonius with Jesus. They took Apollonius and let him eat meat, drink wine and approve of having sex.

This Apollonius—Jesus Comparison fills volumes of books and space on the Internet, but the short version is as follows.

Appollonius was an actual historical figure with numerous credible writers recording his biography at the time he was alive. Jesus was not written about outside the New Testament, there were no historical writers who actually witnessed the acts of Jesus, he is a myth.

Apollonius was similar to Jesus in miracles and spirituality but unlike Jesus he traveled all over the known world and unlike Jesus, his life was documented by living credible writers of the time.

And one of his most famous documented acts was to REALLY go to Rome, get an audience with Nero and scold him publicly for his bad treatment of Christians, doing this soon after the fire of Rome! It is also written that shortly after his visit, Nero stopped the persecution of the Christians.

He lived the story I wrote, or close to it but the incredible thing is that I had already finished the novel before I had even heard of Appolonius.

The further amazing thing about the Appollonius connection is that I had invented the poet character, Demetrius two years before in my previous novel, The Last God.

I was finishing this book, Savior's Quest, with the same poet character when I discovered that the actual historical friend and sidekick of Appollonius was named Demetrius.

It knocked me over.

JESUS AND MARY MAGDALENE

The close relationship of Jesus and Mary has been discussed for centuries.

Any index or reference in a Bible will tell you that Mary traveled with Jesus and the disciples, was closer, spiritually and physically, to Jesus than the others and that the disciples were jealous of Mary because of this closeness. It is written in the Bible more than once that Jesus "kissed her on the mouth."

The entire premise of the popular novel, The Da Vinci Code, and it is well documented that Jesus and Mary Magdalene could have been married with children.

She was the first and last one to see and talk to Jesus after his resurrection.

THE PRAYER OF THE PRINCE

The ancient language that Jesus spoke was Aramaic, it was the common language of most of the east at that time. It was written and sounded very similar to ancient Hebrew which, of course, is still spoken today. In the story when Prince Jezep said the grace at his farewell dinner those were the actual words and sounds of the Lord's prayer spoken in Aramaic.

That is how Jesus actually sounded when he spoke.

CUTTING OFF THE EAR OF THE ROMAN AND CAIPHUSES' HAND

The night Jesus was arrested a disciple cut off a Roman soldier's ear and Jesus placed it back on his head, this scene is from the Bible. Jesus had the power to wither hands and tree branches; this is also in the Bible.

FURTHER NOTES:

THE FIRE

The fire of Rome actually happened. It started in July, 64 AD and burned much of the city.

The emperor Nero blamed the Christians when it was (probably) he who started the fire to make room for his own temples. He built a great palace for himself called The Golden House, dug a giant lake and erected temples and statues to himself in the same area that was burned.

It is also true that (like my story) he hired thugs to roam the city and harass the citizens.

He did feed Christians to lions and other beasts pretty much as I describe it in the book. Christians were also crucified and torched on crosses.

He eventually stopped the execution of Christians because of pressure by the Roman people (and perhaps Apollonius) that could not stomach it anymore. Emperors were very concerned with public opinion that's how they retained their power and when killing Christians got unpopular he stopped doing it.

As for the animals, as strange as it sounds there were hippos and rhinos and elephants let loose in the arena along with lions, leopards, tigers, hyenas, wolves and bulls.

THE SEX SCENES

The sex orgy described in the story was tame compared to what Nero and the previous emperor Caligula actually did.

The mass sexual exhibitions put on by Roman emperors at this time— reported by credible eye-witnesses—were so perverted they would not be believed even as fiction. As wild as it is in the book, my version is toned down compared to the strange sexual things they did at this time.

Find a biography of Nero, check in the index under sexual practices and it will describe a typical orgy of thousands having sex. During the orgies a person would walk up the steps toward Nero and perform sex acts upon him at the climax (no pun) of the orgy. My portrayal of the fat lady in the story climbing toward Nero is loosely copied from history, he did this although usually it was a young boy.

To report any more true history would be pornographic to publish. Sex orgies were mostly centered on public homosexuality, private bizarre sexual practices and much creative bloodshed.

Tiberius, the ruler at the time of Jesus, Caligula, the immediate previous emperor, Nero himself and Vespasian, who ruled shortly after Nero were all known to have had bizarre sexual practices.

The wild sex orgy I described was to give a feeling of how strange and twisted some of the Roman emperors really were.

NERO

The emperor Nero did play "the fiddle," actually the ancient version called a lyre. He is said to have been singing at the time of the Great Fire, but he probably was not actually near the flames. This is poetic license putting him at the fire "fiddling while Rome burned."

He was known as the worst, most cruel emperor in the first two hundred years after Christ.

The devil's number 666 came from the numerology date of Nero's Birth.

He was hated for having his mother killed and for crucifying Christians, he was eventually overthrown by the army.

Nero was deposed by a military coup but not until 68 AD. I felt my version might be accurate in that the people were dissatisfied with his cruelty to Christians and also the jailing of the emperor in my story actually happened only four years later.

After Nero there were three military dictators each lasting a few months to a year and after a few more petty emperors the pagan empire that had lasted a thousand years turned into the Holy Roman Empire.

And in the end, over half of the citizens of the Roman Empire worshipped Jesus Christ.

The bare bones of my story are real and actually happened.

There really was a great fire, the evil emperor who started it blamed the Christians and fed them to the lions, a holy man named Apollonius, who may or may not have been Jesus, is documented to have scolded Nero to his face for his treatment of the people and he stopped the killing shortly afterwards. The emperor was eventually deposed for his evil doings.

So my story actually happened in a loose sort of way.

History is far more exciting than any fiction. Historical Fiction is just writing down actual events in the past, throwing in some dialogue and adding a little color.

—DG
Kona, Hawaii,
June 15, 2009